Daughter of Grace

G·K
Hall
&C°.

Also published in Large Print
from G.K. Hall by
Michael Phillips and
Judith Pella:

My Father's World

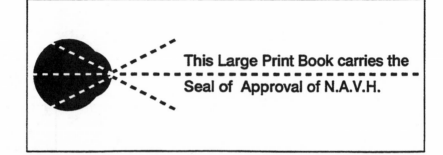

This Large Print Book carries the
Seal of Approval of N.A.V.H.

Daughter of Grace

Michael Phillips
Judith Pella

G.K. Hall & Co.
Thorndike, Maine

Published in 1995 by arrangement with Bethany House Publishers.

G.K. Hall Large Print Inspirational Collection.

The text of this Large Print edition is unabridged.
Other aspects of the book may vary from the original edition.

Set in 16 pt. News Plantin by Warren Doersam.

Printed in the United States on permanent paper.

Library of Congress Cataloging in Publication Data

Phillips, Michael R., 1946–
  Daughter of grace / Michael Phillips, Judith Pella.
      p.   cm.
    ISBN 0-7838-1179-9 (lg. print : hc)
    1. Frontier and pioneer life — California — Fiction.
  2. California — History — 1850–1950 — Fiction. 3. Large
  type books. I. Pella, Judith. II. Title.
  [PS3566.H492D38   1995]
  813'.54—dc20   94-42305

To
Robin Mark Phillips

CONTENTS

Prologue

Well, I suppose Uncle Nick was right.

When we let Mr. MacPherson, the publisher from the East, make a book based on my diary of our life in Miracle Springs, I didn't know what would happen with it. But Uncle Nick said folks would like reading it, and I guess he knew what he was saying, judging from all the mail I've received.

Pa's kind of proud, too — not just of being in a book, but seeing that folks admire him and his family. He walks around town with his head up high, knowing he doesn't have anything to be ashamed of anymore. And I think too, though he's never said it, that he hopes some of the folks back in New York might get hold of the book and read it, and will find out he wasn't as bad a man as some of them might have thought.

Of course Mr. Kemble still blusters around like the whole notion of a book's a crazy idea. And he still tries to talk to me in the same gruff way. But things are different now, and he knows it. Sometimes I can see a little light in his eye when he's looking me over that says he's almost proud of me, though he would *never* say it! I think he's a little proud of himself too, because he's the one who's pretty much responsible for getting it made into a book. But he won't admit that, either!

All of them have been hinting at me to tell more about what happened after we found the gold, and about how Miracle started to grow, and about Uncle Nick and Mrs. Parrish and Pa. And I did have to agree with them. When we were first talking about the idea of a book, it seemed like a mighty farfetched notion. But now that I've done it, there's an incomplete feeling about it all. The story is only partway told. So *much* happened after my birthday when Pa shaved off his beard, and that spring day early in 1853 when we watched the wagons heading East. It hardly seems right that I should tell only part of it, and not what came afterwards.

So that's what I'm going to do now. I'm going to try my hand at a second book, picking up where I left off with the first.

I hope you like it!

Corrie Belle Hollister
Miracle Springs, California
1863

CHAPTER 1

THE DEDICATION . . . LOOKING BACKWARD

In September of 1853, the first service was held in the brand-new Miracle Springs church, and the dedication was followed by a big town picnic and celebration.

It was a warm, beautiful, fragrant day. As I sat there in the freshly painted new building, with Pa on one side of me, and Zack, Emily, Becky, and Tad on the other, my sixteen-year-old heart was full of happiness as Rev. Rutledge led us in the singing of the morning's hymns.

Then he said he had a special addition to the morning service. He asked Mr. Peters, a German man who had settled in the area recently, to come to the front with him. "Hans asked me if he could read an old German hymn for us today," said Rev. Rutledge. "And I told him we'd be delighted."

"This is my favorite hymn," said Mr. Peters in his thick German accent. "It maybe is because I like animals. This song vas written by St. Francis of Assisi, who loved all God's creatures. I loved in ta old country to sing it, but I think no one knows it here. So I make ta vords into English

13

so gut as I can, and I read them to you for ta church dedication today."

He stopped to adjust his spectacles and take a breath, then began to read from the piece of paper he was holding. As he went along, my mind started filling with all kinds of memories of everything that had happened. All the words of the song, and Mr. Peter's explanation of how he'd turned it into English, reminded me of little parts of last year.

All creatures of our God and King, lift your voices up and sing with us, Allelulia . . .
You, the sun that burns bright and gold, and you silver moon with soft gleam . . . praise Him! O praise Him!

All the memories weren't happy. That sun in the desert had been *so* hot. There'd been times I'd cursed God for that sun, burning down day after day, infecting Ma with its heat, till she couldn't cool off — even at night.

Heat . . . heat. Every day her hands and forehead got hotter, her voice weaker, till there was no voice left but Captain Dixon's, trying to comfort us kids, trying to help us in the only way he knew.

I remember walking a little ways away from the wagon camp the night Ma died. Walking, stumbling aimlessly, I hardly had strength to put one foot in front of the other. Ma had been my whole world, and now she was gone. I couldn't even stop to think what we were going to do now. There was nothing but emptiness inside, not even sadness at first . . . just an awful empty feeling.

I looked up and there was the moon — about half a moon, staring silently down at me. Everything around me was quiet. The desert sounds were way off in the distance, and I didn't even hear them. Back where the wagons were, everyone knew about Ma and they were being real subdued. I guess death always makes people quiet. All I could hear was some of the horses shuffling around, and Becky and Emily still crying once in a while back where I'd left them. Tad hadn't cried yet. But he'd understand later, and then the hurt would catch up with him. Zack wanted to cry, I know, but something in him couldn't let it out.

I looked up at that moon, quiet and cold, with the cool of the summer night closing in all around us. I wanted to yell up and curse that moon for not bringing its coolness sooner! The cool had come to the desert, and Ma's face was cool now, too. But the cool had come too late!

How could I praise Him, how could I sing? Ma was dead! Didn't God know what He'd done? I was angry and hurt. The last thing I could do was praise Him!

Tears filled my eyes out on that lonely, quiet desert. *Why, God . . . why! Was it my fault, for not praying enough? Was Ma a sinner that You had to take her away? Why, God? Were You angry with us . . . with Ma . . . with me? Was it on account of Pa that You took Ma away out here in this hot, horrible, empty, lonely desert?*

And still that silent, silver moon looked down, mocking me in my misery. It was blurred now, and my eyes were all wet. "Go away!" I shouted. But then quickly I stopped, shocked to hear my own voice in the middle of all the stillness.

Hearing my outburst sobered me for a minute. I took in a deep breath, trembling like I always do when I've been crying. But I got the air all the way in, and then I looked up at the moon again.

It was still there, still the same, quiet and bright and cool. But now there seemed to be a softness in its gleam. A peaceful feeling gradually came over me, a feeling that maybe God was like the moon, looking quietly down on us, that He hadn't forgotten after all, and that maybe His coolness, His peace, His tenderness would be there even through all the pain we were feeling. I didn't actually think all that right at the time, out there in the desert as I stared up at the moon. But there must have been a feeling in my heart that maybe God hadn't forgotten us, and I wrote it down later.

You fast-blowing wind so strong, and you
clouds blowing along through the heavens, O
praise Him, Allelulia. . . .
Rejoice in praise, you morning rising up . . .
You flowing water, clear, pure, make music

16

for our Lord to hear, Allelulia, Allelulia. . . .

I looked up at Mr. Peters reading, with Rev. Rutledge standing beside him smiling, and I quickly wiped the sleeve of my dress across my eyes. Thinking about that day the year before had brought tears back to my eyes without my even realizing it!

God *had* watched over us. I know that now, although I didn't at the time. He had blown the past away with his strong wind. We couldn't realize it then, but as my sisters and brothers and I continued our journey over that desert, and then over the Sierras and down into California, not knowing what was to come, the clouds above us and the winds blowing about us were God's way of brushing away our past life and getting us ready for everything He had for us there.

A new morning had come to us in Miracle Springs. Suddenly there were new people, like Mrs. Parrish and Alkali Jones and some of the neighbors and townsfolk. Best of all, there was Pa, and of course Uncle Nick. It was like God's way of letting the sunlight that had died with Ma rise again — as the sun does every new morning — on Pa's face. I don't know if it makes sense. Sometimes when people try to use words to say something they're feeling down inside, it doesn't always come out quite right. But I felt like in Pa and in the other folks in Miracle, and in everything that happened, a new morning came

17

to our lives, and maybe I could learn to rejoice in it.

And the water — the wonderful, bubbling, sparkling water! How many walks alone had I taken this year up that stream by the cabin, where the deer came down to drink? Beside that stream I first talked to Little Wolf. Pa and Uncle Nick worked there every day, and we all carried that water up to the cabin in buckets to do the cooking and washing.

Most folks from around here, and from all over the country, praised the water only because it carried the gold from inside the hills and mountains out into the light of day where they could see it and mine it and sell it and make their fortunes with it.

If it weren't for the water, pure and clear, and the shiny gold it brought with it down to Sutter's Mill, Mr. Marshall would never have found what he did and no one would ever have found out about all the riches filling the veins that criss-crossed these hills and mountains of California. It would all have sat there for years and years, maybe forever, and no one would have ever known it. But the water changed history, and made California a state, and Miracle began to grow so fast there were new folks coming to town every day on account of the strike. And lots of the other men hereabouts dug deeper into the hills than before, following Pa and Uncle Nick's example, and some of them found new veins too. Folks said ours was one of the most famous new strikes around, because so many of the original places had started to run out of gold.

But even if it weren't for the gold, even if little Tad hadn't found anything in the mine after the cave-in, and even if we were poor as could be, the water flowing in that stream outside the cabin would be just as musical to me, and I would be just as content. It isn't the gold that makes folks happy. The Lord knows how many around here *aren't* happy for all the bags of gold they've taken to the bank!

If a person's going to be happy, it's got to come from somewhere else. That's one thing I've learned this year! It comes from having a family, and friends, and probably more than anything from learning to be thankful for whatever comes your way.

But the next words Mr. Peters read both filled me with joy and made me have to fight back the tears. They showed me all over again how much had changed, and how thankful I was to God for making us kids part of our father's world, and for making him part of ours, too.

Mr. Peters' words set me to thinking so deep that I didn't come back to myself till he was sitting back down and Rev. Rutledge was talking again.

CHAPTER 2

A MAN OF TENDER HEART

These were the words Mr. Peters was reading:

Allelulia, O praise Him, all you men with tender hearts. . . .
Allelulia, forgive others, you who must bear sorrow and pain, Allelulia. . . .

When it came to changes in our lives, I doubt anything could match the change in Pa! These last months with him had been wonderful.

Nothing could make up for Ma being gone, and I still missed her, but not as much as at first. In my head, I still missed Ma just as much as ever; I doubt I'll ever get over loving her till it hurts. But my heart was getting used to the idea of going on in life without her. I knew it was hard for the three younger kids not having a ma around the place. Pa wasn't a woman, and never could be. And though I did what I could, I was only their sister after all.

But Pa was real kind, even more so to the younger ones, I think, because he knew they needed mothering. I know he loved Ma, but now I think he missed her more for the kids' sake than his own, because he felt so helpless to give them all they needed. Mrs. Parrish would come out once a week or so, and I think she might have liked to help more with the younger kids, but Pa seemed kind of reluctant — as though it was his duty to take care of his family and he didn't want help. He felt that he had to do more for us now on account of his being gone from us and leaving Ma alone for so long.

So Pa'd tuck Emily and Tad and Becky under their covers every night. And though he never said much about religious things, he took us into Miracle nearly every Sunday for Rev. Rutledge's church services, because like the rest, he thought getting some religious teaching was important for us kids. He wouldn't have gone if it hadn't been for us — it was simply one more way he was trying to be a good Pa.

Pa and I never had another talk like that one outside the cabin after last Christmas. Since that day, we'd had a silent understanding between us. And because of it, Pa treated me more like one of the grown-ups around the place.

The change I noticed most about Pa had to do with Uncle Nick. They still worked and laughed and talked together like the friends and partners they were. But there was another side of Pa that I started to see, a little part of him that seemed to think of himself as Uncle Nick's pa, too. In so many ways Uncle Nick was still a kid at heart. He'd do silly things and chase off after ideas Pa called "just a blame fool ridiculous notion!"

Now it was like the partnership and older-brother was only half of Pa's relation to Uncle Nick. The rest of the time he was his pa, just like he was Pa to all the rest of us — a pa who had to tend his family, work his mine, be careful with his money, see to our training, fix up the cabin, and sometimes read us stories. He never gambled or drank any more, and he took his fathering duties as seriously as any man ever could.

More than once or twice those last months Uncle Nick would come home after squandering some of his gold in a poker game or on something he didn't need, and Pa would get after him like he was an irresponsible little kid.

"Don't you know no better'n that!" he'd say. "Those fellas in town see you coming and say to theirselves, 'How can we fleece ol' Nick today?' Sometimes you're just a downright fool, Nick! That mine could dry up any day, and then where'll you be?"

"But, Drum," Uncle Nick would whine like a whipped puppy dog feeling ashamed of itself, "I figured maybe you'd ride into town with me and help me win the money back."

"You figured wrong!" Pa would answer, and that would be the end of it. Uncle Nick wouldn't say much for a day or two, and would try to work harder at the mine. But then he'd just go out and do something foolish again a little while later, and they'd have the same argument, but over something different.

I can remember two conversations I heard, one the previous May and the other more recently, that really showed me how much Pa'd changed. The first was a conversation with Mrs. Parrish and Rev. Rutledge one Sunday after Pa'd taken us in for the little service in Mrs. Parrish's house.

As we were getting into the wagon to head back home, while Pa was tightening a strap on one of the horses' necks, Mrs. Parrish and Rev. Rutledge came up to him.

"Could we have a few words with you, Mr. Hollister?" said the minister.

Pa turned to face them, gave a nod, and continued fiddling with the strap.

"Mrs. Parrish and I have been thinking a great deal about your children and their future," Rev. Rutledge began. Pa shot him a quick glance, and I think the minister figured Pa was going to light into him like he had that day of the Christmas dinner. But before anything else was said, Mrs. Parrish jumped in.

"It isn't what you may think, Mr. Hollister," she said quickly. "Actually, Rev. Rutledge and I've been commenting on what an admirable job we think you are doing with your family. We think it's a fine thing you're doing, and both of us are proud of you. We consider you a real example to some of the other men of the community."

Pa didn't exactly seem comfortable with the compliment, but it did settle down the irritation that seemed ready to rise up. He just nodded and said, "I'm obliged to you for thinking so."

"We really mean it, Mr. Hollister," added the minister. "And with more men like you, and women too — you know, family folks — coming to the area, we've been thinking that we should be giving more attention to the future of our young people. The church is going to be up before you know it, with facilities for a school during the week, and we think it's high time something was done in the way of preparing ourselves for the changing times that are coming. We'll need books and desks and paper and supplies. It'll take a fair sum of money to outfit a new school."

He paused, and Pa, thinking they were finally getting around to the point of what was on their minds — that is, asking him for money — started to reply.

"Well, I'm as much in favor of educating my young'uns as the next man. You can count on me to give my share. As long as our mine's producing, I don't mind contributing what I can. Tad's the one that found the gold, and if he's gonna be schooled, then I figure —"

Mrs. Parrish interrupted him with a laugh.

"You misunderstand us, Mr. Hollister! We didn't come asking for your money, although the time for that may come later."

Pa stared back at her with a confused expression.

"We think you're doing such a fine job with your children, and being one that the men of this community look up to, we wanted to ask if you'd be on the committee to help get the Miracle Springs school organized, and to help us locate a teacher."

"Me? A committee? Why, I don't know nothing about such things, and I ain't —"

"You don't have to *know* anything special, Mr. Hollister," she went on. "You're a man of character, and whether you like to admit it or not, you're one of this community's leaders. You have children who will be directly involved in the outcome of whatever decisions the committee makes, and we think you are a logical choice and would do a fine job."

Everything was silent for a moment.

Sitting in the wagon, we were hanging on every word, as still as a robin listening for a worm under his feet. Rev. Rutledge and Mrs. Parrish had said what they had to say, and Pa just stood there, his right hand hanging over the horse's neck, staring off in the distance as if he was still shocked by their request but was thinking it over real seriously at the same time. The silence only lasted a minute.

Then all of a sudden he turned his head back toward them. He had a look on his face I can't even start to describe. I'd never seen quite the same expression from him before, though as I thought about it later I realized it was that look on his face that showed me Pa was changing. It was such a different expression than what I'd seen that first day we got to Miracle Springs and he came walking out of the saloon.

"I'm right honored that you'd ask me," Pa said. "And I figure I owe it to the kids . . . so I'll do it."

He turned toward the wagon, jumped up onto the seat, flicked the reins and gave a click with his tongue, and with nothing more than a "Good day to you both," we were suddenly on our way back home. I turned around to wave to Mrs. Parrish. She had a smile on her face, but she wasn't looking in my direction. She was smiling at Rev. Rutledge.

After that a committee was formed, and besides Pa and Mrs. Parrish and the minister, there was Mrs. Shaw who lived nearby, and Mr. and Mrs. Dewater from over on the other side of the valley. They met a few times and started sending out notices advertising the need for a teacher in Miracle Springs. And Mrs. Parrish, from her business contacts in some of the nearby cities, got information about desks and blackboards and schoolbooks.

The kids were all excited because there was even talk of the school starting up this year, as soon as the church was finished, and getting to go to school again and see other kids every day was just about all the younger three could think about. I was getting a mite old for school, though I still thought some about being a teacher when I grew up. And Zack didn't say much.

But being on the committee wasn't the only change. The way Pa helped with the building of the church and school showed me, too, that he was determined to be different than he had been for so long, that he wanted to be the family man Ma had known him to be. I'm sure he remembered that argument he and Rev. Rutledge had had last Christmas when they'd got to talking about the building of a church. Pa'd gotten mad when the minister started saying Pa was a fine Christian man who he was sure would help support a new church. But in spite of their differences, all through the summer Pa *did* help, probably more than any other man besides the minister.

The second conversation that showed how much Pa was changing happened about two weeks before the dedication of the new church and school building. Pa and Uncle Nick were just cleaning up from a day's work at the mine, and I was fixing to put supper on the table for them. All the rest of the kids were still outside. It had been a beautiful fall day and none of them were anxious to stop their playing and come inside. Maybe the sounds of them laughing and yelling outside, and me keeping quiet toward the kitchen end of the cabin made Pa and Uncle Nick forget I was there. I'd never heard them talk quite like this before, though from their words I gathered it wasn't their first time.

"Ya wanna come into town with me tonight, Drum?" Uncle Nick said while he washed his hands in the big porcelain bowl.

"Don't think so, Nick."

"Why not? We'll quit plenty early."

"No, it's not the time. I just don't want to go, that's all."

"Why not?" insisted Uncle Nick. "You got other plans?"

"Nope."

"Then what's so blamed important to keep you here? There's a big game tonight. What're you gonna do at home?"

"I don't know. Read, fix that loose hinge on the door."

"Read? Tarnation —"

"Maybe read to the kids some."

"What in blazes has got into you, Drum?" exclaimed Uncle Nick.

"How many times I gotta tell you, Nick?" said Pa, his voice finally starting to rise a little. "Things are different now."

"Aw, come on! You ain't no fun no more! Why, back in the old days, you —"

"This ain't the old days, Nick!" interrupted Pa, and he almost shouted the words. I wished I could slip out of the room, but I couldn't help wanting to hear the rest of it too. "I rode with you, and we did lots of things. I tried to do some good, and I reckon I did a heap of things that wasn't so good. But the whole time I was ashamed of leaving Aggie, and so now maybe I got the chance to make a little of it up to her by being a better Pa to her kids than I was when I was trying to take care of you! I ain't your riding partner no more, Nick! What do I gotta do to get that through your thick head? I may be your partner in running this mine. But other'n that I'm the husband of your sister, and these are my kids, and I aim to do the best for 'em I can, though Lord knows there ain't much a man like me can do all by himself."

He stopped and took a breath, and Uncle Nick, like he always did when Pa got after him, got quiet and looked down at the floor.

"So I ain't going to town with ya! You can throw away your hard-earned gold, but not me! I gotta think of these kids' future. And if I wanna read to my own kids, then you can keep your thoughts on the matter to yourself!"

Uncle Nick sort of slunk toward the door and went outside. About five minutes later I heard his horse coming out of the barn. Pa ran outside.

"Where you goin'?" he called out.

"I don't know, maybe down to Barton's."

"No you ain't, Nick! You stay away from Dutch Flat! Them's a bad bunch down there and I half suspect Jed o' knowin' more about us than I like. You keep away from 'em, you hear!"

"You think ye're my ma now too?" Uncle Nick shot back.

"You just keep clear o' those varmits, that's all," said Pa, and came back into the house. A minute or two later we heard Uncle Nick's horse gallop away toward town, and none of us saw him again for five days. Supper that night was quieter than usual, and Tad asking Pa every three minutes where Uncle Nick was didn't help Pa

29

feel any better about yelling at him. Whenever Uncle Nick went and did something foolish like that I think Pa blamed himself.

But however Pa felt, it made me warm inside to think of Pa's words, and how much he cared about us as a family. And as I thought about it over the next two weeks I began to think that maybe all the change wasn't in Pa after all. I recalled Ma's words when she said he was a good husband and father, and that she couldn't have asked for any better. What I got to thinking was that maybe I was just starting to see some of what Ma had seen all along. Maybe this was how Pa had always been deep inside, or at least had wanted to be.

Whatever it was, it sure pleased me to think that he'd rather stay home and be with us than go into town for a night of poker with Uncle Nick. So when I heard those words, "You men with tender hearts," I immediately thought of Pa. More and more I was seeing how good a description of him that was.

The next words Mr. Peters read made me think of Pa too, but in a different way. "Forgive others, you who must bear sorrow and pain." There was hurt in Pa's life. He had allowed me to share a little of it with him, though now that I'm older I understand more than I was able to then. A lot of wrong had been done, and he'd suffered and had to bear pain and sorrow for long years. And there were a lot of people Pa knew he had to try to forgive before the hurts from the past would go away — the bad men of that gang, probably Uncle Nick, and old Grandpa Belle, who never thought of him as anything but a low influence on his daughter.

Most of all, I reckon, Pa had to learn to forgive himself. That was the hardest thing, especially with Ma dead and Pa feeling like he had done her such wrong never to come back to us. That's why he wanted to be a good pa, so maybe it all had a way of coming together for good. I'm not sure I understand all of what he was going through because fathers are harder to really know than mothers. But I did know that Pa was trying hard to get rid of his past, and I loved him for it.

More than that, I just loved him for the man he was. He really was a man of tender heart! Whatever the men in town might have thought, and however much Mrs. Parrish might have preferred a religious man like Rev. Rutledge to an uneducated, hard-working man like Pa; however much Grandpa Belle may have thought he shouldn't have married Ma, as we sat there that day in September hearing those words in the new Miracle Springs church building, I couldn't think of anything I was more thankful for than my Pa sitting beside me. *He's* the one I would thank God and say *Allelulia* for!

CHAPTER 3

THE DEDICATION . . . LOOKING FORWARD

"My friends of Miracle Springs . . ." Rev. Rutledge was saying, and I glanced up in surprise to see that Mr. Peters had finished and was just settling back into his seat. "My friends, this is indeed a great day for all of us! This is far more than the dedication of a new building. Of course, I would not downplay the importance of what a new church can mean to a community, nor what having a school building right here in our town will mean to the future of our young people. But this is more than the dedication of a building to these noble and worthy ends, for we stand embarking on a new era. . . ."

I know I was distracting Pa, and I hoped Rev. Rutledge didn't see me, but I had brought paper and a pencil with me, and I was trying to write down some of what the minister said. I knew this was a big day for Miracle, and I wanted to be able to put as much in my journal about it as I could. Pa didn't cotton to the idea of my writing so much, though by then he was starting to get used to it.

Rev. Rutledge was still talking ". . . it's a

time, my friends and neighbors, when many communities around this expanding nation, communities like our own, are growing, a time when
families are putting down roots. The pioneering
days of uncertainty and lawlessness are drawing
to a close. The statehood of our great California
symbolizes the westward reach from shore to
shore of a destiny that surely can be seen as in
the Almighty's plan to tame this land and make
it fruitful and prosperous among the nations of
the world.

"And part of that destiny is surely the estab-
lishment of churches throughout the land, and
the education of our young people with schooling.
Therefore, I count it a privilege and a blessing
to stand here today, as one of God's represen-
tatives, in this building erected with the toil and
sweat and the hard-earned money of a good number of you men, and to take my share along with
you in dedicating it to God's purposes, and to
the future generations of Miracle Springs. . . ."

As he spoke, I thought about how much Rev.
Rutledge also had changed in the months since
he came. That first day he spoke to the townsfolk
in the saloon, he seemed none too sure of himself.
After yelling out his first sermon, even us kids
could tell he was more than just a little nervous
when the men started to rile him. And afterward
he left the building like a dog with his tail between
his legs.

But he'd gradually improved since then, and
tried to say things so folks could understand them

better. He still sometimes talked with a lot of religious words, and Mrs. Parrish had a way of saying things I could grab onto better, but I was getting so I could follow him easier than before. As I watched him today, speaking out with confidence and all the folks listening to him, I realized that he'd become a part of the community too. Men like Pa might not have thought of him as a friend exactly, and everybody wasn't in favor of a church building coming to town, but I guess they were used to the minister enough to tolerate his staying around. Most of the grumbling about "too much civilization" had nearly ended by the day of the picnic. Even the men who were set against it at first managed to have a happy time too.

I glanced up and realized I'd been daydreaming again.

"So I thank you personally for your support of this building project," Rev. Rutledge was saying. "Men of stout heart and vigor have given a great deal to this school and church, and you can all be proud of them — men like Mr. Hollister there —" Pa squirmed a little as he said it — "And Mr. Shaw and Mr. Timmons, and so many others of you. And not just the men, but you women too, with food and drink and encouragement — and some of you even drove a few nails!

"But in addition to the construction of this church, I owe you thanks for the support you have given me as your minister. When I came to Miracle Springs last November there were a good many of you unsure whether you wanted a parson in your midst! And I must admit to being disheartened at times along the way. But owing to the encouragement of the faithful among you, I think we have managed to become accustomed to one another, and can now begin to move forward, growing together spiritually."

I knew he meant Mrs. Parrish. She had been his only friend for the first several months, and even now was the only person in Miracle Springs who was with him very often. Some of the other folks would have him over to their place for a Sunday dinner, but you'd see Mrs. Parrish and him together during the week, and it seemed like every time I went to visit her, he was either coming or going or staying for supper. Folks more-or-less figured that someday they'd get married. I guess I figured that too, because Mrs. Parrish had wanted him to come to Miracle so bad and had seemed more than just a little partial to him since then.

And Rev. Rutledge was softer-spoken now on account of being around Mrs. Parrish so much. He didn't preach about hell hardly ever anymore, and he seemed glad to have some of the rowdy men come to meetings on Sunday even if he knew they'd be drinking and fighting again later in the week. So it seemed Mrs. Parrish was taming Rev. Rutledge, and I suppose that's part of what a woman's supposed to do when she marries a man.

I could see why he'd admire her, for Mrs. Parrish was a fine lady. She was always thinking of others and trying to do what she could to help them. I knew how much she'd done for me in just a year. Even as I scribbled down what I could of what the minister was saying, my mind went back to that day a few months earlier when she'd come back from Sacramento. She rode all the way out to the cabin to see us, and when she got me alone for a moment she handed me a little package, wrapped up in pretty blue paper.

"Open it," she'd said as I stared back at her, not exactly knowing what to think.

I untied the ribbon, then slipped my finger through the edge of the paper and unfolded it. Inside was a gorgeous little book with green and orange flowers designed on a cloth cover, bound together by a tan leather spine.

"What *is* it?" I asked. "It's beautiful!"

"Open the pages," she said, smiling so big she could hardly contain it. I opened the book right in the middle and found nothing but blank pages staring back at me. I flipped all through it and there wasn't a single word anywhere.

I must have looked puzzled because she started laughing.

"It's for your journal, Corrie," she said. "I had it specially bound for you in Sacramento."

"But it's . . . it's — it's just like a book!" I exclaimed in disbelief.

"It *is* a book. Real book pages, bound in calf-leather. I had it made at a bindery."

"Oh, Mrs. Parrish!" I said. "I don't know what

to say! How can I ever thank you?"

"I thought it was high time you graduated from that tablet I got for you last Christmas. But look inside the front cover!"

I did so. There, embossed in gold, just like it was the title of a book, were the words — *The Journal of Corrie Belle Hollister*.

I treasured that volume, carrying it with me wherever I went for the next two weeks, being extra careful over everything I wrote in it, trying to make it as neat as I could so the inside would look as good as the outside. Pa was probably right about me being a mite fanatical, and when Mrs. Parrish gave me the book, it only made me think about writing things down all the more.

So I could see easily enough why Rev. Rutledge would be taken with Mrs. Parrish, and would want to say his thanks to her, even though he didn't do it in so many words. For the way I figured it, that church building was as much *her* doing as it was Pa's or the minister's or anybody else's. If it hadn't been for her, there wouldn't have been a Rev. Rutledge in Miracle, and no church built either.

As I'd been thinking about him and Mrs. Parrish, the minister had gone right on talking.

"So let us be hopeful as we move into the future together — hopeful that blessings will come as a result of this building we have built. Let us now join our hearts together in prayer to the God who has given us strength to accomplish this task in His name."

He paused, and throughout the small building everyone bowed their heads.

"Almighty God, we thank thee for blessings thou abundantly bestowest on us thy servants and children. And now, our Lord and our God, we dedicate this building to thy service and thy glory. May we be ever mindful of thee when we enter herein, and may this church be a light to the lost and weary of the world. We pray, too, that the school which will also utilize this building will be a beacon for the light of truth for every child who comes here to learn. Let those of this community support both this church and this school with our time and our resources and our energies for the ongoing work. May both the church and the school of Miracle Springs grow to influence this town and this community for good and for thy glory. In the name of the Father, and the Son, and the Holy Ghost we pray. Amen."

CHAPTER 4

THE TOWN PICNIC

As we rose from our seats and walked outside, everyone had a smile on his face. It was such a good feeling to see the whole town friendly and together. For once there were no bickerings or disputes or differences. Even the saloons had agreed to close down for the whole day. Of course, not everyone was in church, but many were, and I figured there'd be a lot more at the picnic.

As we made our way to the door in the slowly moving crowd, folks were talking and laughing and visiting. Pa came behind us, chatting a bit with Doc Wiley. Up by the door Rev. Rutledge was shaking people's hands as they left the church, and I could see that Mrs. Parrish had joined him and was on the other side of the door doing the same. I found myself wondering if she hadn't wanted to be a minister's wife instead of a business woman — she looked like she enjoyed it. I steered the kids in her direction.

"Well hello, Tad!" she said as we reached her. "Becky, how are you today? And Emily — how bright you look in that pretty dress! Zack, it's nice to see you," she said, giving Zack a firm handshake. Then she turned to me. "Oh, Corrie," she said, giving me a hug, "isn't this a great day? We've waited for it so long!"

I can't even recollect what I said — it must not have been anything too important. There was a lot of noise and folks were pressing all around us. And the other four kids were already out the door and running off yelling like dogs that had been cooped up in a shed for two days.

"I have something I must talk with you about later," Mrs. Parrish said softly into my ear, ". . . maybe during the picnic." Then louder to Pa as he came up behind me, she added, "Perhaps your family can join Avery and me this afternoon."

I glanced back hopefully at Pa, but he just gave her one of his in-between sort of looks and answered, "We'll see, ma'am." Before anything else could be said, we were out the door and Mrs. Parrish was greeting the people behind us.

The town picnic! The images of that day stood out in my mind so clearly I could hardly go to sleep that night. It wasn't so much that any single thing happened. It was more the *picture* of the whole day — the sounds, the faces, the food, the kids all running about, the fiddle music and dancing, and most of all the togetherness of the townsfolk. It was one of those rare moments when people put aside their differences and came together in friendship, as a community instead of a bunch of separate parts squabbling about things that didn't even matter.

I couldn't get out of my mind the picture of

Pa and Mr. Royce, the banker, shaking hands, or Rev. Rutledge helping one of the saloon ladies to her seat. The looks on the faces — most of all, the smiles and laughter — were so vivid! I didn't want to ever forget that people *could* be this way to each other. I wanted to remember every detail of the day — every face, every sound, every bit of laughter, every smell, every taste.

Sometime around two o'clock in the afternoon, I went off by myself for a spell. I walked up the sloping hillside east of the grassy meadow next to the church building. I must have walked five or ten minutes, while the shouts and sounds behind me were gradually growing fainter in the distance. Finally I sat down next to the big trunk of a gnarled old oak tree and turned around to look back.

It was just like I'd hoped it would be! There was the church, white and shining in the sunlight, off to the left. Then all over the meadow below me were the townsfolk, in big clusters and little clusters, men talking, kids running about playing games or chasing a dog or each other. Two long rows of tables had been put up with boards where the ladies were spreading out enough food to feed an army. We were supposed to start eating in about an hour, which was just enough time for what I wanted to do.

I opened up my satchel and pulled out a big sheet of drawing paper and my drawing pencil. Once Mrs. Parrish found out I liked to draw as well as write, she got me some sheets of extra big paper, and now I spread one out in front of me, trying to capture the picture of the picnic. I'd be able to write about the day in my journal later. But to make a memory I could see — that was something I had to do right then!

I started with the church building. I guess that was the natural place to start, because that's what the picnic was about in the first place. Then I drew in some trees, a few of the town buildings in the distance, the tables with the food on them. And then it was time to start trying to fill in the people.

I couldn't help noticing Mr. Alkali Jones first of all. Even way up where I was sitting I could hear the high cackle of his voice, although I couldn't make out what he was saying to Patrick Shaw. He was probably giving him some kind of advice on how Mr. Shaw could get more gold out of his mine. The Shaw claim ran over the hill right next to ours, but up till now Mr. Shaw hadn't found nearly the rich vein folks thought he should have from the way Pa and Uncle Nick's vein ran. Mrs. Shaw was over by one of the tables cutting up a turkey she'd roasted, and her two children, Sarah and Josiah, were nearby with Tad and Becky, throwing a stick out for Marcus Weber's dog Mutt to fetch. I didn't see Zack right then. Emily was sitting down in the grass a ways off with Amanda Jenson, who was a couple of years older than Emily. Marcus Weber was just driving up with one of Mrs. Parrish's wagons. I guess his dog had jumped down off the back early and had come running and barking to join the fun. The wagon Mr. Weber was pulling was empty, and he drew it to a stop at the far end of the meadow, away from the tables, and proceeded to unhitch the horses.

Pa was with a group of men talking. I could see Mr. Dewater, Doc, Mr. MacDougall, and Mr. Larsen. They were probably talking about mining. Just then Uncle Nick walked up. He hadn't been at church and was just now arriving. Mr. Larsen gave him a big slap on the shoulder, and whatever Uncle Nick said in reply must have been funny, because I could hear the laughter that burst out from the men all the way up where I was.

Mrs. Parrish was carrying a ham over to the table from her basket. I couldn't see the honey dripping from it or the pieces of clove stuck into the sides, but she'd told me how she baked hams. I could practically smell it.

A little ways off to one side three or four men carried a big chest of ice they'd brought from the icehouse, then set it down with a heavy thud. A little dog cart sat nearby with four big milk cans standing in it. I knew they'd been brought by Mr. Peters, who didn't care about gold nearly as much as he did about his dairy cows. In the short time since he'd immigrated from Germany, his farm had come to supply folks thereabouts with nearly all their milk and cheese, and he'd brought thick cream today for the ice-cream freezers later in the day.

All around the meadow were other folks. There

must have been two hundred altogether, maybe three hundred. Most of them were standing around, a few sitting on the grass or leaning against trees. There weren't many chairs, not even enough for the ladies with dresses, though I saw Mr. Bosely and Sheriff Rafferty carrying a few chairs Mr. Bosely'd brought from the back room of his store. Some other men were setting long planks of wood on chair-height wood chunks for benches.

Even Mr. Singleton showed up for the day. His *California Gazette* paper had started up as sure as he promised, although he never got around to doing all the stories he talked about at first. He was mighty interested in the new strike at Pa and Uncle Nick's mine, and when I went to talk to him about writing something for his paper, at first his eyes lit up as though he liked the idea. But when I told him Pa wouldn't let anything get printed that used any of our names, his interest fell mighty fast. I tried to write something for him too, but when I showed it to him, he just handed it back to me and said, "Well, we'll just have to see." He was nice enough, but I could tell he didn't like it much and I was too embarrassed to try again anytime soon.

Mr. Singleton went out to talk to Pa a time or two about letting him write the story, but Pa was firm with him that he wouldn't let a word be said about *us*. And that pretty much doused Mr. Singleton's enthusiasm for it, because by then there were other men finding gold all

44

around and he had plenty to keep him busy.

By summertime (the summer of 1853), Mr. Singleton was printing his paper every week. But he was printing it in Sacramento, so it didn't really turn out to be a Miracle Springs newspaper after all. It was the *California Gazette* of Marysville, Oroville, and Miracle Springs. Most of the news seemed to have to do with the other towns, and the paper didn't get to Miracle until two days after it was printed. Besides that, Mr. Singleton set up the office for the paper down in Marysville.

So by the time the paper was established, folks in Miracle Springs figured they'd had a big celebration for Mr. Singleton the year before for nothing, and some of them were downright perturbed at him. Most of the articles and advertisements were for the other towns too, though Mrs. Parrish would put in a notice about her freight service every month or so.

I kept secretly hoping someday I'd get a chance to see my name in the *Gazette* no matter where it was printed and no matter what anyone around Miracle may have thought of its owner!

My sketch was about as full as I had time to make it. The hour had gone by quickly, and I could hear the bell down below signalling dinnertime.

CHAPTER 5

MIRACLE'S SURPRISE GUEST

About an hour later — after most folks were done with their fried chicken and baked ham and turkey and rolls and all the other stuff that had been brought, and the kids were off yelling and romping again, and most of the men were standing around with tins of coffee in their hands — we heard horses coming through town.

At first the sound was just in the background. As it came closer and closer, folks started turning their heads to look. The horses and riders were coming right toward us, and everybody got up and started making their way in the direction of town.

I didn't recognize the name *Grant* at first, though after I thought about it, I did seem to remember hearing it someplace before that day. But at the time it was just a name, nothing more. My first reaction to the man leading the small procession of soldiers wasn't on account of recognizing his name, but because of the look and bearing of the man himself.

He sat up tall and straight on his horse, a rugged, almost stern man with a short sandy beard. Wide-eyed sixteen-year-old girl that I was, I was impressed. I didn't exactly fall in love, but I sure stared a lot. Then he got down off his horse and began shaking hands with the men, and there was lots of talking and laughing. The women hung back and the kids just gawked.

Most of us had never seen men in uniform before. The bright blue shirts and trousers, with yellow stripes down the side, and their yellow scarves and big wide hats — it was a sight to remember! I was already starting to think I should make another sketch of that picnic day to include the army riders and their horses!

Then the handbell started ringing again. I looked around and saw Sheriff Rafferty swinging it, trying to quiet everyone down. When he finally had folks' attention, he shouted out so he could be heard.

"This here's our special guest!" he called out loudly. "My friend, Captain Ulysses Grant! I'm sure most of you men heard of him from the fracas with Mexico a few years back, where he and I served together."

A few cheers went up, followed by everyone clapping their hands in welcome.

"Well, Captain Grant wanted to see some of the gold fields in California, and I invited him up here to see ours."

More applause and shouts.

". . . so after a bit we'll all gather round and listen to what Captain Grant might have to say to us!"

The noise and hubbub broke out again. The

captain and the eight or ten soldiers with him got down and tied up their horses. Several of the women went over and invited them to sit down and eat, and that didn't take much persuasion! For the next thirty minutes the whole sound of the picnic changed. The high-pitched shouts of small children running and playing were gone. Now the kids were standing around just watching the men talk. I was real curious, but I didn't dare get too close. I could see Pa in the center of the crowd, and once or twice I saw him talking to Mr. Grant himself.

A while later everyone started moving toward the edge of the meadow. The sheriff jumped up onto the back of the wagon Mr. Weber had brought, then Captain Grant joined him, and all the folks gathered around in front of the wagon and sat down on the grass.

"Well, folks," the sheriff said, "the captain's just been promoted from being a lieutenant in the Mexican campaign, and he's now on his way to a new duty up north of here."

He turned and spoke to Grant for a minute, then faced us again.

"He's going with the 4th United States Infantry to be stationed up overlooking Humboldt Bay. That's where he's headed. But now I'm going to let him tell you what it's like being a genuine army hero!"

Some cheers went up while Sheriff Rafferty stood back and Captain Grant took his place.

"I ain't much at speechmaking," he said, "and

I ain't going to get up here and pretend to be a politician! And if Simon here hadn't saved my life once down in Mexico, I wouldn't have agreed to do this at all. But I would like to visit some of your mines and like I said, I owe your sheriff my life, so here I am!"

He was a shorter man than I'd figured from seeing him on his horse, three or four inches shorter than Pa, who was six feet. But he was so stout and rugged that he seemed big. His nose was large and straight, his eyes firm and steady.

"What's up north that they need an important man like you?" shouted out Uncle Nick. "I ain't heard of no gold up there."

"No gold," he answered, "just Indians. There's a lot of trees up there as good as gold, some folks think. So they built a fort to protect this little lumber port town, and I guess they figure I'll be able to keep the Indians from burning it down."

The talk and the questions went on for a while, mostly settling around the captain reminiscing about the Mexican War during '46 and '47. After a while I wasn't paying much attention to the words anymore. I heard them off in the background but wasn't focusing on what they were saying. Instead, I was trying to sketch the scene on my paper.

On one side of it I tried to draw the captain and his men as they had ridden up on horseback. I'd practiced a lot on horses, and could draw a decent one. But a group of eight or ten, with

49

men on them, with people gathering around as they came, was harder. It wasn't much good as a drawing, but at least it would remind me what the scene had looked like when I wanted to remember it. Then on the other side of my paper, I drew Mrs. Parrish's wagon with the sheriff and the captain on it, talking to everyone sitting around on the grass.

Well, the day went on, the speeches, music and ice cream ended, and we didn't get back to the cabin until nearly dark. The three younger ones were sound asleep in the back of the wagon even before we got there, because it had been a long, long day. I was wide awake though, and lay in my bed later for two more hours with my eyes open, thinking about lots of things, none of which was going to sleep! Mrs. Parrish had had her talk with me later in the day, as she'd promised at church, and I was so excited I could think of nothing else.

But before I say what she asked me, I want to tell what happened to the sketch I'd made. I showed it to Mrs. Parrish a few days after the picnic.

I knew it wasn't a great picture. But when she saw it she got all in a dither over it. I figured she was just trying to make me feel good. But then she asked if she could put it up on the board outside her office, for the men to see who hadn't been to the picnic or those from out in the hills who hadn't heard about Captain Grant's visit.

"And, Corrie," she said, "why don't you write something brief on the bottom of it. Just explaining the picture, you know. You have such pretty writing. It'll make it all the nicer."

Well, if Mrs. Parrish was trying to make me feel good, she sure was doing a good job of it! Who can turn away a nice compliment like that? I tried to act nonchalant about it, but inside I was happy that she liked my picture.

I asked her if I could borrow Mr. Ashton's desk for a minute, seeing as he wasn't there, and a pencil. She cleared a place for me, and then I sat down.

I wrote on the bottom of my drawing:

On September 17, at approximately 3:30 in the afternoon, the mining town of Miracle Springs, California, was honored by a visit from United States Army Captain Ulysses Grant, shown here on his horse with his men. The visit took place during the town picnic in honor of the newly completed church and school building. Captain Grant spoke for a while to the people in attendance, also shown in this picture. The Captain was on his way to his new duty at Fort Humboldt, at the northern California lumber town of Eureka.

I couldn't help adding at the bottom of that, but in smaller letters: *Picture by Cornelia Belle Hollister*.

It was sure no photograph. But we didn't have

photograph machines in Miracle like they did in Sacramento. Mrs. Parrish liked it all the same, and she marched outside with my picture and tacked it up with a hammer right then for the whole town to see.

Mr. Singleton saw it the next time he was in town and asked Mrs. Parrish who wrote the brief article on the Grant visit. I laughed when she told me about it — him calling it an "article"! And I do have to admit that he treated me a little more like a grown-up next time we talked about my working on something for his paper.

For the time being, about all that came of it was that every once in a while Mrs. Parrish'd ask me to draw something for her board — sometimes just for fun, sometimes showing the men some new mining contraption she had for them to buy. And always she'd ask me to write something to go along with the picture.

Pretty soon the writing part of it got to be more than the drawing part. She'd ask me to just write up a notice about such and such a thing for the board, with no picture. And by the time she thought about printing up a little flyer about her company, well I guess I was the natural one she thought about to do most of the writing for it, even though she told me what to say.

So as it turned out, my first chance to see my words in a real newspaper was in an advertisement for the Parrish Mining and Freight Company. And by the time Mr. Singleton and I talked again about real article-writing, he'd gotten used to my being someone who could write a little, even if up until then it had just been little advertisements.

Captain Grant, I read later in one of the San Francisco papers, hated the cold and wind and rain and fog at Fort Humboldt so much that he got despondent, and some folks said he started drinking real bad. The *Alta* article in 1854 ended by saying, "Captain Ulysses Grant resigned at thirty-two years of age. He has now left the army, apparently for good, and returned to his family in Ohio."

Ever since his first visit to Miracle, whenever I saw news about Mr. Grant, I copied it down. And, of course, he didn't stay out of the army forever, but came back to become one of President Lincoln's generals in the Union army. But I didn't know that would happen when I read of his resignation in the *Alta* in 1854, and the news made me sad.

CHAPTER 6

THE ADVENTURE

Even though I'd lain awake in bed long after everyone else was asleep the night after the picnic, I was the first one up the next morning.

Pa was still snoring in the other room, all the kids were quiet and still, and it was just beginning to get light. I got out of bed quietly, dressed, and went outside. I was too keyed up even to think about staying inside! Mrs. Parrish's words of the previous afternoon had been ringing through my head all night.

The minute Pa came out of the cabin half an hour later, I ran toward him. I guess I didn't exactly use a subtle approach to get him to agree to what I was about to ask. I'm afraid I didn't even give him the chance to get to the outhouse!

"Pa, Pa, can I go to San Francisco with Mrs. Parrish?" I shouted, running up to him.

Poor Pa! I don't think he even knew I was out of bed!

He glanced up, bewildered. "What're you talking about, girl?" he said as he fiddled to straighten one of his suspenders.

"San Francisco, Pa! Mrs. Parrish asked me to go with her!"

54

"If that woman ain't always —" Pa muttered to himself. But then he stopped and said to me, "I don't know, Corrie. I ain't heard nothing about it till just this minute, and —"

"She asked me yesterday at the picnic, Pa, and —"

"Tarnation, girl! Hold on to your britches! Just gimme a minute to take care of myself!" As he was talking he hurried off toward the outhouse at the edge of the woods.

When he came back a few minutes later, he looked considerably more relaxed and ready to listen to me.

"Now, what's this all about, Corrie?"

"Mrs. Parrish has to go to San Francisco for some meeting or something, Pa. Some place where they show off new stuff for folks like her to buy to sell the miners."

"Something like a fair or exhibition?"

"I don't know, Pa. I reckon. But she asked *me* if I could go with her! Can I, please, Pa!"

I was trembling inside. I could hardly stand the thought of getting to see the great city and the Pacific Ocean! But Pa just stood there still for a minute thinking. He was such a kind man, and I loved him. But sometimes I couldn't help being just a little afraid too. This was one of those times, and I was so afraid I'd start crying or something if he said no.

"Well . . ." he finally said, although his tone showed he was still in the thinking stage and hadn't really made his mind up yet. "Well, I

55

reckon I don't see no reason why not, just so long as —"

"Oh, thank you, Pa!" I shouted, and gave him a big hug. "Thank you! I'll be real good, Pa, and you won't have to worry on account of me!"

And without realizing I hadn't even given him the chance to finish his sentence, I turned and ran off up toward the mine. I wasn't going anyplace in particular — I just had to run to get out all the excitement that was built up inside me.

Pa never did get a chance to tell me what he was going to say. I guess he figured he'd said enough to get the idea across that he wasn't going to oppose the idea. And he always stuck by his word.

I could hardly wait for the next two weeks to pass! Every moment, every hour was a torture. I couldn't think of anything but getting to go to San Francisco. For a girl who'd come all the way across the country, it might seem that the thought of visiting one more city wouldn't be so exciting. But San Francisco was different. Sitting right there on the Pacific Ocean, it was growing just about faster than any city in the country because of the gold rush.

And to get to stay in a hotel with Mrs. Parrish! Why, I'd never dreamed of such a thing! The other four kids were full of envy, but I reminded them that I was the oldest and that maybe when they were my age *I'd* take *them* to the city for a visit. That seemed to satisfy them, and no one really begrudged me in my enthusiasm.

Pa couldn't see what the fuss was about. He'd been to San Francisco, he said, and it wasn't so all-fired special. I asked him if he'd stayed in a fancy hotel, and he just laughed and said, "Not exactly." But he was glad I could go, and when we left gave me a kiss and a wink, and said, "Have fun, Corrie!" Then he said to Mrs. Parrish, "You keep her away from the docks!" with a serious voice, but as I looked at him I think he might have been joking.

Mrs. Parrish laughed real loud. "Don't you worry about a thing, Mr. Hollister," she said. "Corrie'll be with me the whole time!"

"Maybe *that's* what I'm worried about!" Pa answered back.

Mrs. Parrish laughed again, then flipped the reins, gave a "H'yaah!" to her two horses, and we were off!

Mrs. Parrish said Sacramento was about sixty miles — one day for a man on a horse, three or four days by mule or wagon train. She said we'd make it in two with the new surrey she'd just bought pulled by her two best horses. It was early in the day when we left, and we first returned to Miracle Springs to fetch Rev. Rutledge, who was riding with us as far as Grass Valley. Then we'd go on to Auburn where we'd spend the first night.

I sat in the back seat, but my hindquarters

didn't get sore like on the wagon coming out west last year; Mrs. Parrish's new surrey had padded black leather seats. The minister and Mrs. Parrish talked most of the morning about wanting to get churches started in Grass Valley and some of the other communities around the gold-mining region. I suppose I should have been interested, but my mind was filled instead with the week ahead of us.

Mrs. Parrish was quiet for the hour or so after he left us, but by mid-afternoon she was back to her old self and we were laughing and talking about all sorts of things. I imagined we'd have some serious talks too. We always did when I was with Mrs. Parrish, and I liked that. But that first day of my big adventure was mostly just fun, and when we got to Auburn I hardly even felt tired.

The next day wasn't quite so long, and we arrived in Sacramento before suppertime. We stayed at a boardinghouse where Mrs. Parrish knew the landlady. I was hoping I'd get to see Miss Baxter, who had been so kind to us all a year ago, so after supper Mrs. Parrish took me to see her.

"Why, Corrie Hollister!" exclaimed Miss Baxter after I reminded her who I was. "I'd have never known you! You done a heap of filling out in the year since you was here!"

"Have you seen Captain Dixon?" I asked. "Has he been back again?"

"He's due just next month — maybe even in

58

two weeks. Land sakes, wouldn't *he* enjoy seeing you!"

"Oh, I wish I could see him again!" I said. "There's so much I'd like to tell him about how we're getting on."

"Well, you'll just have to come back . . . and bring that parcel of sisters and brothers with you!"

"I'm afraid it might be a little farther out to Miracle Springs than you realize, Miss Baxter," put in Mrs. Parrish. "Nevertheless, perhaps you could have word sent to me when Captain Dixon does arrive. It might be that I can schedule a freight pick-up for that time." She wrote down something on a piece of paper and gave it to the landlady, and after a few minutes' conversation we left and went back to our boarding-house.

The next day was the most exciting day I'd ever had in my life!

Bright and early we took a horse-cab down to the river landing. There, waiting to take us down the Sacramento River was the most beautiful white steamer I could have imagined! Walking on board, I felt as if I were stepping into a fairy tale adventure! The deck was full of people waving and shouting and jostling about, but by the time the captain shouted "Cast off!" and his men below unhooked the big ropes, I was in a world of my own. Slowly we inched away from the dock, and gradually I could feel the swaying motion beneath my feet as the captain guided us out into the middle where the current began to take hold.

Beside me Mrs. Parrish was saying something about never getting over the thrill of being on the water and feeling the motion underneath her, but I hardly heard the words.

CHAPTER 7

THANKFULNESS FROM BEHIND THE CLOUDS

Floating down the Sacramento River, I got to thinking about the new church in Miracle Springs. I thought about the building of the church, and how much Pa had helped with it.

After Rev. Rutledge came to Miracle Springs, he held services of some kind every Sunday, usually at Mrs. Parrish's. When summer came, work got started on the new building that was going to be used both for a school and the church. By then there were enough new folks in town that it was crowded in her house. But that just made Rev. Rutledge and Mrs. Parrish all the more enthusiastic for the work that was going on at the building site.

And I think it gave them both a quiet kind of good feeling to see Pa and Uncle Nick helping with the new building more than all the other men, even though Uncle Nick might not have done it on his own, without Pa making him.

They provided lots of the lumber too. Pa said the Lord gave us that gold in the ground, and he figured he should give some of it back. So whenever they needed more boards, he'd hitch up the horses and go into Sacramento to buy a wagonload. And some of the big beams and timbers he cut right from trees on our own claim.

Pa still never said much out loud, but he was thinking about a lot of things, I could tell. I knew Rev. Rutledge was downright thankful for Pa's support with the church building, though the two of them still were formal to each other. I doubted they'd ever be friends, but at least they were able to work side by side without arguing. And probably it helped Pa in his impression of the Reverend to see him with his shirt off in the hot summer sun, sweating with the rest of the men, helping to hoist a beam into place or driving in the nails of the wall supports or climbing up on top of the roof to help steady one of the joists. I think he was a little surprised that Rev. Rutledge was such a hard worker, and it gave him more respect for him than he'd had when we first went to Mrs. Parrish's for dinner.

All through the summer months, the men of Miracle would get together two evenings a week and most of Saturdays to help with the church. By the middle of the summer it was looking like a real building.

Rev. Rutledge was excited about a place to hold church services, of course, but some of the other folks in the community — mothers of young children, mostly — were thinking of the uses for the place during the week. Mrs. Parrish organized a committee of seven people in Miracle to start looking for a teacher to come, and they wrote to papers in Sacramento and some of the other cities and towns around to advertise their need.

Mrs. Parrish was excited about helping civilize this rough and wild place, and gave more and more of her business affairs to Mr. Ashton to run while she spent as much of her time as possible on "community affairs," as she called them. Pa wasn't about to pack up and go someplace else, because the mine was doing well, but I couldn't help thinking he wasn't altogether in favor of the changes. At the same time, I know he was trying his best to put his past behind him and to be a good family man to us kids. So he helped with the church and was civil to Rev. Rutledge and downright friendly at times to Mrs. Parrish. Some of the folks around Miracle were beginning to look to Pa as one of the town's leaders — though Pa himself would have hated to hear me say such a thing!

"What does 'Alleluia' mean?" I asked Mrs. Parrish all at once.

"What makes you think of that as we're floating down the river Corrie?" she said, turning to me.

"Oh, I don't know," I answered. "I was thinking about the church getting built. That made me think of Easter day and that hymn we sang, you remember, *He Is Risen! Alleluia!* I've been wanting to ask you ever since. Then that song Mr. Peters read said *Alleluia* a lot too."

"Hmm," she said, "what would be a good way to explain it?" She thought for a minute, placing one of her slender fingers across her lips, between her chin and her nose like she always did when she was thinking real hard.

"You know how it is, Corrie," she finally went on, "when something is just so wonderful you want to tell everybody? Like a beautiful sunset, or some idea you've had, or maybe a precious possession — a favorite doll or a piece of fine jewelry?"

"Like Pa and Uncle Nick always talking about mining every chance they get?"

"Yes. That's the idea. And when you talk about something you treasure like that, when you can't say enough good about it, then you're *praising* it. That's what 'praise' is. And *Alleluia* is a word of praise — it's a way of saying that you think God is wonderful and loving and kind. The word means *Praise ye the Lord.*"

"I think I see."

"There is another side of it, Corrie," said Mrs. Parrish. "It's easy to give praise to God when you are *feeling* it inside. There are times when the sun is bright and you're happy inside, and you know God is out there making the world beautiful and keeping you safe in His hand. But there's even a better time to thank Him for being such a good and loving God. And that's when it's gloomy and cold and cloudy, and maybe you're sad, and you're *not* feeling like God's anywhere around at all."

"Why's that a *better* time?"

"Because that's when it takes *faith* to praise

64

God, to thank Him for being good, to tell Him 'Thank you,' for taking care of you and watching over you and loving you. It doesn't take any faith to do it when you're feeling it inside. But when your mind and heart try to tell you it's dreary and that life is sad and that maybe God doesn't care about you after all, that's when it takes faith to believe that He still is there just the same."

She paused, and then her face lit up. "Think about your father's and uncle's mine," she said. "It was the same mine two years ago, wasn't it? The same hillside, the same dirt. The gold was even there back then, wasn't it?"

I nodded.

"But your father and uncle didn't know it! To them it *looked* like a worthless, played-out mine, when really it was a wonderful mine full of gold."

"I see," I said, but I didn't really see what meaning she was intending. I guess she saw the confusion on my face despite my words.

"You see, Corrie, it doesn't take any *faith* now for folks to believe your father's mine has gold in it. Anyone can go up there and look and see it with his own two eyes. There doesn't need to be any faith, because you can *see* it! But two years ago, if someone had said, 'This mine has a rich vein of gold in it,' back *then* it would have taken faith to believe such a statement, because no one could *see* it."

"I understand that."

"It's the same with God! If the sun hides behind the clouds for a few days, we still know it's there.

But sometimes when God hides himself behind a cloud, we let ourselves start thinking He's gone, instead of using our *faith* to remind us He still *is* there, and is just as good and loving as always. That's why it's best to give God thanks when we don't feel especially thankful. That's how we learn not to trust our thoughts or feelings *about* God, but to trust in God himself. We can even trust Him when we can't see Him!"

"That seems hard," I said.

"I don't know why it should be harder than believing the sun is still in the sky even when we can't see it," she answered. Then a look of thoughtful sadness came over her face briefly. "But it *is* hard sometimes, Corrie, you're right. And it can be a very painful lesson, learning to say *Alleluia* to God in trying circumstances."

She said nothing more, and I looked out the window at the passing landscape again. One thing I was sure thankful for was Mrs. Parrish. She treated me like a grown-up and never seemed to mind my questions. I was learning so much about life and God from her.

"It won't be much longer now, Corrie," said Mrs. Parrish after a bit. "We'll be to Richmond in two or three hours. We'll stop there to take on some more passengers, and then it's across the bay to the great city!"

San Francisco! I could still hardly believe it! It's more than I would have dreamed or hoped for a year earlier, to see the big ocean that went all the way to China!

66

Mrs. Parrish then tried to explain to me about San Francisco Bay — she said it was shaped like a huge, tall, skinny ear — with towns and harbors all around it where ships came in, and with San Francisco itself sitting on a little piece of land on the other side. "It's the bay that makes it possible for the ships to come in to the city from the Pacific," she said, "but it also makes getting to and from the city kind of difficult if you're not coming by boat."

I couldn't really get a picture of it in my mind, but she said I'd understand when we reached the pier in Richmond and could look out across the bay to see the opening into the Pacific where the ships go through, and see San Francisco on the peninsula, she called it, just to the left.

We finally did get to Richmond in the early afternoon, where we docked for about an hour. But we couldn't see San Francisco at all. There was fog so thick we could hardly see the water in front of us, although I could hear it slapping up against the wood of the pier and the rocks on shore. And when we started moving out across the bay, going slowly through the fog, it was an eerie feeling.

The chilly fog was full of the smell of water and fish, and I could imagine we were sailing out to sea to unknown places. Even though Mrs. Parrish pointed to me through the fog to show me where San Francisco was on the other side, something in me wanted to make the adventure all the bigger by thinking that the captain of the boat might miss the city and go sailing out through "the gate," as they called the opening, right out into the Pacific!

It was cold standing out there on the deck in the fog, and after a while Mrs. Parrish said she wanted to go inside. But I didn't want to miss a thing, so I stayed outside by myself, leaning over the railing looking down into the water as the boat plowed a furrow through it, then glancing up again at the mists blowing about. Every once in a while a portion of something in the distance would appear, whether the shore or another boat I couldn't tell, and then would fade back into the depths of the white-gray cloud we were going through.

I was gazing again down into the water, deep green with white from the boat splashing through it, when suddenly off to our left the mist broke apart, and through the middle of it, as if I was looking through a tunnel of light, I saw the shore and the buildings of the city scattered about the hills of San Francisco.

I stared in wonder. It was like a vision from God, and as far as I could tell I was the only one who could see it, for all about the boat and the water the misty fog still swirled to and fro. But right at the place where I stood, a bright window through it looked in upon the city. It was there all the time, just where Mrs. Parrish had pointed. I thought immediately of the conversation we'd had earlier about the sun being behind the clouds even when you couldn't see it.

Then just as suddenly, as if God swept a giant curtain over the window He had opened briefly for me, the fog filled up the space again, and I couldn't see past the end of the boat's front. But still I stared, wondering if I had dreamed the whole sight.

I never forgot that moment. And sometimes when I can't see what's ahead, I remind myself of Mrs. Parrish pointing through the fog telling me where the city was, and think that maybe sometimes God's telling me the same thing, that He knows what's up ahead even though I can't see it, that He's steering the ship and knows where it's going. And I think that if I'm paying attention, maybe He'll give me a little sight through the fog to help me trust Him even when I can't see where He's taking me.

CHAPTER 8

SAN FRANCISCO!

There is no way to describe our three days in the great city of San Francisco! I wish I knew more of what Uncle Nick calls "them fifty-cent words." Maybe then I could give a better idea.

The fog seemed attracted to the water, because as soon as we got away from where our steamer landed, the sun started peeking through hole after hole. Before long, everything was shining in the bright afternoon sunlight.

We took a horsedrawn cab from the pier to the hotel, and on the way Mrs. Parrish pointed out many of the sights. She even had the cabman take a short detour up a steep hill so I could look down on the city from the top. She showed me where some of San Francisco's newspapers were, where the *Star* began on Clay Street, and down by the waterfront where the *California's* offices were located.

She pointed out a bookshop — "That's where I go whenever I'm here to see if I can find something for you," she said. "We'll visit it later" — and a dressmaker's shop, which she also said we'd visit.

Everywhere there was building going on. Mrs.

Parrish said San Francisco was growing faster than any city in the country. Although our hotel must have been half a mile or more up the hill, we could see and hear the workers all day long and half into the night working on the huge Montgomery Block. Mrs. Parrish said there had never been anything so big or so elegant built anywhere in California. It was four stories tall and the walls were three feet thick. It was so huge there were going to be offices in it, a big hotel, restaurants, saloons, and all sorts of places. Mrs. Parrish said when it was done it was sure to be the center of San Francisco's business and social life.

I had never seen so many Chinese people as I saw in San Francisco, come to help with the construction. The cab driver told us that hundreds of these Chinese men worked eighteen-hour days hauling big numbered blocks of granite for the new Parrott's bank building. I can hardly believe it myself, but he said every piece of granite came from China — along with the men to put them up — and they all had to go in a certain place. It was a four-story building too, but there were so many workmen it was done in just a few months.

Usually when she came to San Francisco, Mrs. Parrish said she stayed at a boardinghouse. But this was a special occasion, she said, and she intended to treat me first class. I wasn't prepared for all the sights that met my eyes when we pulled up in front and then went inside the Oriental Hotel, a fine new building on Hyde Street.

The foyer was carpeted in a rich red and black carpet. There was a chandelier overhead and velvet chairs and couches all around in the lobby. It was the kind of place I'd only imagined in cities like Paris, France!

A man in a red coat took our luggage right away. Mrs. Parrish spoke with the clerk at the front desk, while I just stood on that thick carpet and kept staring all about me, probably with my mouth hanging open and my eyes full of country-girl wonder!

"Must be your first time in the city," came a voice into the middle of my musing.

"What?" I said, looking around.

"First-timer, eh?" he said again. "I figured — I can always tell."

I saw a boy, around my own age, maybe a little older, standing looking at me. He wasn't much bigger than I was, and since he was slender, I couldn't really tell his age. He looked young, but he sounded so sure of himself and confident that he must have been seventeen or eighteen, though he only looked fifteen. His voice was high-pitched. His eyes were as blue as the night, and looked somewhat mischievous. He wore a dirty, gray hat that was tilted to the right. Out from under it stiff blond curls fell onto his forehead.

"Yes, it is," I answered, finally getting hold of my wits.

"Yeah, I knew it. Being in the newspaper business, you see, I got a nose for people." Now he was starting to sound cocky, and I had the feeling he was looking down on me. But then I noticed the bundle of newspapers he was carrying under his arm and thought maybe he deserved another chance.

"You work for a newspaper?" I said, probably a little too eagerly.

"That's right."

"What do you do? You're not a reporter . . . a writer?" I asked.

"I do whatever they tell me," he answered. "I'm what they call in the business a jack of all trades. So, yeah, I've done a little reporting in my time —" The superior slant of his mouth crept back. "You see, my editor, he knows that a fella like me, out on the streets, is likely to pick up better stories than them desk reporters."

"I'd like to write for a newspaper some day," I said.

"Where you from?"

"Miracle Springs."

His first response was a great laugh. "Boy, are you from the sticks! You ain't gonna do no newspaper writing there! Ha, ha, ha!"

"What do you mean?" I said back, my face getting red. "We have a newspaper there."

"You mean ol' Singleton's rag! Ha, ha! It ain't nothing but an advertising sheet — mining tools, mail-order brides, spent claims, and worn out jackasses! We cover *real* news stories here in the city. You must have just lit fresh from the overland trail! So, what are you doing in San Francisco?"

Even as he asked the question he was still smiling that patronizing smile of his, and I didn't
know whether to be hurt or mad.

"We're just — that is, I came with that lady
over there," I glanced to where Mrs. Parrish was
just finishing up with the clerk.

"Well, sounds to me like the two of you could
do with a guide while you're here, and I know
this city like the back of my hand. Robert T.
O'Flaridy is the name! And besides newspapering,
I offer my services to out-of-town young damsels
such as yourself to keep them out of distress!
My rates are most reasonable, and I —"

He was interrupted, just as Mrs. Parrish walked
up, by the desk clerk's irritated-sounding voice
calling out from behind the desk.

"Robin O'Flaridy, what are you doing accosting
my guests again!"

Robin — that fit him better than his fancy
"Robert T." — flashed a big grin, sheepish, but
with a dash of cunning in it too.

"Just trying to make a living, Mr. Barnes,"
he answered, throwing a wink in our direction.

"Well, your job is not to bother our people,
as I've told you fifty times, but to deliver those
newspapers. If you can't do that properly, you
may well lose that job, too!"

"Okay, okay!" He tipped his cap toward us.
"It was a pleasure meeting you ladies. Remember,
I'm the best guide in this city."

He deposited the bundle of papers on the desk
and made a hasty exit.

"I apologize for the annoyance, ma'am," the clerk said.

"No trouble at all, Mr. Barnes," replied Mrs. Parrish. "Perhaps if he is as good a guide as he says, we might consider engaging his services."

"Believe me, ma'am, the boy is all wind. All he does is deliver papers to a few of the large hotels in town, and he tells everyone he's a reporter."

"He *doesn't* write for the paper?" I said.

"*Write!* Did he tell you that? Ha, that's a good one! He's nothing but a confidence man in the making. No, ma'am, if you employed him as a guide, you'd have to chain your pocketbook to your arm. Nobody even knows where the boy lives. He's always on the streets looking for some likely target to fleece, and an hour or two a day he delivers papers and pretends to be the senior editor's right hand man! No, I've seen him mixing with some bad customers, and wouldn't want you associating with him."

"Well, I appreciate your candid advice, Mr. Barnes," said Mrs. Parrish. "But surely, the boy could be trusted. If you hire him —"

"I don't hire him, ma'am. If I had my way, I'd never see him setting foot in my lobby again. No, he's the newspaper's doing, and I'm stuck with him. But the paper isn't the only outfit he runs errands for, if you get my meaning," he added with a look of significance. "And like I say, some of the other types he hangs around aren't the sort a lady like you wants to have

75

anything to do with."

With plenty to think about, we followed the man with the red jacket up to our room. I didn't realize it, but I must have been so tuckered out that I fell asleep in my clothes almost the minute I lay down on the beautiful soft bed.

Mrs. Parrish had a short nap, too, but when I woke she was sitting at the dressing table fixing her hair. She suggested that if I felt rested enough, we get a little something to eat and then see more of the city. We still had most of the afternoon ahead of us, and her meetings didn't start until the next day. She didn't have to ask me twice! I jumped up and washed my face and was ready in a twinkling.

Mrs. Parrish hired us a carriage, but she didn't need a guide. She knew the city as well as any native, or any guide like that O'Flaridy boy said he was. First she took us up onto Telegraph Hill to see the windmill, and then clear across town to the point overlooking the "Gate," where we could see the Pacific and the opening of the bay on the other side. It was beautiful when the fog still clinging to the water would lift or part. It was pretty windy, though the sun was shining warm. What you could see of the water was so blue, just like the sky, and when the sun was just right, even the patches of fog swirling around here and there could be pretty. I thought San Francisco was about as grand a place for a city to sit as anywhere in the world!

Wherever we went in the city we saw different

sights — fancy business men, Chinese workmen, fishing boats of all sizes, and big ships from all over the world. On the waterfront I heard many strange languages being spoken. And of course, there were lots of saloons with rough-looking men coming in and out of them.

I guess it was what you would call "colorful," but Mrs. Parrish said that lots of terrible things happened around there. They even called one stretch of the waterfront the "Barbary Coast," after the pirate coast of North Africa. She said that there were bad men and women in those saloons and boardinghouses, and I have to admit I didn't like the looks of the ladies who came out of them, dressed in bright colors with painted faces and red lips, sometimes hanging on to men in fine clothes with ruffled lace shirts. Those men had a different look than the businessmen you saw around the Montgomery Building. And after our day's outing when she took me to see the city, I was glad when we got away from there.

Just as we were climbing into our cab, while Mrs. Parrish was telling the driver where to go, I glanced back for one last look at the waterfront, with its saloons and people and the fishing boats and bay behind it. My mind was on the whole panorama of blue sky, clouds, the pretty expanse of water, but my eyes fell instead on a figure just at that moment stumbling out of one of the buildings nearest to where we sat.

My mouth fell open in disbelief. It couldn't be! And just as quickly as I saw him, I turned my head away. Even if it was, I didn't want to see that face a second time. I *never* wanted to see it again!

I stared down at the floor of the cab, afraid to say anything to Mrs. Parrish. Yet, somehow I sensed that, drunk as he was, the man had seen my face too, and was even now walking uncertainly toward us.

What a relief when at last the cabman shouted to his horse and I felt the cab lurch into motion. I didn't look back. I never wanted to see the Barbary Coast again!

I kept quiet most of the way back to the hotel. I wanted to tell Mrs. Parrish, but something inside me couldn't. I was afraid, flooded by so many unpleasant memories so unexpectedly, and I just wanted to try to forget. By the time we got back to the hotel, we were talking again and I tried to put the incident behind me and out of my mind.

I'll never forget that evening as long as I live!

When we got back to the middle of the city, it was late in the afternoon and the wind coming in off the ocean was pretty chilly, but some shops were still open. Before we returned to the hotel, the carriage stopped in front of the dressmaker's shop Mrs. Parrish had pointed out earlier.

She told the cabman to wait, then took me inside and said she was going to buy me a new dress. After all she'd already done for me, I could hardly bear thinking of her doing even more!

But she insisted, and said, "Corrie, you have

to let me do this for myself, for the pleasure it will give *me!* I doubt I'm ever going to know the joy of having a daughter of my own, and you're just about the closest to one I'm likely to get."

As she spoke her eyes started to get big and shiny from the tears filling them, as she sometimes does when a conversation gets real personal, and I knew I couldn't argue with her. I couldn't help thinking about Rev. Rutledge, and I was about to say something about maybe her getting to have a daughter of her own after they were married. Whether she had an inkling of what I was thinking, I don't know, but before a word got out of my mouth, she put a finger softly to my lips to silence me.

"You're like a daughter to me in many ways, Corrie. I'm so thankful to God for you! Sometimes I think maybe it's even more special to have a friend like you I can think of as a daughter in the Lord, than to have a daughter of my own flesh. Because in you I'm always reminded of God's love and goodness and grace. Now, let's have some fun, and find you a bright, pretty new dress — and maybe even a bonnet to go with it!"

And it was fun! We stayed in that shop for an hour, Mrs. Parrish and the woman from the shop holding up dress after dress to me, draping them over my shoulders, having me look in the mirror and asking me what I thought. They made me feel so special that I might have cried if we hadn't been laughing and talking and enjoying ourselves so much. I must have tried on six or seven different dresses in all colors. I forgot all about the cab driver waiting outside and the time passing.

The dress we finally picked was the prettiest of all, mostly a light green. I wouldn't have chosen pink as a color to go with green. A couple of the other ones I tried on mixed yellow with green. But this particular dress had such light colors that the two blended in a way I just loved. It was made mostly out of polished cotton, with a full skirt in green. The skirt was loose and soft, but not so full that I had to wear hoops and petticoats underneath. It felt comfortable, like I could walk around free and easy. Above the waist, the bodice was pink, and a wide collar folded down over the pink all the way around, with a green piping around its edge. They called the sleeves leg of mutton sleeves, the full part from my shoulders down to just below my elbows made of the green, with the tight forearms in plain white. Only the top in front and in back was pink, and little pink fabric-covered buttons stretched all the way down the back, matching those on the sleeves.

Best of all was the satin and lace — dark green, with rows of satin stretching down from the shoulders over the pink and down to the waist where the green began. The wide waistband was dark green satin, with a bow tied in back. In between the satin stripes, which were three inches apart down the bodice, were sewn little delicate strips of lace, a lighter green than the satin, but darker than the dress. The same lace went down the wide part of the sleeves too, all the way to where the narrow white began.

The bonnet must have been made at the same time, because the wide floppy brim was of the exact same light green as the dress. The crown was of the same pink, and around the base of the pink was a wide strip of the dark green satin that exactly matched the waistband of the dress. It was all so pretty, and made me feel so fine and grown-up!

Walking out of that shop carrying that parcel, the smile on my face must've been six inches wide.

When we went back to the hotel, Mrs. Parrish dismissed the cabman. We walked up to the second floor to our room and got ready for the evening. We put our dresses on — Mrs. Parrish had bought a new one for the occasion too. Then Mrs. Parrish fixed her hair up all nice and then helped me with mine, so it would look nice flowing out from under the pink and green bonnet. At last we left the room and walked back downstairs.

As we walked through the hotel lobby, I saw several men's heads turn in our direction. I could feel the red coming up my neck and into my cheeks, but Mrs. Parrish just kept straight for the door without even flinching at some of the calls at her.

I guess that's one of the things I always liked about her, that she could be such a lady, so tender and nice, and could cry with you and talk about girl things. But she could be strong in a man's world like San Francisco too. I'd never yet seen her cowed by anyone, man or woman. And walking through that hotel lobby beside her, I felt as safe as if I'd been with Pa and Uncle Nick and Captain Grant — all three of them!

Mrs. Parrish took me to dinner that night at a fancy restaurant. It was close enough that we could have walked, but she said this was our "night out in San Francisco," and that we were going to "go first class all the way." So she ordered another cab — a covered one, this time, with fringe hanging down all the way around — and we rode down Montgomery Street, lit up with the brand-new gas street lights, to the International House restaurant.

On the way I asked her why we didn't eat at the dining room of the hotel. "The Oriental is one of the city's nicest hotels," she answered, "but there is an element present there which I would rather avoid. Sam Brannan and other of the city's leaders may have suites there, but I do not choose to dine with them, and I do not think most respectable women would care to do so either."

I felt like such a lady that night, sitting there in my new dress in that expensive restaurant, with well-dressed people all about — businessmen, Mrs. Parrish said, from all around the world.

I didn't even know what half the food was that Mrs. Parrish ordered, but she explained it all to me, and everything was delicious! There was music playing as we ate too — real music — and a lady who sang. It was like being part of a world I never even dreamed of seeing but had only read about once or twice in books.

By the time we got back to the hotel I was tired — but happy, too! What a wonderful day it had been! As I lay down in my bed, all the things that I'd seen and heard that evening ran back and forth through my mind.

But not for long, because I was asleep before I knew it.

CHAPTER 9

BRUSH WITH THE PAST

The next day Mrs. Parrish had to go to her meetings. She asked me if I wanted to go with her, but I said I'd rather stay at the hotel and either try to read in the book I'd brought or else write in my journal. There was already *so* much to tell, and I wanted to remember every minute of my visit to San Francisco! She said she had to meet some people in the morning, would be back for lunch, and then would be gone for three or four hours in the afternoon.

The morning passed quietly. I read some, but mostly wrote in my journal. Mrs. Parrish was back almost before I realized she had left. We talked a while and had lunch, and then she left again for her afternoon meetings.

About an hour later, I started to get restless. I'd been in that room most of the day, and I wanted to get a little bit of fresh air. Mrs. Parrish said everything would be fine, but that I ought to stay in the room or maybe go into the hall or down to the lobby to stretch my legs.

But I had too much of the outdoors and the country in me for my own good. I just had to get outside where I could feel the sun and wind on my face and breathe air that had been mixed with the clouds and the trees and the wind, instead of just sitting in a stale room for hours on end.

Finally, I got up and walked downstairs and into the lobby.

I had hardly set foot off the stairs when I heard a familiar voice: "Well, if it isn't the country girl who wants to be a newspaper reporter."

I glanced up and there was young O'Flaridy, again with a bundle of the day's papers.

"Having a pleasant visit in the city?" he added.

"Real nice," I answered, smiling but feeling a little cautious after what Mr. Barnes had said the day before.

"Even without my services as a guide, eh?" he said, with kind of a sly smile as he approached me.

Unconsciously I backed up a step, while I answered, "We saw all kinds of things. Mrs. Parrish knows the city pretty well."

"And where is your lady friend this fine day?"

"She had some meetings to go to."

"What kind of business she in?"

"Freighting and the like."

"Mighty peculiar field for a lady to be in. Say, who is she, anyway? She can't be your mother. She your aunt — your older sister?"

"She's a friend."

"Sort of took you under her wing, did she?"

I wasn't sure I liked his being so nosy about our affairs, but luckily he spotted Mr. Barnes eyeing him, so he made a beeline for the counter to dump off his papers. Then he sauntered back in my direction.

"Say," he said, "maybe with the lady gone to her meetings and you all alone like you are, you'd like me to show you around some."

"No, thank you." I tried to sound confident. "I've got plans of my own."

"Aw, what could —"

"Hey, O'Flaridy!" interrupted a man's deep voice from the other side of the hotel lobby. We both looked around, and the instant he saw who the speaker was, Robin left me and hurried over to him.

"I thought you was gonna run them papers down to McCready's for me," said the man, his voice quieter now, but still so I could hear. I didn't like the sound of the man, and he looked like a rough sort, though he was dressed in a black suit. They spoke a minute in quieter tones and I decided it was time for me to make my exit. I didn't want to have any more to do with Robin O'Flaridy or anyone he knew. I turned and walked through the lobby, past the desk, and toward the exit doors.

"Hey, you're not going out alone, are you?" came the persistent O'Flaridy voice yet again from behind me, just as my hand touched the door.

I hesitated. I still didn't know whether to be frightened or flattered by the attentions of this seemingly worldly-wise San Francisco lad. He hurried up to me again.

"I've got to make a delivery down by the waterfront," he said. "How about joining me?"

"I don't think so," I said. "I really have to be going."

"This is a big city, you know. No place for young girls to be roaming the streets without someone to watch out for them. Why —" His voice got real low and he came up close, like he was letting me in on a secret. "Why, I could tell you stories of that fella there I was just talking to, stories that you'd never believe! It's rough out there, and I wouldn't want anything to happen to you."

"I can take care of myself," I retorted before I knew what I was saying, with more courage than good sense. I wanted to get away from him. He was too pushy! I shoved the door open and walked out onto the street. He'd likely keep after me, so I turned and walked quickly away, without looking back.

It was a little chilly. The fog was just starting to blow away, and there were patches of bright showing through all around, but there was still enough fog to give me one of the best memories I had of San Francisco: breathing in that fresh-feeling fog that made my lungs feel so full and alive. I breathed in a few times when I got outside, then I started to walk down the street.

I went down the sloping hill of California Street toward the center of town. I figured if I walked straight down and then straight back up to Hyde I'd be able to remember where I was, and I'd been that way in the cab a couple of times already.

I had walked for maybe ten minutes, then all of a sudden I felt a strong hand close around my arm just above the elbow.

"I thought it was you, missy," growled a deep, raspy voice. "I knew if I followed you an' that lady an' watched this fancy place, I'd find my chance t' git even!"

I didn't even need to turn around. His was a voice I could never forget! And besides the voice, I could smell him too. In an instant I knew I'd been right in what I thought I'd seen the day before.

It was Buck Krebbs!

"Come with me, missy," he was saying, shoving me forward and toward the side of the walkway where there weren't so many people. "You an' me's got some talkin' to do!" Only later, when my arm got a big purple bruise, did I realize how hard he was pinching me. But at the moment I was much too scared to feel anything. "I wanna know where yer pa hid my loot! An' ye're gonna tell me!"

Not more than five or ten seconds had passed since he first grabbed me, but when you're scared, time seems to freeze as if it's happening to somebody else in slow motion. I've had dreams like that where I couldn't move even though something bad was about to happen if I didn't run away or jump to safety. Those first few seconds I was that way. Like a frog that a snake had just grabbed, I was so paralyzed I couldn't move or scream or even think.

But the second Buck said the word *pa,* something unfroze inside me, and all of a sudden woke up.

I don't exactly know what happened next. I read somewhere that fear makes you stronger than you really are. I guess I must've twisted my arm hard. Maybe that's when I got the bruise, or maybe I was stronger than Buck thought I'd be. I started screaming too. I remember being shocked at the loudness of my own voice! Everything all at once took Buck by surprise. I could feel the pain in my arm stop, and then I was running as fast as my legs would move. I didn't even know where I was going, I just ran as fast as I could, and I could feel my hair flying all about my face. Behind me I could hear the pounding of Buck's boots on the wood walk, and him yelling after me, "I'll git 'im, ya hear me, missy! I'll git that pa o' yours! I'll git the loot! I'll git ya all! I'll git it if I have t' kill ya all first!"

I kept running along the street, then turning, still hearing Buck chasing behind me. I ran past the Armory Hall and turned up Sacramento. I didn't know what I was doing at the time or where I was, or I'd have stopped right there and got one of the Guard men to help me.

A couple of blocks later I was in front of the *Eldorado.* People were staring at me, and some of the men hanging around called out rude things to me. I must have looked like a mess, a young kid of a girl running along the street, all alone in front of San Francisco's most famous gambling house.

I turned again, down the hill this time. I found out later it was Washington Street.

I stopped for a spell, caught my breath, and looked back for the first time.

I couldn't see or hear anything of Buck, and I didn't figure with his heavy boots and the whiskey I could smell on him that he'd be able to run too far. But all I could think of was getting back to the hotel before he did, and safely into my room again. I'd never leave that room alone now, because I was sure he'd be waiting for me if I ever came out of the lobby again!

A few minutes later I found myself back on Montgomery Street, which I recognized. I ran toward where the work was going on for the big new Montgomery Block building.

I went up to a man, dressed real fancy, who was just walking inside. I figured he was probably on his way to one of the lawyers' or mine owners' offices that was already open up on the second floor, and was a safe enough man to talk to. He didn't look too pleased at being accosted on the street by what must have looked like a tramp. But when, all out of breath, I asked him where the Oriental Hotel was, he didn't give me more than a *hmmp* or two as he looked me over, then pointed out the way with a half-scowl on his face. Somehow I got back onto California Street, and then ran all the rest of the way back, not even slowing down as I went through the lobby and up to the desk to ask for the key to our room, panting and sweating like a runout horse all lathered up.

When I'd been running through the streets trying to get away from Buck Krebbs, I'd have probably welcomed the sight of his face, but at the moment I was grateful Robin O'Flaridy wasn't anywhere around to see the fix I'd gotten myself in by not taking his advice! I took the stairs two at a time up to our room, hurriedly locked the door behind me with my fingers shaking, and then threw myself down on the bed and tried to catch my breath.

I didn't get much more reading or writing done that afternoon!

But I didn't start crying till Mrs. Parrish got back and I told her all about it. Having her take me in her arms and say comforting things to me made me feel safe again, and that's what made the tears start to come. She said her meetings were all done and that she wouldn't leave me alone for another minute of our time in San Francisco, and she said that Buck Krebbs would never dare come into the hotel and try to harm us, so we were safe enough.

We were to start home the next morning. The man in the red jacket brought our luggage down to the lobby and Mrs. Parrish took care of her last business at the desk.

I could hardly believe it when I heard a familiar voice once again, "Leaving town so soon?"

I turned around and found myself again staring

straight at none other than Robin O'Flaridy! This time he had no newspapers. If I didn't know better I'd think he was waiting for us.

"Yes, we are," I said, silently thinking to myself, *Not him again!*

"Well, I wish you safe travels all the way back to — what's that town out there in the sticks you say you're from?"

"Miracle Springs."

"Oh yeah, that place. Well, I wish you and your lady friend safe travels back to Miracle Springs. Say, how're you getting back there?"

His voice actually was starting to sound nice for a change.

"We'll take the boat up to Sacramento," I said.

"Hmm," he said with a serious expression, "I hear the bay's been pretty rough these days."

Outside I could see that the sky was blue and it didn't look any more windy than usual, so I decided to pay no attention to his remark. And the more I looked at him the more I realized that he took nothing he said very seriously himself!

"You still hankering to be a newspaper reporter?" he asked.

"Some day perhaps."

"Well, the next time you come to the city, you stay right here and be sure to look me up. I'll give you a few tips that helped me get started in the business. What do you say?"

To my relief, Mrs. Parrish had just finished at the desk and came up to us.

"Our cab is waiting outside," she said. "Good bye, Mr. O'Flaridy."

He quickly hastened to the front door and opened it for us with a flourish, annoying the man in the red jacket.

When we were finally on the steamer heading back across the bay toward Richmond and Sacramento — on perfectly calm waters! — Robin O'Flaridy quickly left my mind. Once again my thoughts filled with what had happened the previous afternoon. I couldn't wait to get back home to tell Pa what Buck Krebbs had yelled after me as I ran away from him. His words were mighty frightening to think about!

Probably because I was so worried about him and talking about it, on the way home Mrs. Parrish asked me lots of questions about Pa. I was glad for the chance to tell her what a fine man he was, though something in her tone made me think she didn't need to be told.

We laughed together about those first few weeks after we'd gotten to Miracle last year and how awkward it had been for everybody right at first. A faraway look came into her eye after I told her why he had left New York years ago, and I think she felt truly sorry for how she had misjudged Pa.

"There appears to be a lot more to your father than just what shows on the surface, Corrie," she said.

"Oh yes, ma'am," I answered. "Why, I'd hardly know him now from that man who first walked out of the saloon when Captain Dixon brought us into Miracle!"

When we got back to Sacramento, we dropped in to see Miss Baxter again at her boardinghouse, and who should be sitting there in her parlor but Captain Dixon himself!

Before I knew what I was doing, I ran toward him, and he stood up and I threw my arms around him and gave him a big squeeze. He seemed almost as pleased to see me too, and hugged me in return. He said his wagon train had arrived early, and then he asked about Becky and Emily and Zack and Tad.

When I told him how well we were doing with Pa and about the gold in the mine, he seemed genuinely relieved. He said he'd thought about us almost every day and was glad to hear everything was working out so well.

Miss Baxter fixed us some tea and we had a pleasant visit. Next to Pa and Mrs. Parrish, I reckon Captain Dixon was more responsible for helping us kids through Ma's death and coming to California than anyone else.

When we left to go, he and Mrs. Parrish shook hands. "I hope you might one day be able to come out to Miracle for a visit, Mr. Dixon," she said. "I know the other children would love to see you."

"I may just do that, ma'am," he answered.

We spent the night in Sacramento, then got Mrs. Parrish's horses and surrey from the livery stable where she'd left them, and early the next morning began the ride to Miracle.

We talked about so many things on the way home! Since that very first day on the street outside the Gold Nugget, I had always felt that Mrs. Parrish was my friend, but she had seemed a mite distant all the same. She never really kept herself aloof from me, but she was just so tall and confident, older, and a successful businesswoman, that it made me feel small by comparison.

But after this trip together, and her asking about Ma and Pa and our family, and with us talking about so many things, I felt that I was her friend too. She never seemed quite so distant after that.

We met Rev. Rutledge again, this time in Auburn, and he rode all the rest of the way back with us. He was in high spirits and talked practically the whole way about people he'd spoken with and the great opportunities he said existed for "the field of harvest." I didn't know what he meant by that, and I must admit I didn't pay much attention to him. It just wasn't the same after he joined us, and I was disappointed that my time alone with Mrs. Parrish had to come to an end. Mrs. Parrish was unusually quiet that day too. She didn't seem quite as enthusiastic about the minister's plans as she had been several days earlier.

CHAPTER 10

TROUBLE AT DUTCH FLAT

As we approached the cabin, I hardly waited for the surrey to come to a stop before I was out and running toward it yelling.

"Pa! Pa!" I called out. "Pa . . . I saw that man Krebbs and he said he's gonna —"

But when I threw open the door I was stopped short by the sight of Zack standing there staring me in the face. The other three were behind him, and I guess the worry in my voice frightened them, cause they were all silent. Even though I'd been gone most of a week, none of us thought to hug or greet each other.

"Where's Pa?" I asked, out of breath.

"He's gone to fetch Uncle Nick outta trouble," piped up Tad.

I glanced at Zack.

"He rode off on Jester this morning," Zack said, but before he had the chance to explain, Emily was adding her version of what happened.

"He was real mad," she said, "and his face was all red. I hope he doesn't hurt Jester."

By now Mrs. Parrish had come up behind me and was listening. I was still waiting for Zack to fill in the details.

"He rode out to Dutch Flat in the middle of the mornin'. He didn't take time to tell me nothin'. He just heard about Uncle Nick, and the next thing I knew he was saddlin' up Jester and ridin' off, tellin' me to keep everyone inside and to go over to Mr. Shaw's if we had any trouble."

I glanced back at Mrs. Parrish. Inside I couldn't help feeling that some terrible danger was approaching. I didn't know what had happened with Uncle Nick, but I was worried something awful about what Buck Krebbs had said. I was afraid seeing me had put it into his evil mind again to come back to Miracle and try to hurt us.

"I've got to warn Pa!" I said, turning and running back out to the surrey to grab up my few things and bring them into the cabin. Then, almost before anyone knew what I was doing, even before *I* knew what I was doing, I ran to the barn and started saddling Snowball.

A couple of minutes later I heard the door open behind me. It was Mrs. Parrish, her voice calm.

"Corrie, please," she began, "let's go inside and talk about this. It might be best if —"

"Don't try to stop me, ma'am," I interrupted, not realizing how rude I sounded, especially with her having done so much for me and just getting back from taking me to San Francisco.

"I won't try to stop you, Corrie," she went on, still calm. "You're practically a grown woman now, and I know it's not my place to tell you what to do. But it's late in the day and it's a

97

long way to Dutch Flat —"

"Only fifteen miles. I can ride that in a little over an hour!"

"But you don't know where your father has gone."

"I'll find him! I know I can!" I said, tightening the saddle straps.

"Besides, Corrie, dear, you don't know what the trouble is. There may be danger."

"It can't be worse than Buck Krebbs trying to kill him! It was only about a month ago that Pa was sayin' the men down at Dutch Flat might know something about the men who were after him and Uncle Nick. I didn't think anything of it at the time, but now I see it could have to do with Buck Krebbs. Don't you see, Mrs. Parrish, I gotta go! I gotta warn him! What if Buck Krebbs is back around here already!"

"I understand," she replied. "But I think it would be best if you waited until tomorrow morning. You and the children can spend the night with me, and tomorrow we'll talk to the sheriff and —"

I don't know why all of a sudden I was acting so ornery and stubborn. But deep inside I just knew I had to find Pa and not wait a second longer. Zack was always telling me I was mule-headed. I figured it was because he was my kid brother. But maybe he was right. Pa had said a time or two that as I grew older I reminded him more and more of Ma. And I knew she could be mighty determined once

98

she set herself to do something.

Anyhow, by the time the next words came out of my mouth, I was getting ready to swing up onto Snowball's back. "I'm sorry, ma'am," I said, "but I just gotta try to find him, and I just can't wait till tomorrow!"

I turned Snowball's head toward the door, but before I was even outside Zack called out, "I'm goin' with you, Corrie!" I hadn't even noticed him follow Mrs. Parrish into the barn, where he went straight to Blue Flame to start saddling him.

"You know the way, then," I called back. "You can catch up!" I knew Blue Flame would be able to catch Snowball in a quarter of a mile once he was on the open road. But even though I was in a hurry, I wouldn't have trusted myself to him. Zack had learned to handle him pretty well, but he was too spirited for me. I dug my heels into Snowball's flanks and was off.

"Corrie, at least take something to eat!" called out Mrs. Parrish's voice behind me.

The words brought me to my senses in the middle of all the emotions that were flying through me. I reined in Snowball, stopped, then turned and trotted back to where she was standing beside the barn. "Let me at least put some things in the saddle bag for you," she said. I nodded, got down off Snowball, and followed her back to the cabin.

By this time Zack was out of the barn with Blue Flame. He tied him to a post and ran inside.

I saw at once that he was thinking more straight than I was, cause when he came back out he was carrying a couple of blankets and his overcoat, in case we didn't make it back by nightfall. He was growing up, maybe in some ways faster than I was!

Five minutes later we were back on our horses again, this time with food to last us a day or two, blankets, and coats. Mrs. Parrish hadn't said anything more about trying to talk me out of going. She looked up at me, straight into my eyes.

"I'm sorry, Mrs. Parrish," I said, "to go running off like this the minute we get back —"

"Don't you worry about a thing, Corrie. I understand! And I trust you to do the right thing. I know the Lord is with you."

"Thank you," I answered. "And thank you for taking me to San Francisco! This isn't exactly how I figured it would end, but I *am* grateful to you for everything!"

She reached up and gave my hand a squeeze, still gazing straight into my eyes. "It was a wonderful time for me, Corrie! But we'll talk about San Francisco more later! Now, you go and find your father! I'll have Tad and Becky and Emily at my place in town when you get back!"

"Come on, Zack!" I said, and we galloped off. But before we were out of sight, I glanced back for a last look at the three young'uns and Mrs. Parrish. I couldn't help thinking how nice it looked with her standing with them in front of our place. I found myself wishing she'd still be there when we got back, instead of in town in that big house of hers.

CHAPTER 11

GRIZZLY HATCH

Zack and I rode hard most of the way, at least where we could.

We went over the hill first, crossing the Allegheny road north of Miracle, then along the trail leading from French Corral to Soda Springs till we were across the South Fork of the Yuba. After that we headed south, up and across Chalk Bluff Ridge, down through Deadman's Flat, then across the Bear.

I was proud of Zack. He knew the way exactly and didn't need my help at all. Not that I'd have been much help. I'd only been this way once with Pa, and then not all the way to Dutch Flat. But I guess Zack had come two or three times with Uncle Nick.

We made good time. I think we were there in less than two hours. But even so, it was late and the sun was starting to think about bedding down for the night. Zack told me there'd be a half moon tonight, though, so if the clouds stayed away we'd be able to make it back home after dark if we wanted to.

There wasn't much to Dutch Flat, that's for sure. All it amounted to was a little valley between the Bear River and Canyon Creek where they'd discovered gold. There were claims here and there on the streams, and a shack or two, one of them a saloon. I don't think there was one respectable family in the whole place.

We hadn't really talked about what we would do when we actually got there, or how we thought we would find Pa. I'd been praying all the way that God would help us. I'd remembered a verse in the Bible that Mrs. Parrish had told me about God guiding someone's footsteps if you give yourself to Him.

Now I remember — if you *acknowledge* Him was the word she used. If you *acknowledge* Him, He will lead you. I asked her what "acknowledge" meant.

"If you say that God is in charge of your life," she answered, "if you agree to go along with His leading instead of you trying to lead yourself, then you're recognizing that He is your Lord. That's what *acknowledge* means — just saying that He is holding the reins of your life instead of you yourself. And when you do that, it's like He tells the horse where to go and all you have to do is follow. If you acknowledge Him, He will direct your path. That's what He tells us in Proverbs."

Now her words came back to me, and I'd been praying that God would help us know where to go and what to do. But riding into that little place was a fearsome moment. All of a sudden we were there and we didn't know what we were going to do. I think we figured we'd see Pa's horse right off and there he'd be. But it didn't turn out that easy!

There were some horses tied up in front of a rundown building, but none I recognized. Voices came from inside. Zack and I looked at each other, sort of half-shrugged, then as if by unspoken agreement went slowly toward it, dismounted, and walked timidly inside.

It wasn't well-lit, but I could make out a table with men sitting around it. It looked like they were playing cards and a bottle of whiskey sat in the middle of the table. Most of them had glasses in front of them half filled with the amber liquid.

A couple of them glanced up when they saw us in the doorway, one leaned back in his chair and tilted his hat back on his head as if taking in the sight thoughtfully. One by one the rest of the card-playing company noticed us, and slowly the game came to a halt. There were some muttered comments and some snickering. "Well, what do we have here, boys?" said a voice, followed by a low laugh I didn't like the sound of.

I stepped farther into the room. "We're looking for our Pa," I said. "We wondered if any of you could help us. His name's Drum. Sometimes he goes by just that. Sometimes by Drum Hollister."

"Ya don't say? Yer Pa, eh?" mumbled another.

"You all the way out here alone, girl?" said another of the men, drawing out the word *alone* with a sinister tone.

"No, she ain't alone," piped up Zack, walking forward to join me. I know he was trying to sound brave, but it didn't work.

"Well, if that don't change everything now!" said one of the men. "You hear that, boys? She ain't alone! She's got this tough gunslinger here to protect her! Ha, ha, ha!"

"Please," I said, starting to get a little scared, "have you seen him?"

"Nobody sees nuthin' in these parts, girl! It ain't healthy to be stickin' yer nose into other folks' business."

"I ain't seen yer pa, girl, but I can't say I'd mind seein' you a mite closer!" said the man with the low laugh, rising up out of his chair and moving slowly toward us.

"You leave my sister be," said Zack, stepping forward and pulling me behind him. It was so brave of him. If we hadn't been in such a fix I'd have hugged him right there! I didn't know what he would do, because the man who was walking toward us was twice his size. But still Zack just stood there waiting for him, keeping me behind him.

I was about ready to bolt for the door and make a run for our horses when another voice interrupted the slowly approaching steps of the man's boots on the wood floor.

"Now just hold on, Barton," the new voice

said. "Those kids don't mean no harm. Leave 'em be."

"You leave *me* be, Duke! Keep to yer own affairs an' let me have a little fun!"

"I've seen what your kind of fun leads to, Jed," said the other voice. "Especially when you've got whiskey in your belly. Now back off, I tell you, or you'll have to go up against me. And you don't want to do that. Just remember what happened last time you tried it!"

The man called Jed Barton stopped, threw several bitter curses over his shoulder toward the voice coming from the dark end of the room, then slunk back to his seat. I heard the sound of a man hoisting himself up from a table and walking toward us. Once I could see him halfway plain he didn't look much better than Jed Barton, but everything I'd heard from him up till now told me this fellow called Duke was our friend.

"Your pa was here, kids," he said. "Leastways I reckon it was your pa. Two, maybe three hours back. But not for long. He was trailing someone else —"

"Our Uncle Nick!" I said eagerly.

"Musta been. He just walked in, called out, 'Name's Drum. I'm lookin' for Nick Matthews. Any of you seen 'im?' and he was outta Dutch Flat in five minutes."

"What did you tell him?" Zack asked.

"That some of the boys there were playing a friendly game of cards with Matthews when ol' man Hatch wandered in and wanted to join in.

Your uncle thought he saw an easy mark, and before it was over he near got his head blown clean off. That Hatch is a looney ol' cuss, and he lit outta here after your uncle, sending every one of us for cover. I don't know how your pa got wind of it so fast. I told him the last I seen of Matthews he was high-tailing it outta here in the direction of Blue Devil Diggings. Course, he mighta been heading for Gold Run. And Hatch was after him with pistol and rifle, both shooting at once!"

"So where do you think they are now?"

"Who can tell? But I know Hatch spends a lot of time in these here parts, and if he gets your uncle — or your Pa, for that matter — boxed into one of them canyons down that way, they'll never be able to outfox him. If he chases Matthews into Squires Canyon, your uncle might already be dead."

"Which way is it?" said Zack, already moving toward the door.

"Southeast of here, off the road to Gold Run," he answered. "You kids be careful, you hear?"

"Don't worry," I said. It was a stupid thing to say, 'cause I was terrified myself from what the man said. But I wasn't about to show it.

He followed us outside and watched us get back on Snowball and Blue Flame, still not believing, I think, that we were really going to chase off in the direction Pa and Uncle Nick had gone.

"Thanks, mister," I called out as we galloped out of Dutch Flat, and as I glanced back he was still standing there staring after us, his hat in his hand, scratching his head.

We ran our horses for only about three or four minutes when Zack, who was up ahead, signalled me to stop. I came up even with him and could tell he was listening for something.

"What is it?" I whispered.

"I thought I heard shots."

We listened again.

"There! Did you hear it?" he said. "There it is again!"

It sounded like a single shot from a rifle, followed by some yelling I couldn't make out.

Slowly we started up again, then left the road off to the right and made our way up a grassy ridge, hoping we could get to a point where we could see further. Every once in a while we'd hear a voice call out and we moved toward the sounds. About a quarter mile off the road I spotted a horse up ahead of us, tied to a tree.

"Zack!" I said, speaking softly. "Look! Isn't that Jester?" I hadn't forgotten what that man Duke had said about Hatch killing Uncle Nick, and I was afraid if he found us sneaking up on him, he'd kill us too.

We got down off our horses and led them the rest of the way. It was Jester, so we knew Pa must be close by. We tied Snowball and Blue Flame, then kept going on foot. We were on the top of the ridge now, but still hadn't seen anyone.

The next time a voice shouted out it was so

close it made me jump nearly out of my skin. I didn't know the voice, so it must have been the one Duke called Hatch.

"Ya might as well come on out, Matthews!" he shouted. "Ya got nowhere to hide!"

There was no reply.

"I know ya's in there, Matthews, ya cheatin' scum, an' I mean to fill ya full o' lead!"

I looked at Zack and he looked at me. Both pairs of our eyes were wide open, but we didn't dare utter a sound!

We crept forward on tiptoes, inch by inch, trying not to let the dry leaves and twigs crack under our feet.

All of a sudden I tripped, but halfway through my fall I felt a huge pair of arms grab around me. I started to scream, but just as suddenly a great hand clamped itself over my mouth and held it fast.

My heart was beating like a frightened rabbit's, but I looked up to see myself safe in the loveliest arms I could imagine.

"Pa!" I whispered as he released his hand, motioning for silence with his finger over his mouth.

He looked us over, from one to the other, bewildered, then whispered, "What in tarnation are the two of you doing here?"

"Oh, Pa," I answered back, "it's my fault. I had something to tell you that I didn't think could wait even another day. But now with that man down there trying to shoot Uncle Nick, it doesn't seem so important now!"

"Yeah, you're right," he replied softly, glancing around again down the hill. "That Grizzly Hatch is just crazy enough to kill us all! Now listen to me, the two of you. I want you to go back the way you came. I don't know what horses you have or how you ever managed to find me out here in the middle of nowhere looking down on Squires Canyon. But I want you to go back and get on them horses and get out of here! If Hatch finds out there's four of us, he's likely to get crazier'n ever!"

"Maybe we could help, Pa," suggested Zack.

"There's nothing to do, boy! I been here two hours already myself. But he's got Nick down there trapped in that little cave at the end of the canyon. He may be crazy, but he ain't stupid. He's got Nick's horse, he's got a full view of the mouth of the cave. Nick can't make a move Hatch won't see, but I can't get a clean sight of Hatch. Now get outta here, I tell you!"

"But, Pa, maybe with four of us . . ." Zack said, letting his voice kinda trail off.

Pa turned toward him, slanting his eyebrows like he does when he's thinking. Then a slow smile spread over his mouth.

"You may just have something there, Son," he said after a minute. "You're right — now there's four of us! Only Hatch doesn't know it! If we can make him think it's still just me and Nick, we might be able to lure him away from that cave opening."

He stopped, thinking some more, glancing

down toward where Hatch was watching the mine, then along the canyon, then back up along the ridge where the three of us sat. "Yeah," he muttered to himself, "it just might be crazy enough to work! Zack, my boy," he said, turning to Zack, "we'll try it! Now — do you think you can shoot my gun?"

"Yes, sir!" said Zack eagerly. "At Grizzly Hatch?"

"No, no! For heaven's sake, we don't want to kill anybody! We just want to give him something to think about. Okay, here's what we're going to do."

Five minutes later, after Pa was done explaining his plan, he stood up. "Now you wait till you hear me throw a rock over in your direction. That'll be the signal I'm in position up behind the cave. The minute you hear that rock, Zack, you start shooting. But aim right where I showed you! I don't want you accidently hitting him. We just want him to *think* we're firing at him! Then I'll yell at Hatch and try to get him to leave his position and come after me. At first he won't believe I'm Nick. But then you gotta call out something from up here. Doesn't matter what, just make your voice sound low enough to be mine. Say something like, 'Hey, Nick, how'd you get outta the cave?' If Nick'll just keep his fool trap shut till Hatch comes after me, this oughta work! Now, Corrie, when you see him climbing up the other side there —"

111

He pointed with his finger and I followed with my eyes.

"— when you see him coming after me, you know what to do."

I nodded.

"But remember, he's got to only think there's me and Nick!"

We both nodded our heads, then Pa went back up toward the horses to start making his way around and down the other side of the ridge to the back side of the cave, while we sat and waited. He said it could take him more than half an hour to get in place.

Silently we crouched where we were and waited. It seemed forever, and we never saw or heard anything more from Pa. Hatch yelled and shot at the cave a couple of times, but that was all. Finally we heard a small stone land not far away from us.

I looked at Zack. He looked at me, then he fired Pa's gun in the direction Pa told him to. Immediately when the echo had died away, we heard Pa's voice shouting from across the canyon, off to the right and behind the cave.

"Hey, Hatch, ya ol' buzzard!" he called out. "Thought you could keep me down, did ya? But ya didn't know that cave had another way out! Nice shootin' Drum! Give him another one so I can get outta here!"

Zack fired two more shots, then called out, trying to make his voice as deep as he could, "Come on, Nick, let's get outta here!"

Then for the first time I saw the man Pa had called Grizzly Hatch. He stood up from behind the rock where he'd been crouched. He looked toward the cave, then up in our direction, then back toward where Pa's voice was still badgering him.

I lay real low so he wouldn't see me, but I could see him looking back and forth and could tell Pa's plan had worked. He was getting confused and really thought Pa was Uncle Nick. He was stocky and squat, not particularly tall, though he looked strong. He wore a beard but not a long one like Alkali Jones' — it looked more like he just forgot to shave for a couple of weeks. His hair was dark black and so long it came down over his ears, and he wasn't wearing a hat. I was too far away to make out much about his features. But even from where I was watching, I was glad I couldn't see them. He looked mean.

"I'll join ye directly, Drum!" Pa was shouting. "Just as soon as I work my way 'round the mouth of this canyon. You just keep that ol' coot Hatch where he is! The old weasel will never catch me!"

Zack fired again.

By this time Grizzly Hatch was downright in a boil, which is just how I figured Pa wanted him so he'd quit thinking about the cave. He didn't seem too worried about Zack's shooting in his direction — or maybe he was crazy like everyone said.

All at once he lit out from where he was, ran down the hill shouting out curses in the direction of the cave. It had been so quiet from inside it I began to wonder if something had gone wrong and Uncle Nick *had* disappeared somehow!

Zack fired again and shouted, "Hey, Hatch, come back here, ya varmint! Look out, Nick, he's comin' in your direction!"

Hatch was now scrambling up the other side of the canyon in Pa's direction, shooting and yelling wildly.

I stood up. Now it was my turn.

"If he comes back, you yell out a warning," I said to Zack. Then I began making my way down the hill toward the cave from the left, where Hatch couldn't see me even if he looked back. When I got to the floor of the canyon I looked around. By now I couldn't even hear anybody else, just an occasional shout in the distance. I ran across the flat ground and up the short incline to the cave on the other side.

"Uncle Nick . . . Uncle Nick!" I said into the black opening as loud as I dared. "You in there?"

All was quiet a moment. Then I heard, "Corrie . . . that you?"

"Yes! Come quick! Pa got the man away from the cave!"

I heard Uncle Nick's shuffling steps from inside, then he stepped into the light, holding his hand up to his squinting eyes. The sun was just setting behind the ridge and shining right toward us.

"How'd he manage that?" he asked.

"Come on, come on!" I said, grabbing his hand

and pulling him along. "I'll tell you later. We gotta get outta here before he comes back!"

I ran back down the way I'd come, still trying to keep as quiet as I could, half pulling Uncle Nick behind me. Finally, he broke into a run himself and we made our way back up the hillside to where Zack still sat with Pa's gun.

"Why, dad-blamed if that don't beat all!" exclaimed Uncle Nick. "I been busted outta my prison by two kids! You know how to use that thing, Zack, my man?"

"Who do you think was doing all that shooting you heard a minute ago?" I said. "Zack used that gun just fine. But now we gotta get back to the horses to meet Pa!"

Zack and I quickly retraced our steps to where we'd left our horses with Jester. Still bewildered by the events of his sudden rescue, Nick shuffled along behind us, asking where Pa was. But we didn't stop to answer. I was still afraid of Hatch sneaking up behind us!

In a couple of minutes we reached the horses. We stopped, breathing hard. My panting was only half from running down to the cave and back up the hill. The other half was from still being afraid for Pa. Now *he* was out there with Grizzly Hatch after him!

It was a terrible wait. Every so often we'd hear an explosion of gunfire or some shouts. Once or twice I heard Pa yell out something too. Then everything was dead quiet for about five minutes.

Suddenly through the brush came a trampling

sound making right for us. Without thinking, I grabbed at Uncle Nick and jumped behind him. But almost the next second Pa broke through the trees running toward us as fast as he could.

"Mount up!" he yelled the instant he saw us. "Let's get outta here!"

"But my horse, Drum! He ran my horse off!" said Uncle Nick, hesitating.

"Dad-blame ya, Nick! It's your own durn fault! Now get up there on Snowball! Having your skin in one piece is better'n a horse!"

"But that was a new saddle, Drum!"

"Get up there, Nick! Hatch is right behind me! I don't wanna tell ya again!"

"Snowball? Why, that's just a kid's horse!"

"After this little escapade, I ain't so sure you can handle anything more!" said Pa, clearly irritated. "Zack, you take Blue Flame, Corrie, you get up on Jester with me, and Nick, *you get on Snowball!*"

We all mounted up, though I could feel Uncle Nick almost pouting as he did, hardly noticing that Pa'd just saved his life by risking his own. Pa jumped up on Jester's back, then reached down and hauled me up in one quick motion. I held on to the saddlehorn as tight as I could, Pa reached around me with his arms, took the reins in one hand and squeezed me tight with the other, dug his heels in, and off we went. Zack on Blue Flame was right behind us, followed by Snowball and Uncle Nick.

As we sped along the ridge, I thought I heard

shouts behind us. A couple of gunshots rang out. Pa'd been right. Hatch was right behind us. But dusk was settling in and Hatch was nowhere near his horse. In another minute or two I knew we were safe.

CHAPTER 12

AROUND THE CAMPFIRE

Pa lashed Jester's rump with the reins and the poor horse galloped for all he was worth.

I was bouncing up and down in front of Pa, and if his arms hadn't held me in on each side, I'd have wound up off in a ditch. Zack didn't have any trouble keeping up, but Uncle Nick fell a little ways behind, though Pa still kept pushing as hard as he could go.

Before I knew it we were speeding through a clearing, then we were on a wider road like before, and a small cluster of buildings came into sight. Pa later told me it was Gold Run, but at the time I was hanging on too hard to ask. A few men were standing outside the saloon watching us as we tore past. A couple of them yelled at us, but Pa just kept on going without even slowing down.

Just past the saloon he turned left onto another road, and in less than a minute we were past the little collection of shacks and racing again through the brush and trees and woods.

After about ten more minutes, Pa finally slowed the pace, though he still couldn't let Jester stop and walk. At last, after another five minutes, he did stop.

By now it was night. The moon was shining on the water as it passed in front of us, but even without the light, I'd have known we had reached a river from the rushing sound.

"This here's the ford across the North Fork of the American," Pa said.

Over the sounds of the river, I could hear the heaving of all three horses. "Once Hatch tracks us to Gold Run and them fellas at the saloon tell him which way we was goin', this is right where he'll figure we're headin'."

"We gonna cross that river, Pa?" asked Zack.

"Naw, but we're gonna make Hatch think we did. Come on, follow me."

Pa urged Jester forward toward the water, then stopped. "No, wait. We've gotta leave him a clue to find — somethin' he'll recognize as ours, somethin' that'll make him know we came by here and went on —"

He stopped, thinking, looking around at all of us. Then he said, "Nick, gimme that hat o' yours."

"Not my hat, Drum!"

"You got us into this mess! Now do I hafta take it from you, or are you gonna give it to me?"

Silently Uncle Nick took his hat off his head and handed it to Pa. "He'll know this, all right," said Pa. "He came near shootin' a hole clean through it!" He tossed the hat down a

119

couple of feet from the water's edge, then continued out into the river.

"It's shallow all the way across," he said to me. "Even in the dark, these horses won't have a problem. But we ain't goin' all the way across."

"Why not, Pa?" I asked.

" 'Cause we're headin' south, Corrie. Can't you tell? Home's back behind us. But I don't want that ol' cuss Hatch findin' out where our claim is. I heard o' him for years, and I heard he's a bad 'un. I don't think he knows who we are or where we're from, and I wanna keep it that way! So we'll make him think we're headin' down to Indian Hill, then we'll double back up by Grass Valley and head home that way."

We walked the horses twenty feet out into the river, then he pulled Jester's head around and began leading him downstream to the right. Zack and Uncle Nick followed. Slowly we made our way, following the shoreline, till we were well out of sight of the place where Pa'd thrown Uncle Nick's hat. Still he kept leading the way down the river for ten more minutes. I could hear louder sounds from the river up ahead when Pa finally turned again toward the bank. "Hear them rapids up ahead, Corrie?" he said. "Time for us to get back on dry land and head back north. I don't think Hatch can track us now!"

"You really think he'd try to follow us, Pa?"

"Fellas like him don't forget when they've been made a fool of! I still gotta find out from

120

Nick what went on back in Dutch Flat, but yeah, I think Hatch'll do his blamedest to find us. I don't doubt he'll be askin' around in Dutch Flat an' Gold Run tonight, an' it won't be long before he's standin' at that ford back there, cursin' to himself as he's holdin' Nick's hat, an' vowin' revenge. Let's just hope he's mad enough to ride across the river an' just keep on goin'!"

"We gonna ride all the way home tonight, Pa?" I asked.

"From where we are now, Corrie," he answered, "with no trail to follow for the next three or four miles, in the dark with only half a moon, we're likely three hours from Miracle."

"Zack and me brought some food, Pa. And blankets."

"And the young' uns?"

"They're with Mrs. Parrish."

"Then maybe it'd be best for us to find some place to bed down for the night. But we better get up past Grass Valley . . . maybe near Nevada City somewhere. Then we'll be outta Hatch's territory."

We rode on in silence for a while, and I leaned back against Pa's chest. I felt so safe and protected with him behind me and his arms around me. Even if he had decided to go straight back to Miracle, I could have ridden with him like that forever! By now nothing could have been further from my mind than what had sent me and Zack after Pa in the first place.

121

A couple of hours later the four of us were sitting around a small fire, munching on the biscuits, dried venison, and apples Zack and I had brought along.

"Wish we had some coffee," said Uncle Nick.

I half expected Pa to make some sour reply. He hadn't been any too nice to Nick the whole time, though I suppose he was right about Uncle Nick getting us into the tight spot we'd been in. But once he had the fire going and I pulled out the food we'd brought, Pa seemed to relax a little.

"Yeah, coffee and some o' them beans ol' Grimly used to make," replied Pa. "That'd be 'bout as good as it gets. How that ol' coot could get so much from a pot o' beans and an old worn out ham-hock, I could never figure."

"Them wasn't all bad times, ya gotta admit — eh Drum?"

Pa half smiled as he stared into the flickering fire. Maybe it was just the dance of the light over his forehead and eyebrows, but a look came over his face that I had never seen before. It was a faraway look. All at once he seemed to be someplace else.

"Yeah, they had some good moments," said Pa after a spell. His voice sounded the way his eyes looked.

"An' you recollect his flapjacks?" Uncle Nick went on. "Can't ya just smell 'em? After a hard afternoon's riding —"

"Likely runnin' from a posse!" added Pa with a little laugh, but not taking his eyes off the fire.

Uncle Nick laughed, too. "Yeah, an' then beddin' down for the night someplace in the hills and sleepin' so hard nothin' could wake ya, till that smell o' his cakes on the griddle worked its way into yer nose, and suddenly you was awake an' the sun was halfway up the sky, an' it was time to eat and get in the saddle again!"

Pa smiled, but said nothing. Zack and I didn't want to say anything. We were both listening to them reminisce about the old days. But after a while I found myself as fascinated with watching Pa's face as listening to his voice.

The light from the flames of the fire seemed to bring different things to my mind as I watched. One moment I saw the hard, stern man I'd been afraid of when I first laid eyes on him that day outside the Gold Nugget in Miracle Springs. The slight squint of his eyes and just the hint of an indentation below his cheekbones made him look cold, as if he didn't care much about feelings. But then when the light hit more full, and I could see *into* his eyes, then all at once I saw that maybe he had felt things *too* much.

Maybe the severe look was really a soberness that had come from years of feeling things so deeply that he tried to keep his face from showing what was going on inside. I thought I could see a tiredness in the eyes, too — a weariness from the unsettled life of being on the run for so long. And now here he was again having to hide from

123

someone who was after them, and because of Uncle Nick, just like before.

It was probably silly of me to sit staring at my own Pa, trying to figure out things like that. But ever since I'd started keeping a journal, I found myself thinking more and more about the inside of people and experiences instead of just the outside. And so I couldn't help doing that when I looked at Pa's face and heard him talk about when he and Nick rode together.

It was a good face, I thought — even with two or three days' whiskers. Rugged, I suppose, but I wouldn't call it craggy or sharp. The cheekbones, the chin, the nose were all hard-edged. Pa didn't have any extra fat on him, although his shoulders were big and he wasn't lean. And his dark brown hair coming down just over his ears and spilling down his sideburns onto his cheeks, with just a little bit of gray showing here and there — all put together, I liked Pa's looks. He showed himself as a man that could take care of things. Yet the few times we'd talked seriously, and the time when he'd first told me about leaving the East, there was an earnest tone in his voice that showed he was sensitive, too. Pa looked like the kind of man who wouldn't be out of place in either a gunfight or a quiet talk with a woman.

I found my thoughts drifting to Mrs. Parrish. I wished she could see the deep look in Pa's eyes that I was seeing right then. I wanted her to know what a fine man Pa was, even though he'd had a past life that was different from her

Rev. Rutledge. I wanted her to be able to see the feelings that were beneath the hard shell that Pa showed to the rest of the world. They were certainly getting along better now than at first, but I wanted them to become friends. Well, maybe someday . . .

"What are you thinking about, Pa?" I said finally, not planning to say it and almost surprised at the words when I heard them.

For a long moment Pa just kept looking into the fire. Then he took a deep sigh, pulled his gaze off the orange and red coals, and looked over at me. "I was thinkin' about your ma, Corrie," he said, then gave me a little smile. Even in the firelight, his eyes were bright with tears. I smiled back.

Then all at once he turned to Uncle Nick and said, "Now, Nick, I wanna know just what the devil happened back there in Dutch Flat to get Hatch so all-fired hot to put a slug through you!"

Uncle Nick laughed. "It was a card game," he answered.

"Somehow I ain't surprised," said Pa.

"But ya shoulda seen it, Drum! It was the perfect setup! I couldn't lose!"

"Except that you were settin' up to fleece Grizzly Hatch! Ain't you heard of him?"

"Yeah, but I never believe half the things I hear."

"Well you shoulda believed it in his case! So tell me what happened."

"Well, Barton was dealin', and he called five

125

card stud. I had the seven of clubs underneath, an' my first up card was the seven of hearts. Well, nobody else had much of anythin', and when the seven of diamonds fell down on my pile for my fourth card, showin' just a measly pair o' sevens, I was high man. Now Hatch, meanwhile, had all spades but nothing else. But he was startin' to put some good-sized money in the pot, an' when the fifth card came his eyes flashed, an' he threw in all he had. That's when I knew he didn't know nothin' 'bout that declarin' rule — you heard of it, ain't ya?"

"Yeah, I heard somethin' about it," answered Pa, "but I ain't never seen no game run that way. I heard there's talk of takin' it outta the rulebook."

"Well, they ain't taken it out yet," said Uncle Nick. "An' so ya see, Hatch had to figure he had me cold. The second his last spade came up, he knew he had his flush and he had to figure me for three sevens at most. He had me an' he bet the pot. But *I* knew I had *him!* My only risk was whether they had a Hoyle around. So I called him, an' the pot musta been two or three hundred. His eyes lit up an' he turned over his last spade, and reached out to scoop in the dough.

" 'Just a minute, Hatch,' I said. 'Far as I can tell, you got nothin' that can go up against my three sevens. That pot's mine.'

" 'What're ya tryin' to pull, Matthews?' says Hatch. 'Open yer fool eyes! I got me a flush.'

126

" 'I can see that,' I said, 'but in this game, three of a kind beats a flush.'

"By this time Hatch was gettin' plenty riled.

" 'Anybody got a book o' Hoyle around here?' I asked. The feller that runs the place said he did. He went behind the counter, got the book, gave it to me, and I found the spot where the special poker rules was discussed. I read it real slow an' deliberate-like: 'In five or seven card stud poker, the flush and the straight are not played unless it is declared in advance by the dealer.'

"Everybody's mouths fell open, an' Barton grabbed the book outta my hand mutterin' that he hadn't never heard o' that rule. But then when Hatch asked him what it said — that fool Hatch can't read a word himself — after a couple seconds Barton just said, 'I'm afraid he's got you dead to rights, Grizzly. That's what the book says.'

" 'An' I didn't hear no one declare it,' I said. 'So I reckon my three sevens is high after all.' "

"And what happened to the pot?" asked Pa.

"Well, it was no secret now that the game was over. I put the money in my saddlebag an' left."

"So now Hatch has his money back, your money, *and* your horse! When are you gonna learn, Nick, that it never pays? And now you got him tryin' to put a bullet in yer hide besides! You don't need that kind of trouble! You're just gonna land us back into the same kind of fix we were in back in New York if you don't cut out that kind of nonsense!"

127

Uncle Nick fell into one of his quiet, sulking moods.

"It's just a good thing these kids showed up when they did! If it hadn't been for them, Nick, you'd be a dead man by now! There was nothing I coulda done to get to Hatch the way he was positioned, and if he'd kept firin' into that cave, he'd have got you sooner or later."

Pa paused, then looked over at me.

"By the way, you ain't told me why you two *did* come, Corrie. And how in tarnation'd ya find us, anyway?"

Suddenly I remembered!

"Oh, Pa, I forgot!" I exclaimed. "Everything started happening so fast after we got to Dutch Flat and those men said you were in trouble. I plumb forgot what I had to tell you!"

"Well, what is it, girl, that's so all-fired important you had to track me all over the country to tell me?"

"It's him, Pa! Buck Krebbs! I saw him in San Francisco!"

A cloud instantly spread over Pa's face that neither the darkness nor the flickering of the dying fire could hide.

"You *saw* him. Is that all?" he asked solemnly.

"No, Pa. He saw me too, and he followed me and Mrs. Parrish to our hotel, and then when I was alone he sneaked up and grabbed me again, like up by the mine, and I think he was going to hurt me, but I got away and ran from him!"

By this time Pa was real serious and staring intently at me.

"Go on, Corrie," he said. "Tell me everything."

"I got away from him. I ran all around through the streets and got back to the hotel."

"Where was the Parrish woman?"

"She was at her meeting, Pa. It wasn't her fault. Please don't be angry with her! She took real good care of me, and she told me to stay in the room till she got back. It was my own doing, going out alone like that."

Pa nodded.

"But, Pa, after I got away from him, he ran down the street after me and was yelling all sorts of awful things, saying he was going to get you and the money, even if he had to kill us all to do it! I was so scared, Pa. I thought he might be fixing to come to Miracle right then! He sounded so evil, and I thought that seeing me again must have put it into his mind to come back here. And I just had to warn you, Pa!"

I stopped, thinking I was going to start crying. But I forced myself to hold it in.

Pa looked over at me. He knew what I was feeling. He reached out, placed his big hand on mine and gave it a squeeze.

"Everything's gonna be fine, Corrie Belle," he said. "Don't you worry none. Buck Krebs ain't gonna kill nobody."

"But the money, Pa! He's not gonna stop till

he gets the money."

"There ain't no money, Corrie."

"But how we gonna convince that loco fool Krebbs o' that?" said Uncle Nick.

Pa sighed again. "All the more reason, Nick," he said finally, "for you to keep outta trouble with characters like Hatch. We ain't out from behind the trouble from the East that keeps on houndin' us, an' it's gonna take all we can do to get rid of it once an' for all."

Again everyone got quiet. Pa stood and grabbed up some more of the wood we'd gathered and threw it on the fire. Then he came back and sat down, staring into the flames again. But this time I didn't see a faraway look. Instead it was a look of worry, concern, like he was thinking about what he ought to do.

The next words out of his mouth caused *me* concern.

"Nope, this ain't no proper place to raise no kids." He said it quietly, as if he were thinking out loud. "Nope, it sure ain't," he repeated. "Not for a man like me, alone, the law after me from the East, crazy men trailin' me lookin' to put a piece o' lead in me. No place at all! My kids in danger . . ."

His voice trailed away. I knew he was blaming himself.

"Pa," I said, "as long as we're together, everything'll be fine in the end, won't it?"

"I don't know, Corrie," he said. "It just seems I ain't no fit pa to take care o' five kids by

130

myself. Buck Krebbs tryin' to hurt you, bullets flyin' outta Hatch's gun. You an' Zack in danger there today! That ain't no way to run a family! And me ridin' off this mornin', leavin' Zack an' the young'uns alone. What if Krebbs'd shown up then? No, I tell ya, things ain't right the way they are! I can't let it keep bein' this way. You kids need a proper bringin' up! And I gotta do something to get you one!"

"We're happy being with you, Pa!" I said, but I don't think he was listening. He stood up again and walked away. If I had learned anything about Pa, I knew he was thinking real hard.

Pretty soon Zack and I lay down on the softest piece of ground we could find near the fire and pulled the blankets over us. If it hadn't been for the last bit of the talking, this would have been one of the most pleasant nights to remember since we came to California. It was so peaceful lying there, looking up into the black sky, the faint crackling of the fire in our ears, and the sounds of the crickets and other creatures of the woods.

After a while Uncle Nick pulled his harmonica out of his pocket and started playing softly. I was glad he hadn't put *it* in his saddlebag! What a perfect way it was to go to sleep. I could hardly believe this day had started with Mrs. Parrish and Rev. Rutledge in Auburn!

Before long I heard Zack's breathing change, and I knew he was asleep. The last thing I re-

131

member was wondering what Pa could mean to do to get us what he called a proper upbringing. I said a prayer for him, wherever he was right then, out alone walking, and asked God to help him do the right thing.

CHAPTER 13

PA'S SURPRISE DECISION

When we got home the next morning, the trouble with Grizzly Hatch died down, and things pretty much went back to normal.

Uncle Nick was upset about losing his horse, and every once in a while he would start muttering about going to get it away from Hatch. But then Pa would remind him what got him into trouble in the first place, ending by saying that if he tried to find Hatch, he'd shoot Uncle Nick himself first.

Everything got back to normal, that is, except Pa. I knew he was thinking about something serious. He'd been different ever since the night around the campfire when he'd gotten up and walked off. Riding home the next day he was quiet, and he'd been like that ever since.

Every so often he'd say something — more to himself than to any of us — like what he'd said that night, about this being no way to bring up a family. But we were all afraid to ask him what he meant or what he was fixing to do. I know I couldn't help wondering if he was thinking again about sending us kids back East someplace. In my heart I knew Pa would never do it, but

133

I couldn't help fearing some terrible change. Sometimes he'd go off alone in the woods and just sit, and once I came upon him alone in the barn. He was sitting there on a bale of straw, holding my picture of Ma in his hand, like he was asking *her* what to do.

When he glanced up at me, I saw one tear roll down his cheek. In that moment, suddenly I wasn't worried about myself any more, but I hurt for Pa. All at once I realized how hard this decision must be for him whatever it was about. Maybe he was thinking about packing us all up — him and us together — and leaving Miracle Springs!

That would sure be hard enough on him to make him shed a few tears, because I know he loved this place and the mine. He'd built a new life here, and now he had his family again, and a good claim. Yet there was Hatch and Buck Krebbs and always the danger of something out of his past catching up with him. And Uncle Nick was still wild enough to get Pa and the rest of us into a scrape now and then.

Maybe Pa was right that this wasn't a proper place to bring up five kids. What if he was thinking about taking us kids and going someplace else, and leaving Uncle Nick behind? Most of the trouble had Uncle Nick's name on it, one way or the other. Even the trouble with Buck Krebbs and whatever else might follow them from the East had all started from Pa's trying to help his wife's younger brother.

But I knew that even though he sometimes treated him like a kid, Pa really loved Uncle Nick. They'd been through all kinds of hardship together, and had been partners together, and sometimes when working at the mine they'd have a good laugh over something. They were friends too.

That would be a hard decision, if he was considering splitting up and leaving. And it was something he might be thinking he had to talk to Ma about, even if all he had left was that picture. After all, Uncle Nick was her brother, and she had loved him too.

All this was just nothing more than speculation in my own mind. I didn't talk to anyone about it. We were all walking around softly, not wanting to do anything to get Pa upset. But many things ran through my mind — like Pa sending us away, or him going away someplace else with us, or making Uncle Nick leave, or changing all our names from Hollister to something else so nobody could find us. I even feared that one day we'd wake up and find Pa himself gone and never hear from him again. I suppose I knew Pa would never do that again. But sometimes fears and hurts come back out of the past to grab at me and make me think things I don't want to think.

Then one day all the fears seemed to come true. I woke up one morning, and Pa was gone.

I was always the first of us five kids awake. I'd get up and go outside for a walk, or I'd read in one of the books Mrs. Parrish had brought me from her trips to Sacramento, or I'd write in my journal. About half the time Pa was up before me, sometimes sitting in front of the fire in the other room in the cabin, sometimes out in the barn or up at the mine.

But on this particular morning, the instant I opened my eyes, I had a feeling that something was different. I got up quickly. Pa wasn't anywhere in the cabin and there was no fire started. With a growing feeling of dread I jammed my bare feet into my boots and ran outside and to the barn. Jester was gone, along with Pa's best saddle.

Panic began to seize me, and as I ran out of the barn and up toward the mine I was starting to cry, but I didn't want to stop and give in to it. I didn't expect to find Pa at the mine, but I had to look everywhere. He hadn't said a word about needing to go anywhere, and now he was gone.

If I had stopped to think about it all reasonably, I'd have trusted Pa, but Mrs. Parrish says that people sometimes think with their hearts instead of their heads. And this was one of those times. As I walked slowly back to the barn I was crying, probably more because of the things *I'd* been wondering than any real fear that Pa had left us. But I wanted to get my crying done and my tears used up before I saw the other kids or Uncle Nick. I didn't want to try to explain to them how worried I was about what Pa might be fixing to do.

Pa came back about the middle of the afternoon. He didn't act different or tell us where he'd been right off. But the second he rode up and got down off his horse, I could tell from his eyes that something had happened. His smile and hug were enough to make all my fears vanish — for right then, at least. It was a smile that seemed to still have some of the same anguish in it that I'd seen in his eyes when he was gazing at the picture of Ma. But at least it was a smile, and I was grateful.

It seemed to say that he'd come to some decision. I didn't know what it might be, but he was more like himself after that and he started talking again to us. I think everybody, even Uncle Nick, was relieved. I hoped by and by he'd tell us what had brought on the change.

But he didn't, and things settled back into their old routine. The other four kids seemed to forget all about Pa's temporary moodiness, and sometimes I wondered if Uncle Nick ever paid much attention to those kinds of things.

But I kept watching Pa, hoping maybe he'd tell me, even if he didn't want to tell everybody. And he kept behaving strangely every now and then, going to town and not telling what for, and once riding all the way to Marysville.

"Where've you been, Pa?" I asked him when he got back. It was late in the day and he'd been gone since morning, and his horse was bushed from hard riding.

"Marysville."

"What for? I never heard you talk of knowing anybody there," I said.

"I had to see your newspaper feller, Singleton."

"Why him, Pa?"

"I had some business with him, that's all."

And no matter what I did, I couldn't pry out of him what he was up to.

But he was up to something, I was sure of it. He went into Miracle more often too, and started paying more attention to the *Gazette* every week than he ever had before, though why the sudden interest in Mr. Singleton and his paper I didn't have a clue.

Most curious of all was my suspicion that he went to see Mrs. Parrish some of the times he rode into Miracle. I found out he'd been by her office by accident once when I was talking to her.

I mentioned it to Pa casually. "Mrs. Parrish said you paid a call on her," I said, to see if he'd say something. But he replied gruffly, "Weren't no *call* on the lady. We just had some things to talk over 'bout the school committee, that's all."

And then a few days later, Pa was sitting by the fire in the evening looking through a Sacramento paper. I couldn't figure any way he'd have gotten his hands on it except from Mrs. Parrish. More and more I just kept noticing things about his behavior I couldn't account for.

Then all of a sudden his interest in newspapers stopped, and so did his rides into town. I would have forgotten about everything, except that about a month later, as the weather was turning cold, all at once his peculiar habits returned. Now all of a sudden he took an unlikely interest in the mail delivery. Every two weeks, regular as clockwork, he'd ride in to the new General Store where the mail came every other Friday, and he'd wait for it.

We'd never had any mail that I could recall. Who'd send us anything? Yet there was Pa waiting for that stage every Friday when it was due!

Finally, in the later fall, as we were thinking about looking forward to our second Christmas in California, whatever Pa'd been waiting for must've come on the stage. That particular Friday he came home from Miracle with a different look on his face — not exactly a smile, and not even a "happy" look, but just a different look, with a light in his eyes, like something good was about to happen.

That evening, I finally got answers to all my questions about the peculiar goings-on for the last two months. Pa sat us all down, Uncle Nick too, took a big deep breath, then told us he had some real important news to tell us. Suddenly, I found myself thinking about all those same fears I'd had after the Grizzly Hatch affair. But I kept still and Pa started talking.

"Well, I reckon you all think I been actin' mighty ornery these last coupla months. An' I'm sorry if I ain't been too cheerful, but I had a heap o' things on my mind." He stopped, took in another breath, then started up again.

"I been thinkin' a lot about this life o' ours here. An' I guess we got a parcel o' things to be thankful for. But I still can't help thinkin' it ain't no way for a family to live. Why, with varmints like Grizzly Hatch wantin' to take their piece outta our hides, and with Buck Krebbs sneakin' around wantin' to put a slug into me an' Nick and tryin' to hurt Corrie, and with us still havin' to wonder every day 'bout the law catchin' up with us from the East an' runnin' us to the pokey — why, it ain't no life for kids! Things are still too rough out here in the West, an' I ain't no sort o' man who can make a good life for the five o' you like things are now."

It sounded like he was getting ready to say something awful, like that we shouldn't be together, and I couldn't keep from interrupting him.

"We don't mind it, Pa!" I said. "As long as we're with you, everything's gonna —"

"Let me finish, Corrie," said Pa, almost sternly. I sat back in my chair and waited for what would come next.

"I tell ya, there's still too much goin' on here, and I can't tell what might happen. What'd you all do if Krebbs *did* kill me? Then what?"

It was terrible to hear Pa talk like this! I looked at all the others and they were staring at him with their eyes wide open.

"I can't take the chance of you bein' left alone again," Pa went on. "I gotta do somethin' to protect you young'uns. I just can't take the chance no longer of trying to do what I can't do myself."

I couldn't help breaking into his talk again. "Mrs. Parrish'd take care of us, Pa," I said, "if something happened to you or Uncle Nick. There's nothing to worry so much about, Pa! And Zack and me, we're practically old enough to take care of the young'uns!"

"Hush, Corrie, let me have my say! This ain't easy for me neither. Now whatever you say may be true, but it ain't enough. Mrs. Parrish ain't kin, an' out here in the West, kin is what matters most. An' you an' Zack are a mighty fine young woman an' young man, I gotta admit that. But this here's the West, and things are different. If I was gone, you'd need help to get by — family kind o' help."

He stopped again and took a deep breath. He seemed getting ready for what he'd been trying to tell us all along.

"Well, ever since that Hatch deal, and Corrie tellin' me about Buck Krebbs tryin' to get her and threatenin' us, I realized I needed help with you kids. I ain't no good as a ma to you. Lord knows Corrie's a fine cook and all, but by the time school starts up in Miracle, she ain't gonna have so much time, and you younger ones is gonna need more tendin' especially when Corrie gets older. Besides that, I can't help worryin' about what might happen some day if our past catches up with me an' Nick.

"So a while back I made myself what folks

call a resolution, that I was gonna do my best to fix it so you wouldn't ever be alone, no matter what might happen, and so you'd have someone to fix your meals an' help you better'n a man like me is able to.

"It wasn't an easy decision to make, and I spent a lot o' time talkin' to your Ma about it, though I don't reckon folks like Rev. Rutledge'd take much stock in prayers prayed like that to someone else! But I can't help what he might think, my Aggie's the one this here decision concerns more'n anybody else, and somehow I had to know what she'd think of what I'm doin'. An' so in the end what I decided was that you kids need a woman around here. I gotta see about gettin' me a new wife. And so that's what I'm fixin' to do."

CHAPTER 14

THE LETTER

The moment the words "a new wife" were out of Pa's mouth, I felt a rush of warmth race into me. I'd never actually thought such a thing could be possible, knowing how Pa had felt about Mrs. Parrish. But they had been getting friendlier, and . . . well, it just seemed too good to be true!

The very idea of her as . . . as . . . the idea was just too wonderful to think about! Both my hands went to my cheeks in shocked reaction. My face was flamed, and in my brain already little bells were going off — wedding bells! I hardly stopped in that passing moment of bliss to remember Rev. Rutledge, and the look I had seen on his face when he looked at Mrs. Parrish. And I didn't hear too well what Pa said next, I was too busy thinking about Mrs. Parrish.

Finally I became aware of Pa's voice again. ". . . so you see, that's why all the fuss with the newspapers, I had to investigate, you know, and find just the right woman. It's always a gamble, because you can't see no picture and you don't know if they're tellin' you the whole truth about themselves. But you gotta do the best you can and hope things'll turn out okay.

"Well, I looked in them papers and sent some letters out to an agency in the East that said they'd advertise for me what I was lookin' for in a woman, and I read about some women whose names were in that Sacramento paper Mrs. Parrish was kind enough to get for me, but none of them seemed quite right. I told 'em not to put my name in any paper within five hundred miles of New York. And, well, this here's finally my answer. I already wrote her back and I told her about the trouble with the law, but that I was a decent man. I don't reckon we'll hear back from her for a couple of months, but after that, if she's still of a mind to come, I figure it'll be the best thing fer all of us."

Pa pulled a white envelope out of his pocket and held it up for us to see. It was rumpled. I could tell he'd read it two or three times already.

Then Pa started to read the letter out loud to us:

Dear Mr. Drummond Hollister,

My name is Katie Morgan. I am from southern Virginia, as you will see from the address on my letter. I saw your advertisement in the newspaper from Raleigh south of here. I have never been married. I am thirty years old and now live with my younger sister. But she is to be married in two months. She and I have lived with an elderly aunt and uncle for twenty years, since our parents were killed in the Black Hawk War in 1832. Our

144

uncle has not been well recently and died three months ago. Our aunt is returning to New York to live the rest of her days with another aunt, her sister. With my sister marrying, I feel it is time for me to seek a new life for myself.

I have not had many adventures in my life, though eight years ago a young entrepreneur (that's what he called himself) from New York asked me to marry him and come to live in the big city. That would have been an adventure, but I felt it my duty to remain with my aunt and uncle. Now, however, I feel perhaps the time for my life's adventure has come. My parents dreamed of settling in the West, but after they were killed by Chief Black Hawk's followers, my sister and I were sent back to Virginia. Now perhaps it is time to realize their hope, and mine. I have dreamed of travelling to California ever since 1849.

I am not beautiful, but neither am I altogether plain. I am quite short, with brown hair, a good complexion, and rather stocky build. I am not accustomed to niceties, for we have never had money to spare. I like children and animals. I know hard work and do not mind it. I am anxious enough to come to California that I will spend the little I have saved to get me there. I have saved only about half the $450, however, required to make the sea voyage by way of Panama. If you would like to see me, and would send the rest of what I need to complete the trip to Sacramento, I will stay for a month. You do not need to marry me if you do not care to. I am determined not to be a spinster, and in California I do not doubt I will be able to find a suitable man. I am not overbearing, but neither am I timid — or so my aunt has always told me.

I would like to know about your children. Your advertisement said you also live with your wife's brother? And of course, I am most interested in you. I hope to hear from you soon.

Very truly yours,
Kathryn Hubbard Morgan.

The room was silent a minute.

I had my own thoughts and emotions swimming around inside my brain trying to get over the shock of Pa getting married again — and to a stranger.

Uncle Nick had got over his initial whooping and hollering and was now sitting quietly, staring down at the floor. I reckon he was thinking about Ma, because he finally said, "It don't hardly seem like the right way of treatin' the memory of my sister, Drum, writin' off for some mail-order bride you never seen!"

Pa took in a deep breath, as if the words stung him a bit. A quick flash of pain went across his face, but it was lost as he answered Uncle Nick.

"I know what you're thinkin', Nick. I been strugglin' with the same thing for weeks an' weeks. But I gotta think this is what Aggie'd want."

He stopped, took another lungful of air, then added, "It's for her kids too, Nick — mine *and* Aggie's — that I'm doin' it. I gotta see to the raisin' of *her* kids — and I gotta do somethin' better'n what you and me can give 'em!"

Again it was quiet and nobody said anything for a long time.

"Will we have to call her Ma, Pa?" asked Becky after a spell.

There was such an innocent worry in her voice. But Pa didn't chuckle or even crack a smile. He just got up, went over and picked Becky up in his great big arms and looked into her face. Then he smiled, trying to put her mind at ease.

"You'll always have just one Ma, Becky, and nobody's gonna ever take her place. You'll call her Miss Morgan at first, and then later maybe Mrs. Hollister, or Miss Kathryn. I don't rightly know, Becky. Maybe you'll even find you like havin' another woman about the place, kinda like an aunt or somethin'. But I doubt any of you'll ever call her Ma."

"What'll she be like, Pa?"

"That I don't know, Becky! That's somethin' we're all gonna just have to wait to find out."

CHAPTER 15

SCHOOL

One of the most important things about to happen in Miracle Springs during this time, at least as far as the kids were concerned, was the opening of the Miracle Springs school.

Pa and Mrs. Parrish and the school committee had met quite a few times, and I'd been hopeful about Pa and Mrs. Parrish as a result of working like that together and seeing each other more regularly.

Pa did go to her house pretty often, and sometimes he'd take me, and it got so they were downright friendly to each other. Mrs. Parrish'd greet Pa with a smile and say, "How are you today, Mr. Hollister?" and Pa'd tell her something about the mine or what we kids had been up to while he handed her his coat and hat.

Of course most of the time Mrs. Shaw and the Dewaters were there. Rev. Rutledge was *always* there, and looking so at home and comfortable you'd think he lived there. He was always the first to come and last to go.

Nobody said anything about it, but I got the notion that people noticed his being with her so much and wondered when the new church was gonna have a pastor's wife to go with the new hymnbooks and freshly painted walls. I *wouldn've* dared ask her something like that, but I had the idea Mrs. Parrish might be wondering the same thing.

That wasn't the kind of thing that Pa and I talked about, but I know it crossed his mind now and then too. Once, coming home from town, he was quiet most of the way, and then finally, like he'd been thinking about them all the way since the meeting, he all of a sudden said, "Yep . . . she's a fine woman, that Parrish lady! I may have been wrong about her, Corrie. Ol' Rutledge's a lucky fella — the two o' them's gonna be a mighty fine thing for this town, though I never thought I'd be sayin' such a thing."

I was dying inside to ask him more of what he meant, but by then we were just coming around the bend and the cabin came into sight, and it was too late. Another meeting was scheduled the following week. Pa was taking me almost every time.

I don't know if his agitation had anything to do with what he'd said to me in the wagon, but when time for that next meeting came round he seemed nervous the whole day and quit work at the mine early so he could wash and spruce up.

When he and I got into the wagon later in the afternoon to go to town, he looked cleaner than I'd remembered seeing him in months — his hair washed and combed back, with a clean shirt and pair of trousers. I looked at him, smiled, and said, "You look real fine, Pa."

"Well, a man's gotta scrape the dirt off hisself sometime," he mumbled. "I just didn't figure I oughta be trackin' it into Mrs. Parrish's place, that's all."

Pa'd gotten ready so soon that we left earlier than we needed to. When we got to Mrs. Parrish's, we were the first ones there, even before Rev. Rutledge. But Mrs. Parrish didn't act at all surprised to see us, and invited us in and had us sit down in her parlor and gave Pa coffee while she drank a cup of tea.

For the first time I can remember, the two grown-ups I cared most about in the whole world were acting friendly toward each other. After a while Pa got to feeling at ease and told her some things about him and Uncle Nick. Mrs. Parrish laughed and laughed, and I found myself wishing there wouldn't be a school meeting at all.

But it had to come to an end by and by. Pretty soon a knock came on the door, and when Mrs. Parrish rose to answer it, into the house walked Rev. Rutledge. He seemed a bit taken off guard to find us there, because he started to say something quiet to Mrs. Parrish after she closed the door behind him, but stopped when she walked back into the parlor. When he glanced up and saw Pa, a look of surprise passed over his face, but it was quickly replaced by a smile as he walked forward and shook Pa's hand.

Pa stood and greeted him cordially. They were

on fine terms with each other by this time. But on Pa's face, too, I saw a brief look as he rose — his face did not show surprise, but rather disappointment. I glanced over at Mrs. Parrish as she watched the two men shake hands from the entryway. Her eyes were fixed on Pa instead of the minister.

Maybe Pa's growing friendship with Mrs. Parrish was why his letter from Katie Morgan took me so by surprise. I figured I was getting old enough to have him think of me as a grown-up, and I did most of the mothering for the young'uns already. As for the rest, why couldn't he hire someone to do other stuff, or ask Mrs. Parrish to look in on us every once in a while?

But I knew what he'd say to those notions — that I would soon be grown and married, and he'd still have the young'uns to take care of, that Mrs. Parrish had her own business and the affairs of the church to tend to, and that she was likely gonna be the minister's wife before long, and didn't have time to worry about us. And then he'd say that getting a new wife was the only decent solution.

Maybe he was right, but it would take some gettin' used to on my part.

In the meantime, during the first week of October Pa came home from town one day with the news that Mrs. Parrish'd gotten a reply back from one of the letters they'd sent out to a lady about being the new Miracle Springs schoolteacher.

Her name was Harriet Stansberry, and she'd been wanting to come to California from Denver with her brother. She said if the town wanted her, she'd like to accept the new teaching position.

Pa seemed real pleased with the news, and I was so happy to see him taking such an interest in the town's growth. Three weeks later, Pa asked me to come to the next school committee meeting with him.

After everyone had sat down, I was feeling strange, because both Mrs. Shaw and Mrs. Dewater were looking at me smiling. Before I had a chance to wonder too long, Mrs. Parrish said, "Your father's told you about our correspondence with Miss Stansberry, hasn't he, Corrie?"

"Yes, ma'am," I answered.

"After receiving her letter, we decided to offer her the job, which she has graciously accepted. She had one condition, however," Mrs. Parrish went on. "Here," she said, taking a white sheet of paper from the top of her oak secretary which stood next to where she sat, "I'll read you what she said."

She cleared her throat, then read: " 'I must tell you, however, that I am crippled in my left leg. It was broken by a carriage wheel when I was a child, and though I can walk on it, it is not without a considerable limp and some pain. Therefore, I make use of a cane most of the time. I am a good teacher, but some people would not be altogether comfortable having someone like

152

myself teaching their children. So I want you to know that I will understand perfectly if you feel you must withdraw your offer.'

" 'If you do want me, notwithstanding this liability, I shall be most happy to accept the position of schoolteacher at Miracle Springs, and my brother and I will plan to arrive in your community by stagecoach, weather permitting, before the worst of the winter snows set in — hopefully before the first of December. We realize the danger in the mountain passes, but we have been ready to leave Denver for some time and are anxious to come to California.'

" 'There is but one stipulation I would like to make regarding the position. Because of my injury, I will need an assistant. This should preferably be an older young person in your town who would like to not only be in my classroom, but would also be willing to help me as the need arises. A boy or girl of fourteen would be fine, although I have had assistants in the past as old as eighteen.' "

Mrs. Parrish put down the paper and stopped reading.

"Well, Corrie," she said, "will you do it?"

"Me? Be her assistant?"

"Yes, of course. We all agreed you are the perfect choice! You'll be seventeen in a few months."

I glanced around at Pa. He was smiling proudly.

"Don't look at me to tell you what to do, Corrie," he said. "This is your decision! Though what

153

the lady says is true enough — everyone here thought of you first off."

"Oh, why — yes! Of course, I'd love to, but —" I glanced over in Pa's direction again. "But what about the young'uns, Pa, and everything I gotta do at home?"

"The young'uns will be in school with you, so you can all go together and you can take just as good care of 'em there as at the cabin. And as for the rest, I'm fixin' to get you some help with all that."

This was before he'd read us the letter from Katie Morgan. In hindsight I know he was talking about her. But I didn't know it then, and I hardly paid much attention to his words at the time because of everything else about the school I was thinking.

"We thought you'd want to do it," Mrs. Parrish said, "as much as we wanted you to. We've been hoping you would be involved with the school as more than just one more of the students, and we've been glad your Pa's been bringing you to some of our meetings here. That's why we've already written Miss Stansberry, and we hope she'll be on her way to California within a week or two."

"I . . . I don't know what to say," I said.

"Just say you'll be her assistant, Corrie," said Mrs. Shaw.

"If it's all right with Pa," I said.

Pa nodded.

"Then it's all decided!" said Mrs. Parrish. She

154

rose and walked over to me and shook my hand solemnly. All the others did the same.

Pa stood back, watching, proud of what was happening, although my face was all flushed, being the center of attention in the middle of all those grown-ups.

Then we all sat down again, and there followed a lot of talk and planning about the school. They had to go to Sacramento to get some more books and other stuff. The desks and blackboards were already in the church building, but now that they'd hired a teacher who was actually on the way, suddenly they realized they had to get everything else ready as quick as they could. And there was talk, too, about the rest of the money they'd need for the books and for Miss Stansberry's salary.

But I couldn't pay much attention to all the rest of what went on that evening. I was thinking too much about what I was going to get to do, and I couldn't have been happier!

CHAPTER 16

THE FIRST DAY

The first day of school was set for December 10, 1853.

Miss Stansberry had arrived two weeks earlier. She and her brother had gotten settled in a two-room cabin at the Dewater place on the other side of town. Then she came and paid a call on us and asked me if I'd want to help her, since I was going to be her assistant at the school. She needed help sending some notices around to the folks telling about the starting up of the school.

That first week of December we wrote out lots of letters and invitations. I got my brothers and sisters to help. They were as excited about the school as I was — all except for Zack. But he did his share too.

Miss Stansberry and I rode around to visit all the families with kids and told them about the school getting ready to start up. Even with her leg being crippled, Miss Stansberry was handy with horses and handled Mr. Dewater's carriage just fine. During that time Mrs. Parrish made a trip with Rev. Rutledge down to Sacramento with one of her wagons to pick up the last of the school supplies. By the time December 10 came, everything was about as ready as a new school could be.

In connection with the school opening, I finally got to write an article for the *Gazette* — my first actual "article" in a newspaper! I don't suppose it was much, but I was proud of it and Mr. Singleton put my name at the end of it. Maybe he still felt bad about not doing the article about the mine after he'd said he would. But I didn't care about the reasons! I got to do it and that was all that mattered, and I hoped now maybe he'd let me write about other stuff too.

When the paper came out on December 8, Pa went to the General Store and bought seven copies — one for each of us, and for the first time I can remember he praised me right in front of Uncle Nick and all the rest of the kids.

"You done good, Corrie," he said. "I'm right proud o' ya!"

What a feeling that gave me! There's nothing in the world like hearing words like that from your own pa, though most folks don't hear them too often. Mrs. Parrish says we have to get from our Father in heaven what our earthly fathers don't know how to give. But for me right then, I was full to the brim with the smile Pa gave me after reading the article.

Here's what I wrote:

On December 10, the Wednesday following

this edition, the doors will be open at the new Miracle Springs School. All children and young people between the ages of five and eighteen are invited to attend. Donations for attendance will be accepted but are not required at this time. The school committee — comprised of members of the community including the Rev. Avery Rutledge, business-woman Almeda Parrish, miner Drummond Hollister —

As Pa read his own name out loud, he paused and glanced around the room with a smile. It was likely the first time he'd seen his own name in print, except on a wanted poster. And Uncle Nick gave him a little gesture of congratulation, like he was now a local celebrity.

— Mrs. Jake Shaw, and farmer Harold Dewater and his wife — have raised sufficient funds throughout the community to finance the school's operation through the Spring of 1854. Hired by the committee as the first teacher of the Miracle Springs School is Miss Harriet Stansberry, who has recently arrived in the area from Denver, Colorado with her brother Hermon. She has had teaching experience, and her classroom will prove an enriching experience for all youngsters in attendance. Miss Stansberry will be assisted by Miss Cornelia Hollister, daughter of committee member Hollister.

Pa couldn't help smiling again, and he looked briefly around at all of us before continuing.

The school building was newly built earlier this year and is also used on Sundays and special occasions for church services officiated by the Rev. Rutledge. Anyone desiring further information concerning the Miracle Springs School should contact Mrs. Almeda Parrish at the Parrish Mining and Freight Company in Miracle Springs.

— By Corrie Belle Hollister

Of course Mr. Singleton helped me with it and made it better. Words like *comprised* and *officiated* and *sufficient funds* and *finance the school's operation* were not things I would have thought of all by myself. And anybody could tell that he wrote "will prove an enriching experience for all youngsters in attendance." But he put my name on it, and just told me that's what an editor's supposed to do — make your writing better than you can make it yourself. For now I accepted Mr. Singleton's words and was happy that something I'd written (most of it, anyhow!) was being read by a hundred people in all the communities where his paper went. That was almost as exciting as the opening of the school!

The first day of school was a day to remember! There'd been some rain the night before, but the sun came out when Wednesday morning came.

We were all up early, hardly able to sleep. Even Zack was excited. Pa had taken us to the General Store and bought Zack and Tad new shirts and me and Emily and Becky new dresses for the occasion.

By now Pa wasn't embarrassed at all to show that he was eager for the school too. Being on that committee had made him feel that he was part of making a good thing come to Miracle. Maybe it made him feel that he was being a good pa to us in this one way, when he felt like he was failing us because of all the problems with men like Hatch and Krebbs making life unsafe for us.

Anyhow, that morning he was up early with the rest of us and said he wasn't going to do any work that day. He cleaned up and put on a new shirt. I felt so proud when we rode into town on the wagon — all six of us, clean and sparkling in our new shirts and dresses, Pa sitting tall in front and me beside him. All the young'uns were talking a mile a minute, and though neither Pa or I said much, we were both thinking that this was an important day and that maybe we had a part in bringing it about.

Pa led the horses right up by the school and church building, set the brake, then hopped down, and we all followed. Miss Stansberry was on the porch greeting some other children, although we were there almost before anyone else. The minister and Mrs. Parrish were there too, standing at the foot of the steps. Pa went up to them and they all shook hands.

The few other families arrived soon after us, though most of the parents just went back to their work after dropping their children off. About ten minutes later, Miss Stansberry and I went inside to get the last few details ready before she rang the bell to announce the start of class.

Just as I walked in the door, I glanced back. All around the building children were running and yelling — the younger ones, that is. The few older ones were standing around awkwardly waiting.

The last thing I saw was Pa walking off toward the main part of town with Rev. Rutledge and Mrs. Parrish. I could only see their backs, and of course I couldn't hear what they were talking about. But it was just seeing them walking along together that struck me. A year or two ago Pa might have been walking with a couple of gamblers toward the Gold Nugget saloon for a drink. Now here he was walking in the other direction — probably to one of their houses for tea and talk about the school or the church and what they had been able to do as a school committee — with the minister and an upstanding Christian lady who would never set foot in a saloon except to rescue five orphaned kids. I couldn't help thinking that maybe our coming to Miracle Springs had been good for Pa too!

The desks in the schoolroom were arranged in rows facing Miss Stansberry's. She sat in front, and behind her was a big chalkboard across the front wall. Most of the desks were double, and some seated three in a row, but there was one single one that she'd put off to one side for me, sideways and between hers and the rest, facing the middle. She wanted me to be able to participate with the rest of the class most of the time, but to be ready to get up and help her easily too. She said I would be her legs when she had things to pass around or needed to erase the chalkboard. I was easily the oldest person in the class. Zack, at fourteen, was the next oldest.

In trooped the small swarm of kids, mostly under ten, talking and buzzing like bees. Many were dressed up and scrubbed for the occasion. They scrambled around for seats, and Miss Stansberry quietly waited for the hubbub to subside before she stood up and greeted everyone.

"Good morning," she said in a cheerful voice. "Welcome to our new Miracle Springs School. I am so glad you've come! My name is Miss Stansberry, and I will be your teacher. Most of you know Corrie Hollister —"

Here she glanced in my direction and I could feel my face getting red.

"Corrie is going to be my assistant," she went on, "because, you see, I am crippled in one leg."

She walked out from around her desk, limping noticeably and not using her cane.

"So Corrie is going to help me when I need a faster pair of legs than my own. I would like you to call her Miss Hollister."

As she said this, some tittering broke out and I glanced over to see Tad saying something to Becky. But Becky wasn't listening because she was leaning in Emily's direction and had been, I think, the cause of the laughter.

"I realize this will be difficult for *some* of you," Miss Stansberry added with a smile, looking toward my brothers and sisters, "and so Corrie and I will forgive you if you forget."

The boys and girls were instantly at ease with this woman who had come from Colorado to be their teacher. I already liked her very much, and I knew they would too.

"Now, we're going to spend most of today just getting to know one another. I'll need to find out about you, and I'll tell you about me. One of the first things I need to know is who is here and what all your names are."

A chorus of high-pitched voices all started talking at once, but was immediately silenced by Miss Stansberry's hand slamming down on her desk.

"Perhaps the *first* thing we need to do is get something straight about talking out of turn!" she said sternly. "There will be no more outbursts like *that!*"

I had just begun to wonder if the older ones like Zack and I would be able to get any learning done in the midst of ten to fifteen five-to-twelve-year-olds. The sudden complete quiet that descended over the entire room was encouraging.

Miss Stansberry didn't have the chance to go on with finding out people's names, because all at once I realized all the kids' heads had turned around toward the back of the room. I followed their gazes and looked toward the schoolroom door, where I found myself gasping in amazement.

There stood a young man of sixteen or seventeen, tall and slender, with muscular, wiry limbs. His face was brown and clear, his eyes looked almost black from where I sat, and his hair was pure black and straight. If I had seen only the face, I might not have recognized him at first because since I had seen him last he had taken on many of the characteristics of manhood. But the tan buckskin shirt tunic he wore, laced up with strips of rawhide, and the braid of his hair, let me know in an instant who this unexpected visitor to our school was.

"Little Wolf!" I exclaimed, jumping up from my seat and running over to where he stood. "Are you . . . are you here for —"

"I have come to go to school," he said in a voice strangely deep since I last had heard him.

He did not smile. At first his face did not even reveal that he knew me. Coming here must have been extremely difficult for him. Seeing the disbelief lingering in my expression, he went on, relaxing somewhat as he did. "It is important that I learn what I can, for California no longer belongs only to the Indian and the Mexican."

"But your father?" I said.

"My father has agreed. Though he still resists the white man, he knows I must be educated

164

if I am to have a chance of succeeding in this new world that is rapidly coming."

As we spoke, the others in the room watched in dumbfounded silence. I then took him to the front of the class and introduced him to Miss Stansberry. She suggested that he take a seat next to Zack.

Before the first week was out, not only my desk but a small cluster including two other double desks sat off to one side of the room for the oldest among Miss Stansberry's students, including Zack and I, Little Wolf, and Artie Syfer, who came three days later and was fifteen. The only other older girl, seventeen-year-old Elizabeth Darien, didn't start in the school until February.

Eventually we had two classes in one, and the five of us older ones took care of ourselves a lot of the time, with Miss Stansberry giving us instruction during times when she'd assigned quiet desk work to the younger class. All us older ones helped her a lot. All three of the boys, even Little Wolf, really got to like her and were almost too eager to help.

But even though we were all just about the same age — Elizabeth was even older than I was, and Little Wolf might have been too — I kept being the unspoken "teacher" of the older ones when Miss Stansberry was busy. I was still her assistant, and none of the other three older ones could read, so they'd often ask me and Zack for help.

It didn't take long for Little Wolf to feel comfortable, and pretty soon he and Zack and Artie and I got to be good friends. I was so happy for Zack to have some boys his own age to be with. He brightened up a lot and started really looking forward to going to school every day. When the three of them would go off together, I didn't mind, because Miss Stansberry always treated me like her friend. She and I always had school things to talk about during free time and at lunch.

Tad and Becky and Emily had the time of their lives, although it wasn't altogether pleasant having the assistant's ten-year-old sister being the class cut-up. But there was no changing Becky! Emily, who was twelve, made up for Becky's rambunctiousness by studying hard. And Tad did what all the other eight-year-old boys in the class did — worked as much as he had to, but spent most of his energy on recess.

Maybe nobody is what you expect them to be like. Miss Stansberry certainly wasn't like I figured her to be. Knowing that she was crippled, and finding out she needed an assistant, made me expect her to be helpless or weak, and maybe not too interesting a person. But once she was in Miracle Springs, once I knew her personally, I realized I had figured on a dull, uninteresting, feeble lady with a soft, boring voice.

I couldn't have been more wrong!

I'm not good at fixing people's ages. One minute I'd almost think Miss Stansberry and I were friends and practically the same age. Then something would happen to make me realize she had taught in two or three other schools before coming to Miracle and was closer to Pa's age than mine. When we knew each other better I finally asked her age. She said she was twenty-nine.

At first glance there was nothing unusual about Miss Stansberry. Her hair was blond and pulled straight back from her face in a bun. She was thin, which made her look taller than she was, although I don't think she was more than 5'5" or 5'6". When I stood facing her she was an inch or two taller than I was. Her skin wasn't pale like an invalid's — it had a good creamy flesh tone. But when she got riled it could change to all shades of pink and red. When she was sitting quietly at her desk, her mouth seemed small, but then when she smiled it widened out, showing her teeth.

At first I didn't even notice the color of her eyes. I think they were blue. Rather than the color of them, I noticed their activity — they were always roving about the classroom, wide awake, taking in more than her mouth or any other part of her features would have told you. By the second day of school, I could tell that nothing would get past this lady! Her voice wasn't loud, but it was a bit on the deep side for a woman, a pleasant voice to hear. That voice made her even more in control when she spoke, and soon everyone in the class learned to shut their own mouths and listen when Miss

Stansberry opened hers.

The first day she was nice, smiling and laughing with us, making the school enjoyable. Early in the afternoon, Jeffrey Hobbes forgot to leave some of his brawling outside after he came in from lunch. He was cutting up and being wild. Miss Stansberry let him interrupt only once. The second time, he turned around to tease little Mary Johnston, who didn't need any help disrupting things despite the innocent look on her face! When Jeffrey turned back toward Mary, Miss Stansberry kept right on talking calmly, while she slowly limped in their direction.

All of a sudden — wham! Down on the middle of Jeffrey's desk came Miss Stansberry's cane with a loud crash! Jeffrey nearly jumped out of his skin!

I watched it all from my desk. The class was totally silent. Mary sat there with her face pale white and her eyes huge.

Miss Stansberry slowly made her way back to the front of the room, then turned around to face the class. She hesitated a minute while every one of the children stared at her.

Then she smiled broadly, showing no sign of anger, and said in a very quiet voice, "When I was young, I was taught that the moment a grown-up opens his or her mouth to speak, all children should immediately close theirs, even if the grown-up is not talking to them. This is especially true with teachers. I do not know if that is how your parents have taught you, but in *this*

168

classroom that is the rule. I hope I do not have to remind you of it again."

Right then I think all of us knew that our new teacher was a lady with gumption and that her being crippled wasn't a handicap at all.

But you'd hardly know any of this about her just by seeing her walking down the street. If you did look a second time, it would likely be on account of her cane, and maybe you'd feel sorry for her. But if you were close enough and looked a second time, her face would draw you back for a third glance. She wasn't so pretty all by herself, but that face needed a closer look.

When Pa was nice enough to invite her out to our place for dinner one Sunday afternoon, I saw Uncle Nick do all that I just described. He looked at her once, kind of glanced down in the direction of her cane, then looked back again, but this time his eyes were drawn to her face. She had brushed her hair down that day and it fell to her shoulders, so she looked different, and in that moment she'd taken her glasses off to scratch one of her eyes. So she looked a little more attractive than normal. But when he thought no one was noticing — and I suppose I was the only one who did — I saw Uncle Nick glance in her direction a third time, and this time he looked straight at her eyes.

After school one day she and I walked over to the General Store together. We happened to meet Rev. Rutledge on our way inside, just as he was coming out the door, and I saw him do the same thing. He already knew her pretty well, but after he first greeted us, he glanced back at her face twice. It was just two quick little looks, but I couldn't help noticing. It seemed everyone found more in her face to wonder about every time they saw it, and they just couldn't keep from going back.

I liked Miss Stansberry, and I think most of the other people around town did, too. Before a month was out, folks forgot all about her being crippled.

CHAPTER 17

OUR SECOND CHRISTMAS

When Christmas came, we had a big dinner at *our* place!

It was Pa's idea. He and Uncle Nick had steadily been working on the cabin all year. Now that they could afford to buy what they needed, and had a growing family of seven in all, the place had kept getting smaller and smaller. Pa added our room right after we came, and by now he'd had also put in another bedroom off on the other side of the cabin for himself and Uncle Nick. He was even talking about a third room, so the two boys could share one room and we three girls another!

In the meantime, though, in the process of putting on his and Uncle Nick's room, he'd redone the main room. It was now a little bigger with more of a separate kitchen-place to work when I was cooking and fixing meals. It wasn't just a *cabin* anymore but a good-sized house. I think Pa was proud of the place and wanted to show it off a little.

Or maybe he just wanted to be hospitable. Ma always said hospitality was what turned a house into a *home,* and Pa had mentioned that a time or two.

Whatever his reasons, one day about the middle of December he said to me, "Corrie, what would you think if we was to have some folks out here for Christmas afternoon?"

"I'd like that, Pa," I answered him.

"I mean a great big fancy dinner. We'll have it right here, and we'll let folks see that we're a family and this is our home."

"Yes, Pa!" I replied, excited already. "You mean folks like Mrs. Parrish —"

"Sure," he answered back quickly, "her and her minister-friend —"

"He's our friend too, isn't he, Pa?"

"Yes, of course — the Parrish woman, Rutledge, maybe your new teacher and her brother — wouldn't want them to have no place to go right after comin' to town — an' Alkali."

"Oh, Pa, I can't wait! Do you want me to tell Miss Stansberry and Mrs. Parrish when I'm in town for school tomorrow?"

"No, Corrie, I'm the man of the house. I'll do the invitin'."

I'd noticed him mention being the man of the house or the head of the family several times lately. I think it was still heavy on his mind, like he'd explained when he'd read us the letter from Miss Morgan that he had a responsibility to provide for us and protect us and all. How Christmas dinner fit into that, I wasn't quite sure, except that I think Pa had been looking for ways to do what I already thought he did better than

172

any man I knew of — being what you'd call a "family man."

He did invite them too, the very next day. He wouldn't even let me go along. Wanted to do it himself, he said. He even took a bath and put on a fresh shirt for the occasion, as if going to Mrs. Parrish's just to invite her to dinner was an event in itself. It looked to me like at last the two of them were starting to get along real well. I found myself secretly wishing something would go wrong with Miss Katie Morgan's plans to come out West.

There was a change in Mrs. Parrish too. I noticed it for the first time when she arrived out at our place that Christmas morning. She'd always been so nice to me and I knew we were friends. Although she and Pa'd had their differences, she was civil to him and they'd been getting along fine for a long time.

But when she came out that Christmas morning, it wasn't just that she was *nice* to me and the kids, she suddenly seemed a part of our lives — all of us, Pa and Uncle Nick too. She wasn't like a stranger helping us out. She looked like she really belonged, like she wanted to belong to *all* of our lives — not just the part of us that came to town and visited her in *her* house.

Of course she came with Rev. Rutledge as usual. But as soon as they got there they went their separate ways, and the minister didn't really seem to know what to do with himself. He tried to talk to Pa and Uncle Nick; they were polite and answered his questions about the mine and what they were doing around the place. But there was a kind of awkwardness too. It was clear he was trying to fit in where he didn't really belong.

I don't fault him for that, because that's what a minister's got to do sometimes — he's got to be interested in what people are doing. And Pa was as polite to him as he could be. Pa had come to respect the minister's willingness to dirty his hands and get blisters building the church and pitching in and helping folks when he could.

Even on that day, I saw them once standing by the creek together talking. The minister was kneeling down scooping up a handful of the gravelly dirt and Pa was pointing to something — probably a flake of gold — and explaining something to the minister. And I knew that the part of Rev. Rutledge that didn't act like a fuddy-duddy about man's work, Pa thought a good deal of. Yet there was still a difference between them — ministers, it seemed to me at least, just couldn't ever *really* be like other men. Or maybe it was just that other men could never completely forget that a man was a minister, and therefore couldn't help treating him just a little different. I won't say Pa put on his good behavior around Rev. Rutledge. Pa wasn't that sort of man. But he didn't talk to him like he would to Alkali Jones either.

The minute Mrs. Parrish set foot out of the minister's buggy that day, it was like *she* was one of our family, and Rev. Rutledge was the only guest. Always before, when we'd visit at her place in town, it was the two of them — Mrs. Parrish and the minister — with us kind of set apart. But this day it was different!

She marched right into the house, greeting everyone warmly, shaking Pa's hand and smiling at him and thanking him for inviting her to be part of our family's Christmas. She carried a big basket in her hand full of rolls she had made and cranberries and several pies. All the kids were clamoring around her as she went in, Pa following too; and when she set the basket down on the table and started pulling out the pies, Pa laughed and said he'd asked for them. It was such a nice friendly atmosphere, just the way Christmas ought to be!

And then as the men looked on, she pulled off her coat, took off her bonnet, handed them to Pa, then looked at me and Emily and said, "Well, girls, what's to be done? Let's get this Christmas feast underway!"

She strode into the kitchen like it was her own with Emily and Becky and me following behind her, proceeding to lift lids and sniff and poke around to assess what I'd already done. Within five minutes we were all working away on different parts of the meal. Mrs. Parrish sure brightened up the place!

When the men started to walk outside, I saw a look of hesitation on Zack's face. Ordinarily he would have gone off with the men in a second, but I think even he could feel the warmth inside the house just from having Mrs. Parrish there. When she asked him if he'd like to help by setting out the plates and silverware on the table, he almost looked relieved to have a reason to stay inside with Mrs. Parrish and the rest of us.

Alkali Jones was the next to show up and not long after him Miss Stansberry and her brother Hermon rode up in their buggy. Miss Stansberry came inside to help us while all the men took a walk up the creek to the mine. It was an hour later before everything was ready. It took the meat a good while to cook — Mr. Jones had brought a salted ham and Pa'd killed four fat chickens for the meal — and we had to cut up a lot of potatoes for that many mouths.

At last we were ready, and how small that house seemed with twelve people sitting around the table, even with the extra planks Pa brought in! Everybody had such fresh and happy looks on their faces — Mrs. Parrish and Miss Stansberry had rosy glowing cheeks from being inside and working over boiling kettles and the hot stove. And all the men had that crisp look of walking into a warm room from the cold outside. But it was the smiles most of all that said to me this was what Christmas was supposed to be like.

When Pa pulled out Ma's Bible, I thought I was going to start crying for joy. I thought he'd forgotten all about it earlier in the morning when we'd given each other our gifts. But he hadn't at all! He'd just been saving it for now, like he really was trying to let all these other folks be part of our family.

"Before we get this eatin' shindig underway," Pa said, "I think I oughta read the Christmas passage. It's somethin' me and Aggie started after Corrie was born. I don't mean to be intrudin' on your territory, Reverend, but I reckon if me and these kids're gonna have to get along without her —"

Pa stopped, but only for a second. I could tell this wasn't easy for him to do, but was something he felt he had to do.

"If we're gonna get along without her, then I reckon there's some things in the way of religious instruction maybe I'm gonna have to start attendin' to."

He stopped again, opened the Bible, and started reading the familiar words from Luke: *"And it came to pass in those days that there went out a decree from Caesar Augustus, that all the world should be taxed. . . ."*

As he read, there was not just a silence in the room but a deep sense of something else too, something like contentment or peace. Even Uncle Nick and Mr. Jones had looks of respect on their faces. A year earlier they might have kidded Pa for being too "religious." But now I think they realized he was becoming even a stronger man than before, that the family side of him was taking a firmer hold on things. Pa didn't seem embarrassed about doing what he was doing in front of the minister. I was so proud of him!

Mrs. Parrish saw it too, because when Pa fin-

177

ished and sat down and closed the Bible, she was looking deeply into his face with a glistening around her eyes.

There was just a moment's hesitation, then she said, "Thank you so much, Mr. Hollister, for sharing that part of your family's tradition with the rest of us! It makes us feel very much included in your family on this holy day."

Rev. Rutledge added an "Amen," and there were a few other comments and thank yous. Then Mrs. Parrish said — and in thinking it over afterward, I'm sure she did it to save Pa being put on the spot — "It looks to me like the food's about ready to eat. Rev. Rutledge, would you be so kind as to offer thanks to the Lord for us?"

I could see that Pa was relieved, for reading from the Bible is a different matter from praying out loud in front of a lot of people. By the time Rev. Rutledge finally got around to his "Amen," Pa probably wished he had done the praying, because it was time to start thinking about how to warm the food up again!

CHAPTER 18

PA'S ANNOUNCEMENT

It was sure a different Christmas dinner than last year!

Everything had been so tense then, with angry words exchanged between Pa and Rev. Rutledge, ending with Pa's leaving the house. Who'd have ever thought that a year later we'd be sitting around a table together again, laughing and talking like everyone'd been friends for years? And by the end of the meal even Mr. and Miss Stansberry seemed like part of our Miracle Springs family.

"So tell me, Mr. Jones," Miss Stansberry was saying, since she happened to be sitting next to the old prospector, "you say you were the first to discover gold in this area?"

"That's right, ma'am. It was all on account —"

"Come on, Alkali," interrupted Pa with a laugh, "we've all heard that story a dozen times, and you don't want to bore the schoolteacher with somethin' she'll see right through!"

"On the contrary, I would like to hear it."

"It ain't nothin' but a parcel of make-believe, Miss Stansberry," put in Uncle Nick.

"Nevertheless," she replied, turning to Uncle Nick, "I think I ought to be allowed to judge that for myself. But before Mr. Jones continues, I must ask you to please call me Harriet."

"My pleasure, ma'am," said Uncle Nick, giving her a nod of the head. "Now please, Mr. Jones, in spite of what your friends say, I want to hear your account."

Pa and Uncle Nick leaned back in their chairs as if expecting a good laugh, and Alkali Jones lit into his story of finding gold in the Miracle Springs Creek. All the others listened in rapt attention, while Pa and Uncle Nick, with Zack joining in their fun, chuckled and winked through it all.

When he was through, the minister said, "Well, I must say that is quite a tale, Mr. Jones."

"Don't you believe a word of it, Reverend," laughed Pa.

"Aren't you being a little hard on your friend, Drummond?"

"Alkali's used to it by now, ain't ya, Alkali?"

"Aw, Drum," shot back Mr. Jones in his high-pitched voice, "you durned newcomers thinks you know everythin', but if it hadna been for us old timers in these parts, there wouldna been no gold for the likes o' you!" Then, so that no one would take him too seriously and think he was really arguing with Pa, he let out with his high cackle, "Hee, hee, hee!"

"An whose claim's keepin' you in beans an' new boots?" put in Uncle Nick, not wanting to miss out on the sport of giving Alkali Jones a good ribbing.

"Hee, hee, hee! I found it, an' the two o' you's makin' me work your claim for my own measly little share! Hee, hee!"

"Is there actually more gold to be found?" asked Hermon Stansberry, to no one in particular.

"That depends on who you talk to," said Pa.

"The hills are full o' it, if ye ask me," said Mr. Jones. "Why, jist the other day I was up on Baseline ridge, an' I seen —"

"Oh, not another strike, Alkali!" said Uncle Nick, shooting Pa a quick wink.

"Jist hold on to your hat, Nick," Alkali shot back. "I seen ol' man Strong, you know the ol' varmint that lives up there in the hills trappin' coons and shootin' bear. He ain't never had no interest in gold. He says you can't eat gold an' it won't keep you warm at night, so he sees no good in the stuff. Well, he told me even *he's* spotted gold in his stream, an' he ain't even lookin' fer it!"

His words silenced even Pa and Uncle Nick for a minute.

"What is your opinion, Mrs. Parrish?" asked Mr. Stansberry. "I understand your business supplies the miners with much of their equipment and supplies."

"Yes, I do," replied Mrs. Parrish, then smiled with fun in her eyes. "But most of the men in these parts do not share their views with me — even their views on the future of the gold rush."

She glanced over in Pa's direction. "Would you say that's a fair assessment, Mr. Hollister?" Still the humor was on her face. "Aren't most miners — men like yourself, for instance — reluctant to make a woman their confidante?"

"Them's your words, ma'am, not mine," answered Pa.

Mrs. Parrish laughed. "Cryptic to the end! Very well, I see I'm going to have to answer Mr. Stansberry's question myself." Then she turned more serious and looked back at Miss Stansberry's brother. "I would say, yes, there is a great deal of gold still in California to be found," she went on. "But that is merely a guess on my part. Opinions vary widely, as you can imagine. There are those who thought it was played out in 1850, yet new strikes continue to be made. Our own town here boomed at first, then slowed down. People left their claims, only to suddenly spring back with new strikes throughout the area as a result of what happened right here on Mr. Hollister's land. My own feeling is that gold still exists in abundant supply, but that in coming years it will be increasingly difficult, first to locate, and then to extract."

"The lady's exactly on the target," added Pa. "Harder to find, harder to get at."

"And it's takin' bigger, more expensive equipment, too," said Uncle Nick. "Big outfits is comin' in from all over the place."

"Squeezin' the little guys like us clean outta the gold fields, that's what they's doin'!" said Alkali Jones.

This time his words weren't followed by a

182

laugh. "Pannin' fer gold in a stream ain't findin' much these days, less ye gets lucky like ol' man Strong! Naw, fer fellers like us it's mostly gone."

"That must be good for you, at least, Mrs. Parrish," said Miss Stansberry. "Selling the new gold companies their machinery?"

"Unfortunately," replied Mrs. Parrish, "the way of the small business is probably doomed to go the way of the little one-man claim. My business has always been with local operations, transporting things for them — supplies, small equipment. But the big outfits that are coming in bring their own machinery. They see someone like me, and a woman to boot, as little more than a General Store for miners — strictly small time."

"But you provide a valuable service for all the miners for miles, Almeda," said Rev. Rutledge. He hadn't said a word during the whole discussion about gold mining. "You mustn't be too pessimistic. I'm certain all the men in Miracle Springs will continue to need the goods and services you offer for many years to come."

"The Reverend's right, ma'am," said Uncle Nick, and for some reason I was surprised by his kind words. "None of us coulda got by like we have if it hadn't been for your company an' the ways you help the men."

Both Pa and Alkali Jones nodded their heads and mumbled words of agreement. Mrs. Parrish seemed genuinely touched.

"There, you see what I mean, Almeda," Rev.

Rutledge added. "These men hereabouts aren't about to desert you after all you've done, notwithstanding what the larger companies may be doing."

"Well, I must say, that is kind of you, Avery," Mrs. Parrish sighed, "kind of you all! But, I don't know — I do wonder about the future sometimes. A woman, alone like I am, running a business that perhaps there won't be a need for one day. Sometimes I think I ought to find a rich miner or rancher to marry, and think about being a wife instead of a businesswoman!"

My head shot up at the words. I didn't know if she was being serious, like her voice had sounded just a moment before when talking about the future of her store, or if she was joking again.

Her words caught everyone off guard. As I looked across the table, I saw the minister, who'd been looking right into her face, glance away and start fiddling with something on his plate. His neck showed just a touch of red in it and he didn't say anything more.

As he looked away, there were a couple of "Ahem — ahem's" around the table, people clearing their throats. But when I saw Mrs. Parrish's face, I could tell in a second that she'd been funning, because she threw me a quick little smile.

Now Alkali Jones's quick wit saved the conversation. "Well, ma'am," he said, and you could almost hear his high cackle ahead of time, "I don't know no ranchers here 'bouts needin' no settlin', but I knows where ye might find yourself a rich miner! Hee, hee, hee!"

Uncle Nick and Mrs. Parrish seemed to appreciate his humor, but neither Pa nor Rev. Rutledge did much laughing.

One thing I was learning from watching Mrs. Parrish around other people was how she was always watching them, always trying to put them at ease, always trying to say or do something that would keep them from being on the spot or from feeling small. She didn't want the conversation to get awkward for anyone — or for herself — and so her next words steered the talk another direction.

"Well, I must admit," she said cheerily, "this is certainly a more cordial Christmas gathering than I was able to provide last year!" She laughed, and gradually most of the others joined in.

Miss Stansberry looked at her with a question on her face, so Mrs. Parrish continued. "The children and Mr. Hollister had not been together long, and Avery had only been in Miracle Springs a month. I had not been altogether gracious in some of the things I had said and done toward Mr. Hollister, and no doubt —" and here she turned an apologetic smile in Uncle Nick's direction — "toward Mr. Belle as well. Anyway, we had what you might call an uncomfortable Christmas gathering at my home, for which I have always felt bad. I am just grateful that Mr. Hollister and Mr. Belle — and the children, of course! —" She looked around at each one of us quickly, then resumed, "I'm glad they have all opened their home to us so graciously!"

"Amen — amen!" added the minister.

But her bringing up last year's Christmas only seemed to deepen Pa's silence and he didn't say anything. Afraid, maybe, that it was going to turn out like last year after all, Mrs. Parrish struck up again, though now I thought I heard some nervousness in her breezy tone.

"And now that I think of it, Mr. Hollister," she said, "haven't we had something like this discussion about the future of the gold fields before?"

But it wasn't Pa who answered, but Uncle Nick.

"That's right! I recollect the day! It was with that low-down Royce back when folks was sellin' off their claims!"

"The weasel!" added Mr. Jones. "Why, if it hadna been fer Tad an' Zack here, the durned varmint woulda had the whole blamed town an' valley by now!"

"What's this? Have two of my students done something I should know about?" asked Miss Stansberry, glancing first at Tad, beaming with pleasure, and then at Zack, who looked more embarrassed than proud.

"Heroes, that's what those two are!" put in Rev. Rutledge.

"I want to hear all about it!" Miss Stansberry said. "It sounds exciting!"

"Exciting's hardly the word for it," added Mrs. Parrish. "These two lads did nothing short, I ven-

186

ture to say, of changing the very course of Miracle Springs' history! And certainly Corrie's part can't be overlooked either. She overheard Royce's plan and then ran into town to —"

All this time since Mrs. Parrish's comment about getting married, Pa had kept quiet. Though the talk around the table had picked back up, he'd just been staring down at the table like he was thinking about something else. Now all of a sudden he looked up, took in a deep breath, and interrupted Mrs. Parrish's story.

"I got somethin' to tell you all," he blurted out. "I'm sorry to break into your story, ma'am, and it's not like I ain't proud of my kids for what they done. But one of the reasons I wanted to have some of you here today — though Nick and the kids, we already talked about this, but you, ma'am, an' the minister, an' Alkali — well, I got somethin' I gotta say and I figured this'd be just about the easiest way to get you all in one place like this, and just say it."

When he stopped to take a breath, it was so quiet around that table you could have heard a sparrow chirp clear up at the mine. Nobody so much as lifted a fork to eat another bite.

"I know I'm kinda spoilin' your nice conversation, but your sayin' what you done, Alkali, put me in mind of what I want to say, so I reckon I just gotta rustle up my gumption and say it."

Again he paused, sucked in a breath of air, and forged ahead.

"Well," he said, "I been thinkin' real hard about the kids here, and about what I'm needin' to do for them, to be the sort of father I want to be to 'em, and what's for their best, an' all. So I talked to some folks and I put an advertisement in some papers out East, an' I got a letter back from a nice-soundin' young lady from Virginia who's willin' to come. So I wrote her, and I'm fixin' to send her some money to pay to get her here, and she's gonna come an' be a wife to me and help me raise my kids like they oughta be raised. There! That's what I gotta say!"

He sighed real big and kind of relaxed back in his chair.

"Whew, Drum!" whistled Alkali Jones. "When you say somethin', blamed if you don't say a mouthful! Ya mean to say you's gonna git yerself married again?"

"That's what I just said, Alkali," answered Pa, sounding almost irritated at having to repeat it.

"Well, if that don't beat all! Hee, hee, hee!"

"Well, well! Ahem — congratulations, Mr. Hollister," said Rev. Rutledge, half rising out of his chair and offering Pa his right hand.

Pa shook it, but his heart didn't really seem in it. He didn't look the minister directly in the eye as he did so.

"Yes, Mr. Hollister," added Miss Stansberry warmly. "Congratulations! That is wonderful news!"

Somehow, though, it didn't feel as wonderful

188

as it ought to. As I glanced around the table, none of my brothers and sisters had smiles on their faces. I suppose we'd get used to the notion of Pa having a new wife, but I couldn't help thinking about Ma.

Mrs. Parrish just looked down at her plate and got real quiet.

CHAPTER 19

A TALK AFTERWARD

It's a good thing dinner was mostly over when Pa told everyone about Katie Morgan, because after that it was quiet with the sounds mostly of forks scratching around on plates and chewing and passing plates around. Pa squirmed in his seat a little. His sudden announcement threw a bucket of cold water on what had been a pretty lively and fun talk around the table.

Miss Stansberry and Rev. Rutledge kept on talking, but mostly about her coming and what she thought California was like and how the school was getting along. She asked him about the church, and they laughed over things having to do with sharing the building for their two "ministries," as they called them.

Alkali Jones tried to get Pa talking about mining again, but without any success. Then he turned to Uncle Nick and was talking away to him, but I got the feeling Uncle Nick was trying to listen across Mr. Jones to what Miss Stansberry was saying, so he was involved in both conversations at once. Neither Pa or Mrs. Parrish said much of anything, so the rest of the meal was a little strange.

I was sitting next to Pa. Finally I asked him, quietly — because I just wanted to know for myself — when Miss Morgan was coming. I guess everyone heard me, because they all turned to listen to Pa's answer.

"April, Corrie, or May," he said, "or whenever she can get passage on a ship. Folks are pouring west now, and I reckon sometimes they're filled up."

That loosened Pa up some, just getting his tongue working again, and gradually the talk started to flow better as we got up from the table. The men went over by the fire and lit up their pipes, the women — including Becky and Emily and me — started clearing off the things from the table. But no one asked Pa the question I wanted so badly to ask: When was he planning to marry Miss Morgan?

"We'll clear up some of these things," Mrs. Parrish announced, "and give your stomachs a chance to rest, and then put out the pies!"

"Now you're talkin'! Hee, hee!" laughed Alkali Jones, and other enthusiastic comments followed.

I looked around at the men standing by the fire filling their pipes and talking, and at us kids and Miss Stansberry and Mrs. Parrish in the kitchen putting the food away and stacking the plates to take outside to wash. Listening to all the sounds and voices, I thought to myself that it had turned out to be a right fine Christmas after all. I was worried there at the table for a

191

few minutes when it got quiet, and I couldn't help thinking about all the trouble a year earlier. But now everyone's good spirits were back.

A few minutes later, while I was taking the leftover chicken off the bones so we'd be able to divide it up for everyone to take home, I realized Mrs. Parrish wasn't in the cabin. At first I figured maybe she'd gone out to the outhouse or to take some dishes to the pump-sink outside, but when she was still gone ten minutes later I thought I'd go see.

By then Miss Stansberry had Becky and Emily organized into a cleaning troop between the table and the stove, and the three of them were chattering away. Mr. Stansberry was showing Tad his whittling knife. Zack was with Pa and Uncle Nick and the minister and Alkali Jones. So I figured nobody'd miss me for a few minutes. I cleaned the grease off my fingers, wiped them off with a towel, and went outside.

It was a sunshiny day, but cold. I could see my breath in the air. I glanced around. Mrs. Parrish wasn't at the pump, and I was already getting chilly. So I went back inside, got on my coat, and came back into the fresh, clean air that felt so good against my face — especially with a full stomach!

I looked up and down the creek as I started walking. At first I didn't know where to go, but then I saw Mrs. Parrish. She was about halfway up toward the mine, leaning against one of the big man-size rocks the creek worked its way around. I walked toward her, not really knowing what I was going to say. Then it suddenly dawned on me that she must have come out here to be alone.

Embarrassed, I started to back away, but it was too late. She'd heard me and turned her head around.

"Corrie," she said, smiling. "You found me!"

"I didn't mean to bother you, ma'am, I just didn't see you and got to wondering if —"

"Oh, think nothing of it, Corrie," she said. "I've had plenty of time alone with my thoughts. I'm sure the Lord knew some pleasant company was just what I needed."

I didn't say anything.

"It's been a wonderful Christmas, hasn't it, Corrie?" she said brightly.

"Yes, ma'am."

"Just the kind of day to remind us of the Lord's coming to earth." She paused a second, then added, "How are you finding this Christmas for *you,* Corrie — after a year here, a year with your father, a year thinking more personally about God's life with us?"

No one would ever accuse Mrs. Parrish of beating around the bush when she had something to say! But my thoughts were still of Christmas and pies, and I wasn't very quick about an answer.

"I don't know, ma'am, I guess I hadn't been thinking just now about it."

"I'm sorry," she laughed. "I suppose I always get more pensive on Christmas day than most

193

people. But I always try to slip away by myself at least twice on days like this, especially Christmas, just to keep myself from being so caught up in the hubbub and the conversation and the food and the merrymaking going on around me, to remind myself of what it's *really* about — that Jesus came to live among us, and to help us be like Him."

"I thought of all that this morning," I said. "I got up early and prayed some — and, of course, when Pa read the Christmas story. I guess I had forgotten about it for most of the day."

"There's nothing wrong with the merrymaking," she said. "Christmas is a festive time, a time to be happy with family and friends. But as I said, I like to remind myself about its true meaning as often as I'm able. Your Pa's voice had a real nice sound to it when he read," she added, bringing Pa up without even a pause. "It must make you happy to have him working to be a good father and family man."

"Yes, ma'am, I reckon," I said. She must have heard the hesitation in my voice.

"You sound a little doubtful, Corrie," she said, looking at me steadily. I didn't say anything right off, and she gave me time to think out my answer.

"I'm pleased enough about Pa," I said finally. "You know that, ma'am. You know I think he's a fine man, and I'm just proud as I can be. Him inviting all you folks here today was such a wonderful thing for him to do! But, I don't know, ma'am, it's just that him getting married again — well, that's a turn of events that's kinda hard to take hold of."

"Ah, yes . . . I know what you mean," she replied with a kind of half smile that seemed to hold back more than it said. "I must admit it took me by surprise, too."

"Do *you* think he ought to marry again, ma'am?" I asked.

"Oh, Corrie!" she answered with a laugh that sounded a little jittery. "That is hardly a question that it seems I have any right to consider. What your father does is his business, after all."

"You're like part of our family, Mrs. Parrish," I said.

"That's kind of you to say, Corrie." She put her hand on mine and smiled.

"It's true, ma'am, and so I think that gives you the right to say what you think."

"Of course, I have tried to do my best for you children —"

"And you have, ma'am!" I said. "You've been just — just like — you've been better for all of us than we deserved!"

Before the words were out of my mouth, I was crying, though I didn't know why. Her hand, still on mine, gave me a squeeze.

"And it just doesn't seem right somehow," I went on, but now the words were getting all jumbled in my thoughts, "for Pa to bring somebody here we don't even know to take care of us. We don't need anybody else! We're doing just

fine the way it is, with all of us and Pa and —
and you, ma'am, and I just don't see why —"

I couldn't finish, because I was sobbing pretty
hard by now.

For a long time Mrs. Parrish just let me cry,
stroking my head with one hand while the other
held mine.

When she finally did speak again, her voice
was so tender, it reminded me of Ma comforting
me when I was little.

"There's an old saying, Corrie," she said softly,
"that wives have to learn and have been repeating
to themselves for years. And until they learn it,
life can be downright miserable for them if they're
going to try to understand everything their man
does."

She paused and looked away. I hadn't seen that
far-off gaze in her face for a long time. The few
times I had seen it, it always reminded me of
someone thinking about something that happened
a long time ago. I didn't know if Mrs. Parrish
was thinking about her husband or about something else, but her words seemed to be coming
out of something that had happened to show her
what an important lesson it was to learn.

"And this is how folks put it, Corrie," she finally
said, turning back toward me. "Sometimes men
have just got to do what their hearts are telling
them to do. Half the time to the women in their
life — whether it's a wife, a sweetheart, a friend,
or, like you, a daughter — it doesn't seem to
make sense, but once a man feels that he's got

196

to do something, he *has* to do it or he'll never be able to live with himself afterward."

"But what if it's something he doesn't need to do?" I insisted. "Like with this Miss Morgan coming? We don't need any help! Pa's a good pa and we're getting old enough to take care of ourselves."

"I think I understand a little how you feel, Corrie. But once a man's set on something, whether it makes sense or not, or even whether it's right or not, he's got to go ahead with it for his own sake. If he's wrong, well, that's something he has to find out for himself, and no amount of female persuasion is usually going to make any difference.

"And, Corrie, who's to say your father *is* wrong? I've never been a father — I've never even been a parent. And though I love you and the others like you were my own, the fact is that I can't really *know* what it's like for your pa inside, feeling the responsibility of caring for a family without a wife, with all the troubles he's had following him around. It must be a terrible burden for him sometimes. And I do know this, that he wouldn't be doing this if he didn't feel it was the right thing to do for all of you."

"Well, if he's gotta find a new wife —" I began, my tears starting up again.

I was arguing with myself, though I didn't really realize that till I thought about it later. Ever since Pa'd read us Miss Morgan's letter I'd been all mixed up inside about it, and now all at once everything I'd been thinking was coming out at Mrs. Parrish. "If he's gotta find a new wife, then what's wrong with somebody around here we know? Why couldn't he get someone like the widow Jackson that lives over by Fern lake? She's nice and comes to church and is always nice to us kids. Or why couldn't he — why couldn't he marry somebody — somebody like you!"

I started sobbing again as the words I hadn't planned burst out.

Mrs. Parrish looked sharply away. Through my own tears I saw her turn her head. My first thought was that I'd hurt her by what I said, and anytime you can get your mind thinking of somebody else, even if just for a second, you forget your own troubles.

"I'm — I'm sorry, Mrs. Parrish," I said. "I didn't mean to say something to upset you. I didn't even know what I was saying!"

She turned back toward me with the tenderest smile I'd ever seen on her face. Her cheeks were a little red and her eyes were blinking a little harder than usual. Right at that moment she looked prettier than I'd ever seen her before.

"Oh, Corrie — Corrie!" she said in barely more than a whisper. "You dear, dear girl!"

She drew in a deep sigh. "You haven't hurt me, Corrie," she said softly. "That was one of the nicest things you could ever have said! But sometimes a woman's emotions can't be trusted. You'll understand that better when you get a little older. Then you'll know what it's like to suddenly find your eyes misting over when you don't know why. But — what am I saying? — I guess you know about that already!" she added, laughing.

"I reckon I do."

"I forget you're already a woman in many ways! I apologize."

"Now it's my turn to say I didn't take offense."

She smiled. "I suppose both of us will have many new things to get used to, many adjustments to make," said Mrs. Parrish.

"You too, ma'am?"

"Well, your father's marrying is bound to change — change . . . the way — well, you and he won't be coming over to my house for tea before school meetings anymore!" This last part she added hurriedly, as if she only just thought of it.

"We'll still be friends, won't we, Mrs. Parrish? You'll still come and visit and talk to me about — you know, about everything?"

"Of course, Corrie! Nothing will ever change our special friendship. But Miss Morgan — I suppose I'll have to get used to calling her the new Mrs. Hollister! — she'll be your friend too, I'm certain of it. And she'll want you to confide in her also."

"But I don't want to confide in her!" I half-shouted back, my anger and frustration coming out again. "I don't need anyone but Pa and you!"

Mrs. Parrish smiled. But she didn't speak immediately. She seemed to be thinking. Then finally she said, "Have I told you about everything working out for good, Corrie?"

"I don't remember exactly," I answered. "I suppose I've heard you talk about it before."

"There's a verse in Romans, Corrie, that says everything will work out for our good in the end *if* we love God and are called according to His purpose. And I think perhaps we need to remember that right now with your pa marrying again."

"But I don't see how *everything* can be good?"

"It doesn't say that everything is good. It says that *in* everything God is able to work out good, to make good come out of it."

"For everybody?"

"No. For those that love God — that is, for Christians who are called according to His purpose — in other words, those whose lives are ordered by God's ways, not their own. It means that if a Christian is trying to live by obeying God's ways and doing what God wants, rather than living for himself, God will be able to make all things work out for good in the end. Even if something bad happens, if you are trying to live by God's principles, not selfishly, then good will come out of it for you in the end."

"What you're saying, then, is that if Pa's going to marry Miss Morgan, good will come out of it."

"Yes, I guess that's what I'm saying. I can't say whether he was right or wrong to write her and ask her to come to California. I only know that for you and me — *if* we are faithful to live as Christians by God's principles — it will work out for good in the end. We don't need to worry about your Pa, except to pray for him. All we need remember is to obey God, and then we can trust good to be the ultimate result."

Both of us were quiet for a spell.

"I guess you're right," I finally sighed. "But it's hard to trust God when things look like they're going in a way you don't want them to go."

"Remember the fog in front of San Francisco, Corrie? Many times we can't see what God sees. He may be doing things we have no idea of. He can see a lot further ahead than we can."

I smiled up at her. "I know you're right. But it's hard to grab hold of the kinds of things you say sometimes."

"It takes time to get some of these lessons deep enough into your heart that you can start living them. And hurts and pains are a required part of the learning too. Nothing much worth learning comes without pain. Maybe now God's giving you a chance to feel some anxious thoughts so you can grow a little closer to Him by trusting Him to work out what's best."

"I hope that's it," I said.

"But don't you think we've been away long enough? They're going to think we skipped out to leave all the cleaning up for them!"

Mrs. Parrish took a step or two away from the rock, then reached her arms high above her head and took in a deep breath of the cold Christmas air.

"Oh, Corrie!" she said, "It's so wonderful here! This is the day of all days to remember that we needn't fear for what lies ahead. You have a home, a family, this beautiful place, and a loving Father in heaven watching over your every need!"

She turned back toward me and embraced me warmly. We held each other tight for a moment, then stepped back. Tears sprang to our eyes again, but neither of us said anything.

Then she took my hand and we began walking back down the slope toward the cabin. I glanced in that direction just in time to see Pa, who'd been standing on the porch, turn and go back inside. I wondered if he had been watching us. But I don't think Mrs. Parrish saw him.

"I think it's time we spread out those pies!" she said. "Knowing how men are, your pa will probably already be hungry again!"

CHAPTER 20

THE REST OF CHRISTMAS DAY

When we got back to the cabin, the spirits inside were high again.

In one corner Alkali Jones was telling one of his tall tales. The laughter of the kids and the gleam in his eye told me he was spinning a good one, probably no more true than his occasional claim that he told Sutter where to build his mill.

Miss Stansberry still held a dishtowel in her hand, but instead of using it on anything she was talking to the minister with Uncle Nick standing to her right, listening to every word. I don't think I'd ever seen Rev. Rutledge and Uncle Nick say two words to each other without Pa or Mrs. Parrish around. Now there they both were with Miss Stansberry.

Pa and Hermon Stansberry were at the fire, and it looked like Pa was explaining something to him about one of his guns. Pa was looking toward the door, and the minute we came in he burst out, as if he hadn't seen us just a moment before, "Where you ladies been? We was about figurin' on diggin' into them pies without the two of you!"

Mrs. Parrish laughed and threw it right back at him, "Don't you dare, Mr. Hollister! When I bring pies to such a festive gathering as this, I reserve the right to cut them myself!"

She came into the room as if it were her own house and marched right over to the basket of pies and started pulling them out. The minute she was back, the younger kids deserted poor Mr. Jones. His best story couldn't hold a candle to being with Mrs. Parrish!

"Now, children, what would everyone like, do you suppose?" she said, testing a knife with the edge of her thumb.

"Apple . . . pumpkin . . . mince!" came the shouts all at once.

"Please, please!" she replied with a pretend scowl and a wag of her finger. "Who do we serve first?"

"The ladies," said Emily.

"No, the company," insisted Tad.

"Well, since I am both a lady *and* company," returned Mrs. Parrish, "as well as the one who made the pies, my answer is that we serve the head of the family first." She turned toward Pa with a little nod and smile. "Mr. Hollister," she asked, "what is your pleasure?"

"Well, ma'am — thank you," said Pa, taken a little by surprise, but pleased at the honor. "I reckon I'll have a slice of your apple."

"Very well. Zack, hand me that pie there, will you?"

"To *begin* with, that is!" added Pa.

Mrs. Parrish laughed. "Yes, of course, Mr. Hollister. I wouldn't want you to go away hungry! That's why I made plenty — I know how fond you are of pies!"

"And how would you know a thing like that, ma'am?" Pa's voice had a tone in it I don't think I'd ever heard before, at least toward Mrs. Parrish. He was always so serious around her and now it sounded like he was teasing her.

"There are ways to learn these things, Mr. Hollister," replied Mrs. Parrish as she handed Pa his pie, then began cutting the others.

"I want to know how," he insisted.

"Let's just say I have my own set of spies."

"My own kids tellin' on their pa!"

"Oh, Pa, I just told her you liked pies!" I said. "There can't be much harm in that."

Pa kind of grunted, but threw me a wink as he did, just to make sure I knew he wasn't serious about being upset, then drove his fork into Mrs. Parrish's pie.

"And right tasty pie it is, too!" he said through his first large bite. "Worth waitin' for, and worth bein' spied on to get a hold of!"

Mrs. Parrish and I both laughed, and by now everyone else was gathered around. While Mrs. Parrish cut, I took orders and handed out the plates of pie. She'd made two apples, so even though there were almost a dozen of us, everybody had enough seconds to stuff themselves all over again, with pie left over in the end.

The rest of the day, both Pa and Mrs. Parrish

were real cheerful and more friendly to each other than I'd ever seen them. I couldn't for the life of me figure what it could have had to do with Pa's announcement at dinner. Maybe it had something to do with Mrs. Parrish's going out to be alone, and the talk she and I had. But whatever it was all about, I liked it real well.

With the warm fire, the food, and all the different people with us, it felt so good that I didn't ever want the day to end. And if Pa's marrying again was what it took to make him and Mrs. Parrish as close to each other as I was to both of them, maybe it was a good idea, after all.

I guess Mrs. Parrish must've thought so too, because she was buoyant the rest of the day. I'd never seen her like that. Maybe when she'd been outside alone thinking, she'd come to the conclusion that Pa's decision to get married was a good one and she was happy about how much better it would be for all of us.

Darkness had already fallen, and before things started quieting down in the cabin, the men had wandered back to the table two or three times to pick and nibble at the leftovers. I was surprised at how long everybody stayed. But there was enough of a moon that evening to light the ride back to Miracle, and everyone was enjoying the day too much to leave.

When it fell quiet for a moment, Mrs. Parrish rose, silently left the house, and returned from her buggy a minute or two later holding a large bag.

"I brought each of you some presents," she said, glancing around at the five of us Hollister kids. "My apologies to the rest of you," she added, looking at the Stansberrys, Uncle Nick, and Mr. Jones with a smile and shrug. "But you know what they say, Christmas is for children!"

"We'll enjoy your giving to them just as much," put in Miss Stansberry.

Then Mrs. Parrish reached into her bag and began pulling out little gifts, each wrapped in bright paper — dolls for the girls, a colorful wooden top for Tad, a pocketknife for Zack, and a new book called *Moby Dick* for me. When all our exclamations and thank-yous had died down some, she pulled one more little package out of her bag.

"I must confess, I have one for you, too, Mr. Hollister," she said, handing it to Pa. "Apologies again to the rest of you!" she added looking quickly around the room. "I saw this the last time I was in Sacramento, and I immediately thought, 'This looks like something Drummond Hollister would enjoy.' So I bought it, and here it is."

"That's right kind of you, ma'am." I could tell Pa was embarrassed by all the fuss, but he didn't show it as his fingers tore off the paper and he took the nice carved pipe in his hands.

"It's a *fine* looking pipe. You really pulled a surprise on me — Mrs. — Mrs. Parrish," said Pa. "I can't figure what to say, except thank you, ma'am."

Mrs. Parrish nodded but didn't reply.

"What's that white stuff there?" asked Pa.

"That's ivory, Mr. Hollister," she said softly. "They carve it from the tusks of elephants in Africa."

Pa gave a low whistle, indicating that he knew the pipe must have been expensive, while he kept turning it over and around in his hand.

Meanwhile Alkali Jones walked over to the corner, picked up his fiddle, and plucked softly at the strings.

"I say, Mr. Jones, do you know any Christmas tunes?" asked Rev. Rutledge. "Perhaps we might sing a chorus or two."

That was all the invitation Mr. Jones needed to begin demonstrating that indeed he did. And if he didn't know a song that Rev. Rutledge wanted, then "if the Rev'ren'd be good enough t' hum a bit o' it," he'd be sure to pick up the tune in no time!

What a perfect way to end a wonderful Christmas day — singing and clapping and smiling, while Mr. Jones fiddled and Rev. Rutledge led us in singing "Joy to the World," "Hark the Herald Angels Sing," and "The First Noel." He even taught us a couple I'd never heard.

But we hardly needed Mr. Jones. We'd sung in the church services plenty of times, but I'd never realized how beautiful a singer Mrs. Parrish was! Her voice was an instrument all by itself! And, of course, Rev. Rutledge could sing and so could Miss Stansberry. It was a lively and pretty sounding music that came from our place that evening!

After the more rousing songs, a quiet came over us all the moment we started singing "Silent Night." After the first verse, Mrs. Parrish interrupted to tell us all the story of Franz Gruber and of the snowy mountain night when the words of the song first came to him. When she was through, we started singing again, with Rev. Rutledge helping us with the words, all the way to the last verse:

> "Silent night, holy night,
> Wondrous star, lend thy light;
> With the angels let us sing,
> Alleluia to our King;
> Christ the Savior is born,
> Christ the Savior is born."

Everything was silent for a long time. No one in the cabin said a word. Then finally Rev. Rutledge looked over at Pa and said, "Mr. Hollister, it just somehow seems fitting for us — would you mind if I offered a Christmas prayer?"

Without a moment's hesitation, Pa answered, "Not at all, Reverend. I think that'd be a mighty fine thing to do."

We all bowed our heads and closed our eyes, then Rev. Rutledge began to pray. For the first time his words didn't sound far off to me. It didn't seem that he was trying to make sure God heard him up in heaven someplace, but like he was talking to Him right in the room with us.

"Our Father," he said, "we are all so thankful to You right now for this day — this Christmas day! We are thankful because of what this day means — that on this day Your Son, God's own Son, became a little baby and was born on the earth. God, we thank You that there is such a day as Christmas, and that there was a baby Jesus, who lived among us and grew up to be a man who would die for us. We know that He came to us on Christmas day in order to teach us how to live, how to behave, how to think, and how to obey You. So God, we pray that You would help us in our daily lives to do those things — not just remembering Jesus on Christmas day, but remembering *every* day that He walks beside us to help us be Your sons and daughters. Help us, our God, our Father, to make *every* day Christmas day in our hearts, a day when the life of Jesus is born ever new to us! Amen."

CHAPTER 21

NEW YEAR, NEW CHALLENGES

The year 1854 opened with a gigantic snowstorm the day after New Year's. It was four days before Pa finally rode Jester into Miracle. When he came back he said that no one else had been able to get to town either, and that Miss Stansberry had cancelled school until the roads were melted off.

The old timers of the area said they never remembered so much snow that low down out of the mountains. Alkali Jones, of course, had stories to top everyone's, and he claimed that long before gold was discovered, *he* had seen snow six feet deep where Sacramento was now. Nobody believed him. But they listened, every now and then throwing winks from one to another to show they weren't swallowing a word of it.

When we finally did get back to school, a lot of things started changing. There are times we look back on as being turning points, and after those times nothing is the same again — like when Ma died, or that first day when we rode into Miracle Springs with Captain Dixon.

This was one of those times. It wasn't sudden, not one particular moment, but a spread-out time of change. I suppose it started with Pa's letter from Miss Morgan. Nothing could be the same after that. And the idea of a second Mrs. Drummond Hollister took a lot of getting used to. I wasn't altogether seeing things from Pa's standpoint. I should have been happy for him, and down inside I knew he was doing it for us kids as much as for himself. But the selfish part of me was afraid of what Miss Morgan's coming might mean.

Christmas day at our house had been a day to stick in the mind for a long time. There had been so many difficulties from the first when we came to California, getting all the people and feelings and relationships figured out — first we found our Pa, but Pa and Mrs. Parrish didn't get along too well. Then Uncle Nick got into trouble. When the minister came, he and Pa did a lot of arguing. Then Pa changed from being so gruff, and his life became different than his rough past. Finally Miss Stansberry came, and the school started up.

There had been so many changes! Yet there we all were in our cabin — together, talking, having fun, laughing, singing — Uncle Nick, the minister, Alkali Jones, Pa, and Mrs. Parrish! It felt like a high point, the perfect end to all the problems we had all had that year.

But it seemed almost fated to end just as it was beginning. The minute Pa told everyone about Miss Morgan and about him marrying again, I could feel that things were going to change again, that we might never again have a day where everything was as good as that Christmas day.

Maybe it was selfish of me, but I didn't know if I relished the thought that a year from then there'd be a new woman taking care of things in the Hollister kitchen instead of me. Mrs. Parrish might not ever spend Christmas with us again. She might not even be Mrs. Parrish the next year, but Mrs. Rutledge instead.

Not all the changes were things I worried about. After that Christmas day, once we got back to school, I started feeling a special friendship with Miss Stansberry. After that day she felt a part of our family, and I noticed her always smiling warmly and taking a moment or two with Tad and Becky and Emily. She knew just how to treat Zack, helping him with his learning, but in a way that made him feel like he was one of the older and grown-up pupils. She had such a knack for making Zack feel like she really needed him in the school that he started perking up, working hard on his papers and reading, doing schoolwork at home, and trying all the time to please her.

Pa'd say things like, "What's got into you, boy?" half joking at Zack working on some assignment, and Zack'd just shrug.

But I could tell Pa was happy about it — though not half as proud as Zack was when Miss Stansberry praised him in front of the class for his hard work and improvement. It wasn't long before she had him helping with the younger boys. Even Little Wolf went to Zack for assistance a lot, and Zack was proud of that, since he was several years younger than Little Wolf.

Miss Stansberry was kind to me too. She gradually quit treating me as one of her students and began treating me like another teacher. Whatever she'd said about *needing* an assistant, all of us knew by that time that she could handle most anything that would come up. No one thought of her as crippled anymore — I don't even think we remembered it half the time. I think she wanted me as her assistant as much for my sake as her own.

In March I turned seventeen, and that had plenty to do with some of my worries. I didn't think of it at the time, because when I'm *in* a situation I don't really know why I think certain things.

But looking back on it now, deep inside I realized that seventeen was nearly grown up. I wasn't a little girl any more. And maybe that's why Miss Stansberry treated me differently as time went on. Late in the spring she even asked me if I'd like to call her Harriet.

Before Miss Morgan's letter I didn't need to think much about what would become of me. There was nothing much to think about except helping Pa with the young'uns, cooking, and keeping the house. I never really thought much about the future. I hoped I'd get to write some more for Mr. Singleton, but I never thought about having to leave Pa and the cabin.

But with Miss Morgan coming, it seemed that Pa might not need me much any more. Being seventeen, I'd be grown pretty soon, and it gets cumbersome with too many grownups in a little house. She'd take care of the kids and the cooking, so there wouldn't be much for me to do. And I was getting too old for school. I couldn't keep being Miss Stansberry's helper for ever!

I had never thought much about my future — just a little about being a teacher or writing some newspaper articles. But now I realized that people would start to figure I ought to get married.

And if I tried to do some kind of work like teaching or working for a paper, they'd start to call me an old maid! I didn't figure I was the marrying kind, and wasn't interested in being one. Yet if I tried to do some kind of work of my own, it might mean leaving Pa and the kids.

I knew Pa was trying to help, but Miss Morgan's coming didn't do much for me except make me afraid of what might happen to me next.

So that spring of 1854 was a hard time for me. I went for lots of walks by myself and wrote lots of thoughts in my journal. I was moody and quiet sometimes, and I wasn't altogether pleasant to the others.

I tried to pray whenever I'd get to worrying, but I couldn't tell if God was paying much attention or not. I knew I ought to talk to Mrs. Parrish about it, but sometimes I was embarrassed to tell her what I was thinking and feeling because it seemed selfish, and she was always so thoughtful of other folks.

But on Easter Sunday afternoon, just a couple of weeks after my seventeenth birthday, I had a talk with her that I'll never forget. And of all the things that made the first part of 1854 so memorable, that was the biggest day of all. It was a turning point that made all the others seem small.

Mrs. Parrish took me for a ride out into the country and told me, "I think the time has finally come, Corrie, for me to tell you something I've been wanting to share with you for a long time."

Pa had gotten a letter from Miss Morgan the day before. It wasn't the first letter we received, and it didn't say anything different from the others. But maybe because of my birthday, because I was thinking about getting older and wondering what was to become of me, that particular letter unnerved me.

Or maybe it was the way Pa seemed to be gradually getting excited about her coming, because from the letters she sounded like a fun lady. And he was talking more regularly about how things would be after she got here, and I was feeling a little hurt that he didn't seem to care much about me and what I was feeling.

The letter said:

I don't know exactly what day I will arrive, since so much of the passage time, I am told, depends on the weather. I will stop over several days at a hotel in San Francisco, and from there I will notify you of my arrival. I will then take the steamer up the river to Sacramento, where I hope you will be able to meet me. If there are other details, I will write again. I will tell you now, so that whenever and however I manage to get there, how you may recognize me. I do not favor hats, but on this occasion I shall be wearing a floppy white hat with a red flower. It is the only hat I own. I am looking forward to meeting all of you — children, brother-in-law, yourself . . . your whole clan. You have warned me to be prepared for a humble mountain cabin. But it will be a pleasure for me to have a stove and kitchen to call my own after so many years with my aunt. Tell Corrie and Becky and Emily that I am so happy to have such big girls for my step-daughters — that is, if you decide to keep me, Mr. Hollister!

That was not all she wrote, but it was enough to bring a lump to my throat, and as soon as Pa was finished reading it I went outside to be alone.

I didn't want to be anybody's stepdaughter! And I didn't want to be called a "big girl," as if I were ten years old! And I didn't want to share *my* kitchen with someone I didn't even know!

I couldn't tell any of what I was thinking to Pa. He'd either get mad at me or else feel bad himself, and I didn't want to cause him any more misery.

I'd already overheard him telling Uncle Nick once that he was having second thoughts about what he'd done. And now that he was planning to go through with it, I didn't want to upset him any more.

Worst of all, I felt so selfish! Why couldn't I be happy for Pa, happy for Miss Morgan, like everybody else? If this was for the best for all the rest of the family, how could I be so mean as to worry about no one but myself? I wanted to be good and I tried to ask God to help me think better thoughts, but down inside I felt miserable.

The next day, Easter Sunday, we went to church. I sat there the whole time trying hard to keep from crying. I didn't hear a word Rev. Rutledge said. I don't even remember what he spoke about. I just sat there glum and staring forward, with my mind tumbling about on all the things I was wrestling with inside, and knowing I wasn't behaving like God would want. It was Easter Sunday, when folks were dressed nice and happy and smiling to one another, and that just made it all the worse!

Some folks have a way of being able to look

at you and know just what you're thinking. Mrs. Parrish was always that way with me. She walked over to me after the service, pulled me a few steps away from the others, and said, "How about if I drive out this afternoon and you and I go for a ride together?"

CHAPTER 22

EASTER SUNDAY – NEW BIRTH

By the time we'd driven out to a little meadow a couple miles out of town, Mrs. Parrish had gotten out of me all the worries that were on my mind, and a few more even *I* didn't know were there!

One or two questions was all it took and I gushed out with it all.

By the time I was done, I was crying and feeling like a baby, and feeling all the more foolish for thinking my anxieties had to do with growing up. Right then I'd never felt *less* like a woman and more like a little girl!

"And you feel both mixed up about all the changes that are coming, *and* a little guilty because you think you're being selfish, is that it?" asked Mrs. Parrish.

"That's about the size of it," I answered. "Just when it seemed my world was getting smoothed out, now all of a sudden I feel like I did after Ma died, not knowing what's to become of me."

"Well, perhaps I can help," she smiled. "Perhaps *the Lord* can help, I should say," she added. "Come, let's go walk. This meadow is one of my favorite places. I often come here when I want to get away and think or pray."

She tied her horse to a tree, then led the way across the grass, greening and now growing briskly in the spring warmth.

"Let's sit over there on those two large rocks, Corrie," she pointed.

When we were comfortable, she took a deep breath, then began.

"I've been wanting to tell you some things for a long while, Corrie," she said. "But the time has to be just right, or else it's impossible to understand them. I could have said all this to you much sooner, and part of me wanted to. Yet I knew it would mean more to you if I waited until the time came in your life when you were hungry to know these things."

She paused and thought a moment. "Corrie, do you remember the conversation we had our first Christmas together — when I took you and Emily and Becky to the dressmaker's?"

"Oh yes, Mrs. Parrish!" I answered. "You told me a lot about what sin means, and how we all need Jesus in our lives to take away the sin. I wrote it all down in my journal."

Mrs. Parrish smiled, then very seriously asked, "You do know that Jesus is still alive, don't you, Corrie?"

"Yes, ma'am. That's what today's about — Easter. Everybody knows that, don't they?"

"Maybe they know it in their heads, but do they fully realize what it *means* — in the daily

221

moments of their lives?"

"What does it mean?" I asked.

"Just this, Corrie — and this is the most wonderful truth in all the world. Since Jesus is alive, He is with us — right now, this very moment!"

"I guess I've heard that, but it's kind of hard to catch hold of — I mean, you can never *see* Him."

"That's because He's not present in His body, but in His Spirit." Her eyes were glowing with excitement. "And there's a very special place God created for the spirit of Jesus to live after He came back to life — to live forever! Do you know where I mean?"

I thought I knew what she was getting at. "Inside us?"

"Exactly, Corrie! In our *hearts!*" she replied enthusiastically. "In my heart —" she laid her hand on her bosom, "— and in yours, Corrie. That's Jesus' home, in the hearts of men and women!"

"Really?" Her excitement was catching. "In everybody's?"

She gave a sigh, and a cloud passed quickly over her face.

"No, Corrie, not everybody's," she said.

"Are there too many people?" I asked, "and not enough of Him to go around?"

"Oh no, that's not it at all! God is so big that He could fill up every heart on ten thousand worlds and still have only begun. No, the problem is that not every heart *lets* His Spirit live there, even though that was the reason it was made."

"You mean God doesn't automatically live in our hearts?"

"Oh no, Corrie. God is such a gentleman that He will never come into a place unless He's invited. So He only lives in the hearts of the men and women who open the door to that little place down inside them. It's like —"

She stopped and thought for a second.

"Well, think back to Christmas day and that wonderful dinner we all had together. What do you suppose Rev. Rutledge and I would have done if we'd driven up, gone to the house, and found the door locked? Then up drove Harriet and Hermon and they came and joined us. They asked why we didn't go in, and we told them the door was locked tight.

"We knew your father was inside. What should we have done — gone out to your pa's tool shed to find a sledgehammer to break down the door?

"No, we wouldn't even have wanted to go in unless he himself, the head of the house, invited us in and opened the door to us. As it was, we went in and enjoyed a day of hospitality, good food, and wonderful fellowship, because your father invited us to come and opened his home to us."

She paused a moment to let it all sink in.

"That's how God is, Corrie. He wants to come in and make His home with us. But He waits patiently and never beats down doors. You see, there's only one key to the door of every heart, and we're the only ones who possess it. God may be all powerful, but on the other hand, that's one thing God *can't* do — force open our doors."

She paused, and the most peculiar smile came over her face. I could tell that the words had sparked some memory in her own life. She said nothing for another moment, and I sat silently, feeling like I was watching her relive some time in her past — a happy moment, but one that carried with it a certain pain as well.

"So to answer your question," she finally went on, "God *wants* to live in everybody's heart, and I hope someday He will, I don't know. But for now He only lives where the doors have been opened from the inside."

Again she stopped and the same odd smile returned to her expression. "Opening the door can sometimes be very painful. I can tell you that from personal experience. I did not always see things as I do now, Corrie. God had to put me through some heartbreaking disappointments, and I resisted for a long while. Perhaps one day I shall be able to tell you about it," she added rather wistfully.

"I would like that, ma'am," I replied.

"But not today . . . to start on *that* story would take all afternoon!"

She laughed. It was good to see the joy return to her face. It seemed she had put her memories back into the closet of the past once again.

"Again, from my own personal experience, I can tell you that after God *has* come inside, everything changes. He helps our inner selves to become more like Him. God's desire — in my heart, yours, your father's, your uncle's, Rev. Rutledge's, or anybody's — is to make us become like Jesus — not just in outer actions, but inside. With His Spirit living inside us, gradually we do become more gracious and forgiving and loving and unselfish and considerate *on the inside*."

Even before she was finished I was crying again.

"And that's what you want, isn't it, Corrie?" she said gently.

I nodded.

"You want to be more like God wants you to be, but with everything making your life confusing right now, you realize you're not at all like you think you should be, like you want to be? Is that something of what you're feeling?"

I nodded again.

"I know that feeling, Corrie," she said. "I know what it's like to feel like you're bad, to feel like you've failed, to feel like you've disappointed the people you love the most. And you see, that's why Jesus wants to live in our hearts. He can help us!

"He can not only help you face your uncertain future, He can help you become the person you long to be deep inside. None of us is what we'd like to be. The Bible says we're sinners. But God can help us. That's why He wants us to unlock the doors of our hearts and let Him come in and live with us there."

"That sounds too good to be true."

"It's just so good it *must* be true! Oh, Corrie, God is so good to us! He loves us more than we can realize and has such a wonderful life to give us! Yes, I'm a sinner, just like the worst man in Miracle Springs. But inside my heart the Spirit of God lives. And He is slowly remaking me, and teaching me to live and think and behave differently than I would if He were not helping me."

"Oh, I *do* want to be good, Mrs. Parrish!" I exclaimed. "I want God to live in my heart, too, and to help me like He is you! Do you think He is there?"

"I don't know, Corrie. He may already be there, drawing you toward Him. One never knows when that little invisible door opens and He slips in. I truly believe that the door of some people's hearts' open before they are ever aware of it, and God's Spirit finds an easy and natural entrance, perhaps in the early years of childhood. Some hearts seem open to God right from birth.

"Others are born with great resistance, and it may take years and years of God's patient knocking before they finally hear Him. For some persons there is an exact moment when they consciously open their heart. For others it is a gradual process. In your case, Corrie, I suspect that God has long been with you without your even knowing it. I sense that your heart is open toward Him, and that you want to be His daughter."

Even as she spoke, I could feel my eyes filling with tears once more.

"I do, Mrs. Parrish!" I said. "I do want to be His daughter and to live in a way that pleases Him — down inside, like you said, not just on the outside!"

She tried to say something, but hesitated. I could see a tear falling down her cheek. At first I didn't understand why, but I did later.

"You . . . you can't know what joy it gives me to hear those precious words, Corrie," she said at last, and her voice was husky with emotion. "And they please God far more than either of us can possibly realize. I sensed when I saw you in church this morning that the day had finally come when you would want to know these things and were really ready to begin living in a deeper way as a Christian."

She paused, then looked into my eyes with the most wonderful smile on her face.

"Corrie," she said, "I love you, and I know you are dear to God's heart . . ."

She stopped, then reached across and took both my hands in hers. Then she closed her eyes and started to pray.

"Oh, loving Father! How I thank You for this dear friend you have brought to me! Show her, Lord, more and more of Yourself every day. Nurture her dawning faith, and let her reflect the image of Your Son. Strengthen her heart's desire —"

She stopped. I opened my eyes to glance at

her. She was softly weeping.

I closed my eyes again. I couldn't help being a little nervous.

"God," I prayed out loud, "I really do want to be good like You want me to be. And I want to be kind and loving like Mrs. Parrish talks about, on the inside. I want to be Your daughter, and I don't know if that door to my heart's open or not, or if maybe You're already there. But if You're not, I'd like you to be, and —"

Suddenly I couldn't say anything more. I felt a rush inside me, like the breaking of a dam on a stream, like something was being pulled out from the very depths of me. My voice cracked and my eyes were full, but I struggled to get out the words —

"Help me, Lord. Help me to live like you want me to. Help me not to resent Miss Morgan's coming. Help me to know what I'm supposed to do."

That was all I could say for a minute. It was already more than I figured I could pray out loud in front of anybody.

But then almost without thinking, I added, "And I pray for Pa too, Lord, that you'd help him to do the right thing. Amen."

Mrs. Parrish added a quiet *Amen* after mine.

I opened my eyes. Mrs. Parrish was looking at me with a radiant smile. Her cheeks were wet with tears.

CHAPTER 23

THE RIDE HOME

I felt better after that.

It wasn't so much that now all of a sudden I figured all my worries would go away. But riding back to Miracle, Mrs. Parrish explained that once I had really given myself to God and asked Him to help me be a person who was more like He wanted me to be, then my whole outlook could change.

"You see, Corrie," she said, "when a person desperately *wants* to walk closer to God the Christian life begins to be so much more thrilling. Most people are content with their lives as they are. They don't think about growth, change, about developing new habits and attitudes. They just take every day as it comes and aren't really trying to be any different from one day to the next. Growth and development toward more godly behavior isn't what they base their lives on. But then from out of nowhere comes some trouble that they don't know how to handle. And then they finally begin to realize that they need some help. They see that they need to open the door and invite someone else into their house, someone who can help them become the kind of person they now see that they want to be. But until that time, they feel self-sufficient and satisfied and content with the way they are, and feel no need for growth and change. It is very difficult for people to be close to God if they are perfectly content to remain locked inside their houses all alone."

"And that's why you waited until today to tell me about opening the door of my heart to let Jesus live there?" I asked.

"Don't misunderstand me, Corrie," replied Mrs. Parrish. "I truly believe you have loved God for a long time. You and I have had many good talks together about being Christians. I would not have you think that I consider all that meaningless. It's just that *now* — now that some of these hurts and frustrations and confusions inside you have awakened a hunger to grow and be better — now you can really begin sharing your life with God more deeply every day. It's not that what came before wasn't good and valuable, but now that you realize your need, you can begin depending on God more, and trusting Him for more and more things in your life."

"Trusting Him — how?"

"Trusting that He will take care of you, trusting Him to work good for everyone out of Miss Morgan's coming, trusting Him for your pa, trusting Him for your future — for everything, Corrie! If you've given yourself to Him as His daughter, then you can trust Him to be a wise and loving heavenly Father, and to take perfect care of you!"

"So I shouldn't worry about my future, or whether Pa will think I'm in the way in the kitchen? Sometimes I just can't help worrying."

"It's all right to be concerned and to think about things. But remember what I told you a while back, about how God can turn everything and make it into good? Corrie, your whole attitude toward life slowly begins to change when you realize that God is with you every moment, helping you grow, strengthening you, helping you know what to do. Pretty soon all those worries don't look so big, because you realize He knows all about them too and has the solution all figured out ahead of time."

"But what if I can't?" I asked.

"Can't what, Corrie?"

"Can't do all those things — trust God better and be nicer and not worry so much. What if God being with me doesn't change my attitude and make me strong like you said?"

"Oh, but it will, Corrie! There is no *what if* to it. When God lives in a heart, things *do* change. He makes sure of that — He helps!"

She stopped, and her enthusiastic look suddenly turned thoughtful. I could tell she was reconsidering what she'd just said.

"Well," she finally said, still with the serious look on her face, "there is one *if* to it, now that I think about it. Not all people do grow and change and get to be strong Christians."

"Why is that?"

"Well, Corrie, I told you that God doesn't force His way into our lives. And He doesn't force us to do His will either. We have a *choice* to accept Him and submit to the changes He wants to work in us. God comes into our lives, saying, 'I'll come into your heart, and I'll give you joy and I'll make you strong, and I'll help you become more like Jesus, and I'll gradually turn you into the person I created you to be.' That's His gift to us, His part. But we have to cooperate. We need to respond to His love with obedience. Our part is this: we have to do what He says. God *will* change us and make us better, but He won't work against our will. He can only work the changes if we are holding up our side and doing what Jesus told us to do. We need to say 'yes' to Jesus — not just to His desire to live in us, but to His desire to rule our lives as well. Our obedience to Him makes it possible for Him to do the changes He wants to do."

"Well," I said slowly, trying to take in all she was saying, "I reckon that's fair."

"Completely fair! Everything God does is fair, though sometimes the fairness is hard for folks to see. And this agreement — God doing His part, us doing our part — explains why some people never change and others do, and why there are nasty, selfish people in the church who think they are good Christians. Being a Christian is more than knowing in your head who Jesus is — it's

232

surrendering your heart to His ways. The changes in our lives depend on whether we are obeying God, not on our religious talk or how much about the Bible we know or whether we go to church all the time."

"So going to church and reading the Bible and praying and all that doesn't matter?" I asked.

"Oh no, Corrie, I didn't mean that! Those things are very important. But they're only important if they help you learn to do more of what Jesus said. Otherwise, I'm afraid they are meaningless. Do you understand?"

"I think so," I answered slowly. "If I open the door of my heart to let Jesus live there — and I think I have, haven't I, Mrs. Parrish?"

"You have, Corrie! Yes, His Spirit *is* inside you."

". . . if I've done that, then He will make me better and will help me have better thoughts and trust Him more . . . *if* I try to do what I'm supposed to — if I obey what Jesus said to do."

"Yes, that's it exactly! And that's why it *is* important to read the Bible — especially the four gospels — so you can find out what Jesus said, and the kind of people He wants us to be."

"I see."

"And then there's one last catch, Corrie."

"Another one?"

Mrs. Parrish laughed. "I'm afraid so! But this is the last one, I promise. After this, I think you'll have plenty to think about for a good long time!"

"All right," I said, returning her smile. "But I've already got more than I think I'll be able to remember."

"Well, this last thing may be most important of all. Do you want me to tell you now or save it for another time?"

"Oh no. Tell me now. I want to hear it! But when I write all this down in my journal, I'm going to have to come and ask you lots of questions to help me remember everything you've said."

"Agreed. Now, Corrie, we must remember that God's work in our hearts takes a lifetime. The changes we're talking about, learning to trust Him, obeying more like Jesus did, being more loving to people — none of that happens to us all at once. We're still the same people. We still have the same bad habits. And though God wants to remake us — and does! — it's a very slow process."

"Because we don't do our part very well?"

"Partly. But even when we are good and *do* what we're supposed to do, it still takes a long time for us to get to be very much like Jesus. So try not to get discouraged if you get to feeling like you're not the kind of person you want to be. It takes years and years of practice — of *trying* to trust God more, of *trying* to have better attitudes toward people, of *trying* to be unselfish — before you begin to feel you're getting anywhere."

"That does sound discouraging."

"Perhaps I'm not explaining it very well." She paused, thought for a moment, and then said, "If we are cooperating, then God *is* bringing about the changes. But they're happening so deep inside us that *we* can't see them for a long time. You *are* His daughter, a daughter of His grace and love. And He *is* gradually making you more and more like Jesus, but way down deep where His Spirit lives — in your heart — and the changes aren't always visible on the surface. Do you see what I mean?"

"I think so. Kinda like when Pa and Uncle Nick are working in the mine, you can't see them when they're way down inside it. They may be digging out all kinds of gold, but if you're standing looking at the outside, you can't see it."

"That's it exactly, Corrie! God is mining for gold inside our hearts, but we can't see how much He's getting, and maybe won't see it for years and years."

"And is it kinda like — from what you said before about it being something both God and us have to be working on — is it kinda like we're doing the gold mining with Him, but can't see it?"

"The great thing, Corrie, is that *we* decide how full of gold our own mine is!"

"How's that?"

"Remember what I said about the years of practice in *doing* the things we're supposed to do?"

I nodded.

"Well, every time you or I do some little act

235

of kindness, even though afterward we might not *feel* any different, a tiny little change happens deep inside us. We've added a tiny piece of gold to the mine! Every time I deal fairly with someone in business that I could have taken advantage of, every act of kindness you do to one of your brothers or sisters, every gentle word, every forgiveness, every unselfishness, every time you or I lay aside what we want for the happiness of someone else, every prayer we utter on behalf of another, every generous act — they're all little nuggets of gold, Corrie. Some Christians are filling their mines with rich veins, while others are letting opportunities pass every day, and their mines are filling up instead with nothing but dirt and worthless rock."

"But when do we find out?"

"I suppose most people won't know until they die. But once you've been walking through life for five or ten or fifteen years, every once in a while you begin to get glimpses of gold coming to the surface.

"You see, Corrie, the Lord is working away in the mine of our hearts all the time, from now until the day we die — all night, all day, every moment. And all those little specks of gold we fill our mines with, today, tomorrow, next week, next year, *every* little kindness and unselfishness for all the rest of our lives — they all add up together.

"In the end, our hearts are either rich with the gold we have put there for God to develop into a Christlike character, or else they are still empty, even though God has been picking away all our lives to find some gold to put to use. We don't see this work going on, but every moment we are either putting gold in the mine of our heart or we are putting dirt and rock there.

"That's why, at the end of life, some people are radiant with the love of God and others are miserable old grouches. It all depends on the millions of tiny choices we make all day long, every day — golden choices of unselfishness or dirty choices that turn out to be worthless in the end."

I looked up just as she finished speaking, and we were driving up the road to our house. I guess the conversation was finished for now, because already I could hear the yells of Emily and Becky and Tad running out to meet us.

It was probably just as well we were home. I had plenty to think about for now!

CHAPTER 24

THE DAY FINALLY COMES

It was May when Miss Morgan got here.

Pa said he'd told her all about his past in New York — actually his words were, "everything she needs to know" — and she still wanted to come. He said, "I reckon she more or less knows what she's gettin' herself into." As much as Pa didn't want the wrong folks to know about New York, he seemed to be trying hard to be honest about himself whenever he could.

There'd been considerable anticipation around town. After all, Pa was well known. With us kids and the gold mine and all, there'd been quite a bit for folks to talk about concerning Pa already. And once word started spreading around about him sending for a mail-order bride, Pa was on everybody's lips. It was the first time around here that anything like that had happened.

Pa hated it, of course. Occasionally, one of the men would come out of a store or one of the saloons with some comment or a laugh and a wink, like, "Hey, Drum, when's yore pretty little catalog bride comin'?" or "I'll tell ya what, Hollister, if she ain't to yore likin', send her my way." Whenever he heard shouts coming his direction, he'd walk on or turn the other way, ignoring them altogether.

Something told me that Pa almost wanted to forget the whole thing. After all, nobody had heard any more of that man Hatch from south of here. Uncle Nick had been behaving himself. And all my worries after going to San Francisco with Mrs. Parrish turned out to be nothing at all. In fact, I was embarrassed to have gotten in such a tizzy about it, thinking Buck Krebbs was going to follow me here just because he happened to see me all alone. After all, he had known where Pa was all the time. Why was seeing me in San Francisco going to make any difference to him?

At the time I was scared that he'd tried to get me when I was by myself, that seeing me might put the idea into his head to try it again. But now I felt foolish for making all the fuss — especially since that was what started Pa out thinking he needed to get a new wife.

But Mrs. Parrish told me there weren't any accidents that happened to God's people. And since I was one of them, then all that was part of "God's story for my life," as she called it, including the new chapter that was about to begin, the coming of Miss Kathryn Morgan.

I couldn't help wondering if Pa wished he'd never written those letters. But he'd already sent the money back East, and maybe he didn't want the men around town to think he was backing down. Before long it was too late, anyway. Miss

Morgan was probably already on her way.

We knew about when she'd be coming, but then came the letter saying she'd be coming into Sacramento on the steamer arriving from San Francisco on May 11th, at 2:45 in the afternoon.

Maybe only Pa and I were secretly harboring our reservations about the whole notion of a new woman about the place. Everyone else seemed excited.

It was such an "event" that three or four hours after the letter arrived, the whole town knew Pa'd be heading down to Sacramento the next day to fetch his new bride-to-be. The more hoopla there was about it, the more reserved Pa got. He seemed mighty anxious inside. Maybe he was thinking more about Ma than Miss Morgan. Sometimes he'd sit up late at night, just sitting beside the fire, holding the one picture of Ma we had, or holding her Bible, although I don't think I ever saw him reading in it. He'd get up or sigh, almost as if he was saying to himself, *Well, sometimes a man's just gotta do somethin' just 'cause he thinks it's the right thing to do, even if he ain't too keen about it.*

At the same time, even though he wasn't saying much these days, part of Pa couldn't help being just a little bit excited too. I think he was hoping that maybe he'd like Miss Morgan a lot.

The whole town would likely have gone to Sacramento with Pa if he'd let them! Pa had become kind of a local hero, and everybody was watching his every move and wanting to be part of it.

Alkali Jones, Uncle Nick, others of Pa's friends — they all would have gone.

But Pa said no — it was just gonna be him and the kids.

Zack and Little Wolf had been getting to be good friends, mostly riding horses together a lot up in the hills around Miracle.

Little Wolf's father was raising horses now, and he didn't seem to mind his son being around a white boy. They'd go up in the hills, high up toward the Sierras, and they'd race and even help break some of the horses. So when we found out about the trip to Sacramento, Zack begged Pa to let Little Wolf come along. Pa said he could. The two boys would ride their horses.

Pa was planning to take our wagon, even though it was just an old buckboard, and clunking along the bumpy roads wasn't any too comfortable. But the afternoon before we were to leave, we heard the hoofs and rattling and clatter of someone coming up the road.

Pa was the first one to the door. All I heard him say was, "What in tarnation . . . ?" The end of his sentence finished up with his mouth hanging open.

Outside sat a new-looking, all-black brougham carriage, covered on top, with a nice little door and a window into the inside compartment. Two of the Parrish Mine and Freight Company's finest looking horses snorted and danced in place in front of it. Mrs. Parrish was just that moment jumping down onto the ground.

Pa walked out with a bewildered expression on his face, followed by the rest of us.

"I hope you won't take offense, Mr. Hollister," Mrs. Parrish said with a smile, shaking Pa's hand. "I well remember when you told me some time ago that I should not interfere with your family's affairs."

While she spoke her face was smiling, like she knew Pa wasn't going to fuss like he used to, and showing that she wasn't afraid to kid him just a little.

". . . but I must say, that old rickety wagon of yours is not the proper coach for a man of your, shall we say, your standing in the community, to pick up his future bride in. No, no, Mr. Hollister, I said to myself that you simply must have something finer on this occasion."

She paused, to give more emphasis to her next words.

"So, as you can see — I have solved that little problem for you."

She held out the reins in one gloved hand.

"But, I — I don't reckon I understand what —"

"Don't worry," she laughed. "It won't cost you a dime. Nor me, either! I have a friend up in French Corral, a wealthy banker who has done a good deal of business with me. I knew he had this brougham and rarely used it. So I rode up yesterday and borrowed it for you. I've taken full responsibility. You don't have to worry about a thing."

"You caught me unsuspecting, Mrs. Parrish," said Pa at last, forcing a smile. "But there just ain't no way I can —"

"Just take the reins and don't say a word, Mr. Hollister." Now her voice was more serious. She was still smiling, but not at all making light of the situation. At that moment I saw how much Mrs. Parrish had come to care about Pa. At first it had been just for us kids that she'd done things and been nice. But this — I could tell as she handed him the reins and looked steadily at him — she'd done just for Pa.

Pa seemed really touched. "Ma'am," he said, "I am obliged to you! That's just a mighty thoughtful thing to have done."

"Not another word about it," replied Mrs. Parrish. "Just bring your Miss Morgan back here safe and sound. Now," she went on, turning back to the carriage, "it's made to seat four inside. With the children, you might squeeze in five. But if not, someone can sit next to you up on the driver's seat. And there's a rack on top for her luggage. Take some rope with you to tie it down."

Pa walked all the way around it, taking in every line and curve, examining the wheels, while Mrs. Parrish undid her horse from the harnesses.

"So I'll just be back off to town," she said, throwing the saddle she'd brought over the horse's back and cinching up the straps. "And I'll see all you back here in four or five days!"

She went around to each of us with a hug and

a personal word. She held me an extra second or two, then just looked deeply into my eyes without saying anything. I knew what that look was meant to say.

Early the next morning, Pa climbed into the driver's seat, and Emily and Becky and Tad and I clambered up into the fancy black carriage. With Zack and Little Wolf excitedly leading the way on their two horses, we were off on our two-day trip to Sacramento.

CHAPTER 25

THE ARRIVAL OF MISS KATHRYN MORGAN

On the afternoon of May 11, we stood alongside the Sacramento River at the same landing I already felt I knew, watching the big white steamer glide slowly up to the wooden dock.

We scanned the deck and the people on it as the boat slid up, looking in vain for a white hat. But none was to be seen.

When the boat finally came to a stop, two men jumped down and tied the huge ropes to two pylons. A third man hauled out a short wooden ramp, banged it down onto the dock while keeping one end hooked to the boat, and the passengers started filing down the incline and off the boat.

I don't reckon anyone would have had much trouble picking *us* out! There we stood, five kids and an Indian, crowded around a big, rugged-looking man, with his hat in his hand, and a look of apprehension on his face.

"Will she be nice, Pa?" asked Tad's innocent voice.

" 'Course she'll be nice. Now just be quiet and help me look," came back Pa's answer — a little too gruff, but I guess both Pa and Tad were nervous.

It didn't take much more looking. The second she came into view we all spotted her. It was the only floppy white hat and red flower in the whole place! She was shorter than most of the other women, which was why we hadn't seen her on deck.

I don't know quite what I expected to happen. There we were, and there she was, all of us frozen in time looking at each other. I suppose it wasn't any longer than a second, but those kinds of moments have a way of stretching out. You can get inside them and think about all kinds of different things, and then come back again, and still only a tiny fraction of time has gone by. This was one of those times. Everything stood still on the outside, while my mind was racing on the inside. And then when I woke up to the real-life present, we were still just standing there staring as she marched toward us, smiling, with her hand stretched out.

"Mr. Hollister!" she said bright and cheerily, "I'm Kathryn Morgan!"

"Er — howdy, ma'am," Pa stammered as he shook her hand, "Drummond Hollister, at your service, ma'am. These here's the kids."

"Let me try to guess," said Miss Morgan before Pa could get around to introducing us. "You're Corrie," she said turning and smiling at me.

I nodded.

"It's easy to see you're the oldest," she said.

"And something else your Pa told me is easy to tell too — you're nearly a grown-up young woman — and a very pretty one."

"Thank you," I said, blushing. "Welcome to California."

"Oh, thank you!" She looked around and took in a deep breath. "So this is the land of fortunes," she said. "Funny, I don't smell the gold in the air. To hear folks back East talk, you'd think the gold was just lying around on the ground. Is there *really* gold here, Mr. Hollister?"

"Oh yes, ma'am," said Pa. "You'll see it soon enough, I reckon."

"Oh, I almost forgot. I brought you a little present, Corrie," she said, looking down into her handbag and reaching around with her hand. "I brought you all something — they're not much. I didn't have extra room, but I thought it might be nice to bring you all a little piece of Virginia. So, Corrie, I brought you a seashell from the Atlantic Ocean."

She handed me a beautiful little reddish-white shell that had a twisted circular pattern on it. Once a sea animal, probably something like a snail, had lived inside it, she said. "If you hold the open end to your ear on a quiet day," she said, "they say you can still hear the sea where the shell came from."

She stooped down next to me and greeted Tad. "Do you know how I know that you're Tad?" she said.

" 'Cause I'm the littlest?" asked Tad, staring

with his big eyes into Miss Morgan's smiling face.

"That's right! And do you know what we say back in Virginia about little things?"

Tad shook his head.

"We say that the best things come in the smallest packages! Here, Tad, look what I have for you." Again she reached into her bag, this time pulling out a shiny green rock. "This is a Virginia rock, Tad, like your sister's shell. Every time you look at it, you can remember how big this country of ours is."

She turned to Becky, standing next to Emily. "Let me see, you two girls —" She glanced back and forth between Becky and Emily. "You are not that far apart in age, but I would say you —" She looked at Becky again. "You look to be about eleven, am I right?"

"In three months," answered Becky.

"So you are Becky!"

"Yes, Miss Morgan, and I drew you a picture!" From behind her back Becky pulled out a folded white piece of paper. "It's a picture of Pa working in his mine," said Becky.

"And you drew it for me?" exclaimed Miss Morgan. "Why, Becky, thank you! That makes me feel very special." Her smile brightened.

"That means that you are Emily," she said, turning to Emily, who only smiled shyly. "I'm so glad to meet you at last, Emily!"

Before she had a chance to say anything more,

she felt a tug on her coat. She turned back toward Becky.

"What about my present?" said Becky.

Miss Morgan laughed. "I hadn't forgotten you," she said. Digging into her handbag again she pulled out two little wads that looked like rags. "Inside these wet rags are a little tuft of grass and a start of some Virginia moss, both packed in good black Virginia soil. I've tried to keep the roots damp in these rags, and I'm quite sure they will both grow. Here girls," she said handing them to Emily and Becky. "I want you to plant a little garden, with these and maybe some other things. We'll water them, and before you know it, you'll have a little patch of green Virginia right in your own back yard."

She stood up and looked around to the other side of Pa, noticing for the first time that there was an extra person. Zack saw the quick look of confusion on her face, and said, "This here's my friend from the school, Little Wolf."

"Which means you must be Zack," said Miss Morgan. She shook his hand. "Why, you're gonna be as big a man as your pa one of these days," she said, "and a strong one, too! You've got a powerful grip for a — let's see, you're how old, Zack?"

"Fourteen and a half, ma'am," he answered.

"Yes, of course. Well, like I said, you seem awfully strong for fourteen."

She was sure doing her best to make friends with everyone right off!

"Little Wolf?" she said, turning to Zack's friend. "Is that a nickname?"

"That is my name," replied Little Wolf. "I am of the *Maidu* tribe."

The smile left Miss Morgan's face. "I see," she said blankly. Then turning again to Zack, she handed him a small, thin piece of light-colored bark. It had some color and markings on it I couldn't make out at first.

"It's a piece of painted bark," she said, "with an Indian proverb written on it in Cherokee. Before they were driven back to Oklahoma, they used to be one of Virginia and North Carolina's *civilized* tribes, not like the Sac and the Fox, who massacred my parents."

I thought her eyes gave a quick glance in Little Wolf's direction, but just as quickly she was looking at Zack again. "The Cherokee's great chief Sequoia developed his alphabet in 1821, the first Indian tribe to have a full written language of their own. So let this always remind you, Zack, of the difference between peaceful and violent ways."

A brief silence followed. Pa'd been standing watching everything without saying a word, and still Miss Morgan kept the conversation going.

"And for you, Mr. Hollister," she said, "I have the best gift of all, a symbol of beginnings, of new life." She reached inside her bag one last time, and pulled out something small and brown that fit easily in the palm of her hand.

"A pine cone, ma'am?" said Pa, taking it from

250

her and looking at it, seeming to wonder what she found so special in an object so common.

"Not just any pine cone, Mr. Hollister. A Virginia pine cone! Oh, I know you have pines in California. But this cone, with the seeds still inside it, has come three thousand miles. And when we plant these seeds and watch the little seedlings grow, they will remind us that it is possible for a tree — and perhaps for men and women as well — to grow in new soils and strange surroundings."

I think Pa knew what she meant and took the pine cone and put it into one of his coat pockets with a nod of thanks.

"Now along that line, just one more thing," she said. "I also brought you all some apple seeds for the very same purpose. You've heard of Johnny Appleseed, haven't you? Well, we'll help him in his work in Miracle Springs! But I've got them packed away someplace safe, so we'll worry about them later."

"Speaking of your bags, Miss Morgan, ma'am —"

"Please, Mr. Hollister," she interrupted, "if we are going to be married, don't you think we ought to get over the formalities? No more calling me *ma'am*, if you please. Call me by my name — my *given* name."

"You want me to call you Kathryn, ma'am?"

"No, I want you to call me *Katie*, without the *ma'am*. That's what everybody at home calls me — Katie. And I see no reason to change it now.

You children may call me Katie, or Kathryn, or Miss Morgan — whatever your father would like."

"You kids call her Miss Morgan, you hear," said Pa.

"And you, Mr. Hollister?" she asked. "How would you have me address you?"

"Well I reckon you can call me Drummond, 'cause that's my name, though most of the boys call me Drum. You can use that, too, if you like."

"I like Drummond. It's a good, strong name."

"Well, Kathryn, ma'am," said Pa, not even realizing he'd ignored both Miss Morgan's requests in one breath, "like I was fixin' to say, you'll be wanting to get your bags. I reckon they got them unloaded by this time."

"Yes, I asked the steward to take care of them for me."

She turned, glanced around for a moment, spotted the steward, and was instantly off in his direction. The rest of us followed.

She was sure lively. She had told us her aunt said she wasn't timid, and I guess her aunt was right.

CHAPTER 26

KATIE

We took two days getting back to Miracle, stopping that first night in Folsom and the second in Colfax at some boardinghouses Pa'd made arrangements with on the way down. It sure was an interesting drive.

There was so much to get used to!

Inside the coach the talk was lively, Miss Morgan asking Emily and Becky and me and Tad all kinds of questions. Emily was reserved at first, although Becky and Tad made up for it, chattering away as if Miss Morgan was their best friend they hadn't seen in a year. Being the youngest, their memories of Ma might have started to get vague sooner than for the rest of us. Or maybe the pain of memories was dimmer, and so that made it easier for them to accept her right away.

It was a little crowded inside, and at first I put Tad up on my lap. But it wasn't long before Miss Morgan hoisted him up onto hers, and there Tad was content to stay. His big brown eyes were glued to her face. And Becky would sit no place but right beside her, talking away, sometimes all three of them at once.

Emily and I sat across from them, listening

and looking out the windows. I was thinking a lot, too. But Miss Morgan didn't let us go for too long without joining in the talk.

There were long periods of quiet when everyone's energy would get used up for a while. Even Tad and Becky needed to rest their mouths and minds sometimes. At such times I'd try to watch Miss Morgan out of the corner of my eye. I didn't want her to think I was staring at her, but I couldn't help wondering what she was thinking about us all when she drew in a deep breath and looked outside at the countryside passing by.

And I wondered what was going through Pa's mind, too, outside up on the box guiding the horses, as he listened to the sounds of laughter from inside. What might a man be thinking, to hear the voice of a woman he hardly knew, a woman he'd brought west to be his wife, laughing and talking with the children of his first wife?

We made lots of stops. It seemed like somebody needed to go to the outhouse every ten minutes or so. But since there wasn't one, we had to make use of the woods instead. And Pa was trying to be considerate of Miss Morgan too, I could tell.

After some of the stops we'd rearrange and shift places. I sat up with Pa some of the time, and so did the others. Miss Morgan sat with him a time or two as well, but I couldn't hear what they talked about.

Halfway through the second day we were

bouncing along during one of those quiet times. Becky was up front with Pa, so the commotion inside was less. Tad was asleep next to me, leaning against my shoulder. Miss Morgan and Emily across from me were each looking out their windows.

She'd been trying to get me at least to call her Katie, but I wasn't quite used to it. I was old enough to be an adult, she said, and if Pa wanted the younger ones to keep calling her Miss Morgan out of respect, that was okay with her. But she hoped to be more like a sister than a stepmother to me, she said, and she'd like me to call her Katie. I smiled and said I'd try.

When we were all being quiet for a spell, I had a chance to look at Miss Morgan a little more carefully than I could while she was moving about and conversing away with us.

The first thing I couldn't help noticing about Katie was her mouth. I've noticed that most people have a particular part that draws my eyes first. When I meet someone new, I find myself staring at one place on them — usually some part of their face. Often it's the mouth or the eyes, of course. But every once in a while I come across someone with an unusual nose or a high hairline or a hat I can't take my eyes off. And sometimes I even find myself staring at somebody's ears!

For as long as I can remember I've noticed people's faces and tried to imagine which part of them was opening into the *real* them, that part of them that thought and felt, their "soul" I guess you'd say. With some people I find myself looking into their eyes and knowing that I'm seeing a little bit "inside" them. Mrs. Parrish's eyes are like that. When they're looking into my face, or filling with liquid because she's feeling something deep, or when they're sparkling with love, I just can't look at anything but her eyes. And when I'm talking to Mrs. Parrish, I talk to her eyes, because that's the part of her that makes her who she is.

With other people I find myself talking to their mouth, and with others I kind of work back and forth between the eyes and mouth. I remember one little boy back in Bridgeville — he couldn't talk at all, so he had to make folks understand him without words. His whole face was moving every second, and I never had any trouble telling whether he was happy or sad or whatever. His eyes and mouth and nose and eyebrows and ears and forehead all moved about, and I knew what was inside his mind. After I knew him a while, I almost forgot he couldn't talk.

Katie Morgan's mouth was what drew my attention first. And always after that when we were looking at each other, I talked to her mouth and watched what it did. Her mouth, like Mrs. Parrish's eyes, was that little window in her face that looked down inside the real her.

It was a wide mouth, that spread out into her

cheeks when she smiled. Her teeth weren't big, but she showed them every time she spoke, nice, even white teeth. It was a mouth that always had something to say, even when she was just quietly thinking. Even then the lips would be subtly moving, shaping themselves with thought, moving this way and that, up and down, sideways. And when she talked — which was a lot of the time — then the mouth was more active than ever. The teeth, the lips, the laughter — everything about her mouth was used when she was communicating.

The voice that came out of the mouth, too, was part of all that. It was a high voice, though not too high, a pleasant voice to listen to, that sounded like it would be able to sing. While Pa's voice sometimes reminded me of a high, rugged mountain, and Mrs. Parrish's made me picture a summer sunset, Katie's brought to mind a cheerful stream, full of clear snow water, rushing down a hillside in spring.

Actually, Katie's whole face was wide, wide enough so it had room for her big smile. Her nose was ordinary and her forehead wide. She had medium brown hair, combed down the middle and falling off to the right and left to just above her shoulders.

Katie's eyes were green, and they opened real big when she was trying to be astonished, so that white spread all around the black and green parts in the middle. At times like that I'd look at her eyes instead of her mouth, because they could flash and show expression too. Her whole face was like that — active and expressive. It wasn't a face I could ignore if she was looking at me. She made sure you looked back.

What she'd said in her letter was true. I don't reckon Pa figured she was beautiful the first time he set eyes on her as she got off the boat. But then when you caught her eyes and mouth in just the right expression, she was pretty enough. I don't suppose Ma was beautiful either, and Pa sure loved her. And prettiness doesn't count for much if it's hiding ugliness down inside. Katie Morgan was average-looking — just like most women, I reckon.

She'd said she was a little stocky, and I suppose that's a good enough word. I noticed her height right off. I was likely two or three inches taller than her, and she was a little on the thick side, though not plump. It was a hardworking sort of build, sturdy and strong. When she shook my hand, her grasp had been firm and her hand large and rough. I didn't see anything dainty about the rest of her. You could just tell by the way she walked and moved, and by the look of her hands and face and arms, that she was a woman who would be able to do what she needed to get by, and that she'd probably get along in the West just fine.

She was dressed in a nice-enough looking dress, blue and a creamy color, sort of between yellow and white. It was probably her best dress. If I were coming to meet a new husband, I'd wear my Sunday clothes for sure. But as we sat in the carriage and I had the chance to take in a little more about Katie's appearance than I had noticed on the dock, I could see that spots of the blue were faded here and there, and underneath the elbows the cloth was wearing a mite thin. It was not a new dress, and not at all fancy.

Funny how you notice little details about people more and more that you didn't see at first — like the dress Katie was wearing. And after two days of being absorbed with her mouth, watching it, listening to it, having conversation back and forth, getting to know her as she talked — as we rode along that second day when it was quiet and Tad was sleeping, I found myself looking at her eyes almost for the first time. She was gazing out the window. Her mouth and whole face was still and calm.

And what I saw — or thought I saw — was a look in the eyes of question and wonder. Looking out over the California gold country for the first time, maybe she was thinking about Virginia, thinking about how far she'd come, thinking about that man up there in front shouting at the two horses. I don't suppose she could help wondering if she'd done the right thing, wondering what was going to become of her in this strange new land, wondering if she — like the seed from the pine cone — was going to be able to grow in this new California soil. I thought I saw a hint of loneliness too, just for a second, like she was already homesick. I'd been worried so much about myself and how hard her coming was going to be on me.

Suddenly I found myself feeling sorry for her.

CHAPTER 27

NEVER THE SAME AGAIN

Eight or ten miles from Miracle, Zack and Little Wolf galloped on ahead.

By the time we reached town, word of our coming had spread and a dozen or so people were hanging around doors and windows, hoping for a sight of the new Mrs. Hollister-to-be.

But Pa wanted none of their gawking faces. At the first sight of them, he could tell what they were up to. He lashed the reins and shouted to the horses, and we flew down Miracle's main street like a black blur. I hardly had time to show Katie two or three buildings, and we were already out the other end, crossing the creek, heading round the bend and starting the long circular climb toward our place.

He slowed down after that, but it was still a bumpy, clattering ride up the hill, across the creek two or three more times, to the claim. We were glad to be home when we heard Pa's "Whoa!" and felt the horses come to a stop.

"Well, here we are!" said Pa, climbing down from the front and opening the door for us.

Katie stepped out, glanced around, and drew in a deep breath with a look of satisfaction. Just then Uncle Nick walked up.

"Nick, this here's Miss Kathryn Morgan," Pa said, as he tied up the two horses to the hitching rail.

Uncle Nick looked Katie over, with not a frown exactly, but a serious expression, and certainly not a friendly one.

"I'm happy to meet you, Mr. Belle," said Katie. "I hope we can be friends. The children have been telling me all about you!"

Uncle Nick didn't say anything.

"And they've been telling me about your sister," Katie added. "They're very fond of her, you know. And I hope you don't think I will ever presume to take her place."

Uncle Nick's face seemed to brighten just a little. "She was a fine lady, Aggie was," he said, speaking to her for the first time. "She made Drum here a fine wife."

"I am so sorry she didn't make it here with the children," Katie replied. "I only hope I can be half as good a wife as she was. I just want to be a help to you all here." She sure knew how to make herself pleasing!

Uncle Nick gave her another look, a little longer one this time, then threw his glance in Pa's direction. "She might do after all, Drum! She ain't no Agatha Belle, but you mighta done okay for yourself!"

Before Pa could answer, Katie said, "I thank

you kindly for your approval, Mr. Belle. I will take that as a compliment!"

"Corrie, take Miss Kathryn inside and show her the place while we get the bags down," Pa said. "Zack, get up on top there and untie that rope."

Katie and I went inside, followed by the three younger ones. Zack helped Pa. Little Wolf had galloped off over the hill to his place just outside Miracle. I don't know where Uncle Nick went. We didn't see him again till suppertime.

It was about four-thirty in the afternoon when we got home. The sun was just thinking about settling down over the hills downstream. So the first thing we did was to start making supper. It reminded me of Christmas day with all three of us girls and Katie in the kitchen at the same time. Pa stuck his head in the door to say, "I'm taking the carriage back to the Freight Company. I'll be back inside forty minutes." I thought it was funny that he'd leave again so soon after getting home. And it was curious, too, that he didn't mention Mrs. Parrish's name about the carriage. But I hardly had a chance to think about it more, and before I knew it he was back and we were ready for supper.

Pa had halfway fixed up his and Uncle Nick's room for Katie to stay in after she got there. He didn't really do much except take their stuff out. He and Uncle Nick were planning to stay in the barn until the wedding, which didn't please

263

Uncle Nick too much. He'd said that he didn't see why Pa didn't just put her up in a boardinghouse in town someplace instead of turning them out of their own home. But Pa said they couldn't tell what kind of woman she was if they were always having to ride into town to fetch her every day. If anyone needed to stay in town, Pa'd said, then Uncle Nick could. Uncle Nick went off in a huff, but he didn't go to Mrs. Gianini's, and that first night he was out sleeping in the barn with Pa. It was a good thing summer was coming and most of the cold weather was past.

Well things were sure different around here after that. And I realized they'd never be the same again.

There wasn't much actual talk about the wedding — not at first, anyway. It was more or less taken for granted, and we just went about living our lives every day, knowing it was out there and the day was steadily approaching. I knew Pa'd been planning on having the ceremony sometime in June, after Katie had been here about a month. He told Uncle Nick once that he figured "a month was long enough to find out if she's gonna take to the kids or not."

In Pa's mind, the marriage was still just mostly for us. But I knew he wanted to make the best of it for himself too, as long as it was something he felt had to be. I didn't know what day Pa was thinking of, but I figured it would be in the middle of June, probably on a Sunday after the church service was over.

He'd went into town a week after Katie got to Miracle to see Rev. Rutledge. I figured it was about the wedding plans.

CHAPTER 28

MAY 1854

Those five weeks between May 13 and the wedding on June 24 were weeks of getting accustomed to new ways.

Every one of us around that place had plenty of change and adjusting to do, getting familiar with having Katie around. It was like when we'd come and had had to get used to Pa. Now that we were used to him, everything was changing again. Now that I think of it, I suppose it was hardest of all for Katie. But she hardly ever showed it.

I wrote a lot in my journal that month. With Katie there, I had more time because I wasn't having to do as much work myself. So I had a chance to write and read more than usual, and take some long walks.

Actually, it wasn't as hard for me after Katie got there as I'd thought it would be. Katie must have known that there'd be things I'd be struggling to get used to. She seemed to go out of her way to be nice — and not just to me. She was nice and cheerful to everyone.

We'd get up in the morning and she'd send us off to school with lunches and a wave. I still helped to get the younger ones ready to go, but it was nice having help with the breakfast and lunches. When we got home, she'd always say something like, "Well, Corrie, what do you think we should do about supper tonight?" still halfway treating me like I was the woman in charge of the house. I wasn't, of course, but she was considerate and that made me feel a mite silly for all the worrying I'd done earlier.

All in all, the first week or two wasn't so bad. It was like having a maid around the place — which was a peculiar enough thing for folks like us!

We were gone at school most of the day, till midafternoon, so I can't say what things were like then. Pa and Uncle Nick kept working away up at the mine pretty much as usual. Alkali Jones was here probably half the days. Katie kept busy in the house and I could see things she'd done — cleaning and arranging — when I got home. It had looked all right to me before, but she seemed to find ways to make it look better. After a while the cabin started to take on a more homey look. She started working on curtains for the windows and would ask Pa for this and that — some shelves here, some new linen or bedclothes there — and Pa would oblige with whatever she wanted.

Miss Stansberry sometimes talked about wishing she could be "a fly on the wall" listening to somebody else's conversation. I laughed when I first heard her say it, but I wished the same myself

267

when we were at school — to be a fly on the wall of the cabin!

Did Katie and Pa ever have lunch alone? What did they talk about? Or did they ever go on walks or rides in the wagon alone together, as if they were courting? Those were the kinds of questions I couldn't help wondering about.

But I didn't know any of the answers. I never saw them alone together, except by accident. From looking, you'd never have known they were planning to be married the next month. It still seemed like a "business" kind of deal, like she was going to work for Pa instead of be his wife — tend the cabin and kids and keep the place clean.

Pa was as nice to Katie as he'd be to anyone. He'd show her consideration and compliment her on a nice meal. And lots of times he'd say, "Thank you," to her for different things. He seemed like he was trying to act like a good husband ought to.

I think Pa wanted to be nice to her, maybe even for Ma's sake, to do some things better now that he hadn't done with her. But he didn't touch Katie or put his arm around her — and as long ago as it was, I can still remember him putting his arm around Ma almost every day. And they didn't laugh or have fun together or go outside alone or anything. She called him Drummond. He still called her Miss Kathryn. After a while she kept pestering him about it. I thought of her as *Katie* in my mind, but to her face I still called her Miss Morgan like the other kids.

Tad and Emily and Becky all loved her, of course — she saw to that. If Pa'd brought her all the way from Virginia mostly to be like a nanny to his children, then she was up to the task. At first little Tad had followed Uncle Nick around like a puppy dog. But now that there was a new person around, the luster was gone from Uncle Nick's shadow. Tad and Becky were Miss Morgan's constant companions, and she didn't seem to mind. The three of them were always talking. Emily kept to herself a little. I think she would take longer to accept a new stepmother, just like Zack and me.

I wish us three older ones could have talked about the feelings we were having, and how Ma and Pa fit into them. But there's a big difference between seventeen and fourteen and thirteen. Brothers and sisters aren't always accustomed to talking to one another about important things, anyway. So probably even though we were sharing lots of the same feelings, we didn't really talk about them to each other.

I wasn't the only one who was growing. Zack would be fifteen in the summer. He was shooting up, getting tall and lanky and his voice was getting deep. It wouldn't be long before there'd be three grown men up there working the mine.

Emily, too, was getting shapely like a young lady. I wish Ma had lived to see quiet little Emily gradually blossom into a woman. Right now she was sort of in between. The little girl would laugh

269

out in the merriest way, but suddenly without warning that part of her would hide and out of her rich, blue-green eyes would come a glance that made her look for an instant to be twenty years old.

I was amazed when I saw it. Emily had always been my kid sister, and now all at once I began to realize that we'd both be women before we knew it. On her face I could almost see the two parts of her — the woman-child and the childlike-lady — going back and forth, neither quite knowing which was supposed to be in control.

I wish Emily had someone to help her through the growing-up struggle, like I'd had Ma and now had Mrs. Parrish. Maybe one day I could be a little like that for her. Or perhaps she and Katie would hit it off like I had with Mrs. Parrish — though I couldn't tell if Katie would understand things in the same way Mrs. Parrish always seemed to.

Uncle Nick seemed to get accustomed to Katie pretty quickly. He didn't complain about the barn much after the first day or two, and he acted more friendly toward Katie, even on the second day. It wasn't long, in fact, before he and Katie seemed to be pretty good friends and would laugh and talk together. They were a little closer in age than either was to Pa, and Uncle Nick was pretty rambunctious himself, like Katie seemed to be, so I expected they would get along fine.

Once Uncle Nick realized that Katie was going

to be a help around the place and that he didn't need to be jealous of Ma's memory on account of her, I think he decided to accept her as part of the family.

He started making an effort, just like Pa, to be a mite more gracious, with a woman around the place now. He and Pa'd make a point of washing their hands before supper or of cleaning the mud off their boots before coming in the cabin. They even started taking regular baths in the creek, and with Katie washing their clothes, it smelled more pleasant when everyone was inside.

The townsfolk and the people in the shops liked Katie right off. Nobody in Miracle Springs knew Ma, so they were all just happy for Pa and they all said Katie seemed like she'd do just fine in California. There was talk about several other men writing for mail-order brides too, now that they saw how well Pa had done!

It was a Tuesday when we got home from Sacramento. The following Saturday evening Pa was talking after supper about going to church the next day and seeing folks for the first time with Katie with us.

"It's only fair that I warn you, Drummond," said Katie after she realized what Pa was talking about, "that I'm not a religious person. I don't intend to be going off to some church service every Sunday."

Her statement took Pa by surprise. We all

271

waited to see what he'd say, but he let her go on.

"Oh, I don't mind going with you once in a while. And I'll do my duty to you and the kids. I won't stand in the way of them getting their proper share of religious training, if that's what you want for them. It's just that for me, church is not something I have much use for."

"Mind telling me why?" said Pa.

"My aunt was a devout lady. She went to mass every week, and had the priest come over to the house after she was sick. But I never saw any good it did her — just a bunch of rituals that wasted half her life. And a long time ago I decided I was going to make better use of my time than that."

"There's a lot of decent folks think church holds folks together and makes a community work better," said Pa.

"I don't doubt the church has a function," Katie answered. "But all the priests and preachers and half the church people I ever met were just as hypocritical as the crooked shopkeepers and land swindlers, so I never saw much use of getting involved."

I was just about to say something but Pa spoke up again, and his words surprised me.

"Well, here in Miracle Springs we got a decent man for our preacher, and I don't think anyone for miles would say he's a hypocrite. There's as much difference between Rev. Rutledge and

Royce as day and night."

Good for Pa! I thought, *sticking up for the minister.*

"Royce?"

"The banker. He's our local version of what you call land swindlers."

Uncle Nick laughed from over by the fire. "Don't you know, Drum, he's just trying to make an honest profit like any businessman!"

"Who've you been talking to, Nick?"

"Royce has changed," laughed Uncle Nick. "No more shady land deals. Now he swindles folks the honest way! If you wanna know my opinion, Katie, I can abide preachers a lot sooner than I can bankers! Them's the ones I don't trust!"

Now Pa laughed. "You're right there. Royce woulda had this whole claim of ours if Corrie and Tad and Zack hadn't foiled him. Low-down clean through. But talking about that minister again, I helped him build that church of his and he proved himself a worthwhile man in my book. And he's got some other good folks in that church too."

"You may be entirely right. I'll go with you tomorrow and you can depend on me to do my duty as your wife and for your children. Just don't expect me to become one of this man Rutledge's followers."

Nothing more was said. Pa settled back in his chair and was even more quiet than usual for a spell.

CHAPTER 29

AN AFTERNOON IN MIRACLE SPRINGS

We all piled into the wagon the next morning to go into town for church. Uncle Nick didn't usually go with us, but he did that day, and it was nice, feeling like a whole family.

It's funny I would say that with Katie there, but that was how I felt. And naturally everybody was all eyes as we rode up.

Katie must've known everyone was curious about her, but she just walked into the church like there was nothing out of the ordinary and she did this same thing every Sunday. Pa led the way in and didn't stop to make any introductions, just nodding to his friends here and there.

We took up a whole row of chairs, the eight of us — a Belle, six Hollisters, and a Morgan-soon-to-be-a-Hollister. I don't suppose he could have helped noticing it, but Rev. Rutledge didn't say or do anything out of the ordinary, and the service went on pretty much like always.

The minister did say one thing that stuck with me. He was talking about how it was when we expect things to go a certain way and then all of a sudden our plans are upset. Or when we think we're supposed to do one thing and find out we can't.

He said that God never blocks one path unless He's got another one for us to take. He said it was like walking through a forest and all of a sudden finding a huge tree fallen across the way. Sometimes God puts those trees there to make us move in another direction we might never have discovered otherwise.

What he said reminded me of Mrs. Parrish talking about everything always working out for the best if we're doing our best to obey God. Katie's coming was like a tree across the path of *my* life. It might not have been how I wanted it to be, but if God really was the one who was behind everything that happened to me, then it was bound to turn out good in the end.

Right then I realized I ought to try to think of Katie not like something that had come across my path that was intended to hurt my life, but as a tree God had sent to move me in a new way — maybe toward something that wouldn't have been able to be otherwise, something that was even *better* than the first path through the woods.

Anyway, I think that's what Mrs. Parrish would have told me. She was forever looking for the good side of things that happened. She said it was more than just being optimistic. She said that's what God *wanted* us to do — to always trust Him to work everything out in the best of all possible ways.

I sneaked a peek around to where Mrs. Parrish was sitting listening to Rev. Rutledge. She smiled at me as if she knew what I was thinking. *It must make her proud,* I thought as I turned back and faced the front again, *seeing this church and all the people in it, knowing that she was the one who got it going, and who first wrote to Rev. Rutledge.*

I never heard anyone say it, but I guess she was the most influential person in Miracle Springs. I couldn't think of anyone whose life hadn't been changed in some way on account of her — her business, the money she helped folks with, the church, the school. I wondered if *she* even knew all she'd done! I found myself wondering, too, if there were any trees in her path.

My thoughts drifted to Katie again, then back to the tree and what Rev. Rudledge was saying.

Lord, I prayed silently as I sat there, *I do ask You to make Katie's coming be a good thing for all of us, especially for Pa. I want him to be happy and to do what he thinks is best. I pray that You'd make everything happen just like You want it to, and help me to be loving and to help Katie if I can, even though I didn't like the idea of her coming at first. And help me to do like Mrs. Parrish says and trust You for everything, and to know You'll make it for the best.*

After the service was over, we went slowly out, shaking the minister's hand. He was all smiles to Katie, welcoming her to Miracle and telling

276

her that Pa was a fine man and had a wonderful family. She smiled back and was pleasant, but recalling to mind what she'd said about ministers the night before, I wondered if the smile on her face was real, or just put there until church was over.

I'd always heard folks say things to Rev. Rutledge as they shook his hand and went outside, "Fine sermon this morning, Reverend," or maybe, "Your words blessed my soul, Reverend." Mostly it was the older women who sometimes came who said things like that. But this morning as Rev. Rutledge took my hand and smiled at me, I suddenly found myself saying almost that very thing. "I want to thank you for what you said about the trees falling across our path, Rev. Rutledge," I said. "I think that is going to help me with — with —"

Suddenly my words dried up. I was embarrassed and hoped Uncle Nick behind me hadn't heard.

But Rev. Rutledge smiled broadly at me. "Are you saying there's been a tree across your path, Corrie?" he asked.

"Yes, sir, I reckon that's it."

"Well, just let the Lord help you get around it, and you can count on Him to set your feet down on an even better path than the first one."

"Thank you, sir," I said. "I'll remember that!"

When I got outside and down the steps, Pa and Katie were already with Mrs. Parrish and the two women were shaking hands for the first time.

"I am so happy to meet you at last," said Mrs. Parrish warmly. "This is quite a man you've come to California to wed, Miss Morgan! One of this community's leading citizens!"

Pa mumbled something, but I didn't hear it. Mrs. Parrish threw back her head and laughed.

"Leading citizen, you say?" said Katie inquisitively.

"Oh yes!" answered Mrs. Parrish, loving every second of putting Pa on the spot. "Why, the stories I could tell you!"

"You don't know nothing to tell about me!" exclaimed Pa. I couldn't tell at first if he was riled, but then I realized he was just joining in the fun.

"I *would* like to hear it all!" said Katie.

"I had hoped to talk you all into coming over to my house this afternoon," Mrs. Parrish went on, "so I could get to know Katie a little better. What do you say, Mr. Hollister?"

"*Mr.* Hollister?" said Katie. "You know him as well as you say and you still address him so formally?"

"He's not given me leave to do otherwise," responded Mrs. Parrish.

"Surely, Drummond, if you allow me to call you by your given name after only one week, this lady who has been your friend so long deserves no less."

"You can call me whatever you like," said Pa, not exactly getting upset now, but not liking it too much having two women talking about him.

"Then, Drummond," said Mrs. Parrish, "would you do me the honor of a visit this afternoon? Perhaps you could stop over now and we could have tea and coffee and some biscuits."

She drew his name out slowly, like she enjoyed saying it. "I'd like to have you for dinner one Sunday after church," she went on, "but I'm sure you already have plans today."

"I have a lamb leg on the fire," said Katie.

"Well then, you'll just have time for a nice visit and then you can go home to it."

Without any further discussion, in five or ten minutes, after Pa was through seeing and shaking hands with the other folks wanting to meet his mail-order bride, we were back in the wagon on our way to Mrs. Parrish's.

She must've been planning on us coming. She had several trays of crackers and little biscuits out, and she made coffee and tea and was very hospitable.

Mrs. Parrish was our best friend in town. And now it seemed Mrs. Parrish wanted to make herself a friend to the newest member of the family, Katie Morgan.

They chatted freely. "Every time a new woman joins the community," said Mrs. Parrish, "I am so thrilled. When I first came, it sometimes seemed I went for weeks on end without seeing another one of our kind! Now at least the men don't outnumber us more than twenty or thirty to one. And our numbers are growing fast!"

After a while Mrs. Parrish got up. "Corrie,"

she said to me, "I have something for you. Would you come into my room with me? We'll just be a minute," she said to the others. "You all go ahead and have something more to eat."

I got up and followed her.

When we were in her room with the door closed, she turned and said with an expectant look, "Well?"

"Well, what?" I returned.

"What do you think? How are things with Miss Morgan?"

"Oh, fine, I reckon. She's nice enough."

"She seems very nice, Corrie. I think you should be pleased."

"I'm trying to be, Mrs. Parrish. I prayed for her during church a while ago. But it still takes some getting used to."

"I know, dear. And it probably will for quite a while. But give the Lord time. Remember what I've always said, He not only brings good, He gives nothing but the best."

"You keep reminding me, and I'll keep trying to believe it more."

She smiled. "That is a fair deal. I agree. But — here!" she reached toward a little package on her dresser, "this is what I brought you in to give you." She handed it to me. It felt like a book.

"It's brand new — just published. I had it sent to me from a bookstore in San Francisco."

I unwrapped it. It was a book, bound in cloth, with the simple title *Walden* in gold across the cover, with the words underneath, and smaller, "Life in the Woods."

"I think you'll like it," she said. "It's by a man named Henry David Thoreau. I've been following his writings for some years. When other men were fighting the Mexicans and discovering gold and making fortunes here in California, do you know what he did?"

I shook my head.

"Thoreau went out into the woods all by himself, taking virtually nothing, and lived alone by a lake near Concord, Massachusetts, called Walden Pond. Like you, he kept a journal, and this is the result."

She pointed toward the book. "Something tells me you and Thoreau have a lot in common, Corrie Belle Hollister. He loved nature, as you do. He found nature speaking to him. He discovered much about himself and about God's world and his fellow man, all from his unique ability to find quiet and calmness within himself.

"He was then able to hear voices speaking to him — God, nature, and his own inner being. And he possessed the God-given talent to make his thoughts and observations known. He reminds me of you, Corrie. I do not doubt that the world is going to know your name one day, and that you will be telling the world many things. Who knows — someday people may even be reading a book with *your* name on it!"

"That *would* be something!" I said.

"You can never tell what God might do, Corrie.

Sometimes those trees across our path, like Avery was talking about today, are thrown there by God because He has some wonderful *new* thing to do in our lives that we'd never see with our eyes fixed straight ahead. I have no doubt at all that He will take you on *many* interesting and un-expected paths, and as long as you are obeying Him and trusting Him, they will be wonderful ones! But I suppose we had better not leave my other guests alone any longer!"

"Thank you for the book, Mrs. Parrish. I'll treasure it!"

"I just pray it encourages you to be faithful to your journal and your other writing. I feel God is going to use your writing, Corrie. And perhaps making a friend of Thoreau will help."

CHAPTER 30

A DETERMINED LADY

Katie's talkativeness and cheerfulness came into our house like a summer wind.

She was the kind of person I couldn't help liking. And I think Pa liked her, too. But after a couple of weeks, I found myself starting to wonder what it was going to be like having her there forever. Gradually she stopped being just a visitor. Our home began to seem more like it was *her* home, where *she* was in charge.

Maybe she figured that was how Pa wanted it. That was why he brought her here, wasn't it, to manage the household? That's how wives did it.

And maybe that's how Pa *did* want it, how was I to know? But to my eyes it began to look like she was getting pretty determined about how things were to be done, when it wasn't even her own place yet. But then again, in less than a month it *was* going to be half her place, so maybe everything was just as it ought to be.

One afternoon Uncle Nick and Pa were later than usual coming down from the mine. Uncle Nick was the first to come inside, and he no more than stepped foot inside the door when Katie half-hollered over her shoulder to him, "Come on, Nick, get washed up. Supper's ready and I don't want it getting cold. You too, Drum," she added to Pa as he walked in. "Come on, kids, everyone around the table!" Nobody thought to say anything, we all just did as she said. Pa and Uncle Nick turned right around to go back out to wash their hands. I guess it was a little thing, but I noticed.

From the very beginning she was always cleaning up around the place. At first it was nice. I thought I'd been doing pretty good filling in for Ma, but once Katie arrived, with her sweeping and dusting and scrubbing, I realized how little I really had done.

What Pa noticed, I think, wasn't the cleaning so much as the straightening and rearranging. Often I'd see him stop and look around for something that wasn't where he kept it. She'd see the puzzled look on his face, ask him what he was looking for, and then go get whatever it was for him.

One night he and Nick were sitting in front of the fire smoking their pipes, their feet up on a low table in front of them. They still had their boots on, and they weren't any more clean than boots generally are. As Katie approached I saw Uncle Nick give Pa a quick wink, then scrape his boots together so that some of the dirt fell off onto the table.

Sure enough, Katie saw it and marched right over. "I just cleaned that table today, and I'll thank you to keep your boots off it and your dirt outside!"

"Aw, for crying out loud, woman," said Uncle Nick, "this is our cabin, not no fancy hotel!" He was joking with her, but she didn't realize it. Her next words were heated.

"Now you look here, Nick Belle. Your brother-in-law brought me here to keep a nice and tidy house for him. If you don't like the way I do it, then I suggest you find another."

Uncle Nick was so shocked at what she said he didn't say anything more for a minute. The smile stuck on his face for a moment, then slowly faded.

"Now hold on there, Miss Kathryn," said Pa. "Nick didn't mean no harm. But he's right about what he said. This is our place, and we ain't used to trying to keep every speck of dirt out of it. I reckon you'll just have to get used to a little dirt here and there."

Katie looked at Pa, seeming surprised for a moment, but with no intention of backing down.

"I see," she said slowly. "Well, if that's the way you want it, I'll comply somehow. But that's no way to run a house, Drummond Hollister, I can tell you that."

She turned and walked away, leaving Pa and Uncle Nick exchanging looks that said more than they'd have wanted Katie to see. Nick was smiling and winking again. Pa was serious.

And despite what she said about complying, when Pa and Uncle Nick finally got up, I saw her go over, pick up the two pipes lying there, empty the tobacco from them into the fire, and then put them up on a mantle shelf. Later, before he went out to the barn, I saw him walk over that direction looking for it.

"Where's my pipe?" he finally said, half-muttering, to no one in particular.

"Up on the mantle," said Katie.

Pa located it, then headed for the door.

"You're not going to smoke out in the barn, are you?" Katie asked.

Pa half shrugged that he was.

"Oh no, Drummond. Not with all that straw out there, and the children and me sleeping so close by. It's not at all safe. No — you do your smoking in here."

I thought Pa was going to say something, but then he apparently thought better of it. He turned around, strode quickly back to the fireplace, tossed his pipe back on the mantle, and left the house without another word, not even a good night to the rest of us.

Five minutes later, from out in the barn I heard a loud laugh from Uncle Nick and I knew Pa'd told him what had just then happened over the pipe. Uncle Nick got a kick out of Katie's ways. I think sometimes he even goaded her on just to rile her. But it seemed it was starting to annoy Pa.

Even though Katie may have been a mite bossy, we sat down to nice meals together like a family ought to, and everybody's manners improved, especially Zack's and Uncle Nick's. Pa was pretty mannerly anyway. But Uncle Nick was noticeably cleaner, and he started shaving more regularly. He hardly ever went into town in the evenings after Katie got there. He just seemed to like being around the place.

After a week or two, he and Katie were getting along real friendly, although he teased her something awful — like with the boots on the table — causing little scuffles between her and Pa. But that was always Uncle Nick's way — teasing, kidding, laughing, causing trouble, having fun — and I could tell he enjoyed having somebody new to do it all with, especially a woman only a few years younger than him. When he realized Katie was strong-headed enough to throw it all right back at him, I wondered if he'd finally met his match. Katie would come right back with a remark to one of his wisecracks, sometimes with a quick glance or smile in my direction to say, "See, men aren't so tough. You just have to know how to handle them."

Well, she might have had it figured out how to handle Uncle Nick, but I wasn't sure her way was going to work with Pa. Maybe on account of Pa knowing she was going to be his wife, everything was more serious. Marriage must do that to folks.

The third Sunday after Katie got there, Pa was moving around getting himself and the wagon ready to go into town. Then as we were getting set for breakfast, he said, "You kids get dressed in your Sunday duds soon as you're done eating, so we can get into church on time."

"I didn't know we had plans to go into town today, Drummond," said Katie, pausing and looking up at him as she stirred the eggs scrambling on the stove.

"Well, it's Sunday, ain't it? I just figured that we'd —"

"I told you before, Drummond," Katie interrupted, "I do not intend to make a regular ritual of listening to that man's religious pronouncements about trees and paths and God and forests and whatever else it was he so enlightened us about two weeks ago. And last week wasn't much better, though I put up with it. But I told you I wasn't going to make it an every-week thing."

"You tell him, Katie!" kidded Uncle Nick, giving her a little jab in the ribs. Uncle Nick was always trying to protect folks from getting too serious.

Katie's eyes flashed and she glanced at Uncle Nick. At first I thought she was going to lash out at him, but it wasn't anger gleaming out of her eyes.

"You shut up and stay out of this, Nick," said Pa. "This is between me and Miss Kathryn and the kids. I'm telling you all that I'm taking *my* family to church this morning. Be ready, all of you, after breakfast!"

He turned and left the house, and we didn't see him for half an hour. It was a pretty quiet meal. We'd all heard every word and I think the argument frightened us. Uncle Nick did his best to cheer us up around the table by saying it was all going to work out fine.

We went to church, just Pa and us five kids. Afterward, we played for another half an hour while Pa and Rev. Rutledge talked about the wedding. When Pa came outside and climbed back up in the wagon, he said, "Well, it's all set — the fifteenth, after the service."

"That's in just two weeks, Pa," I said.

"Might as well get the thing done, Corrie. She's doing all the things a wife's supposed to do. Might as well make it official and get on with it. Where's Becky?" said Pa, suddenly looking around and realizing he was one youngster short. I hadn't even realized she'd slipped away.

"She's over in them woods, Pa," said Zack, pointing out behind the church building. "There's a little grove of firs and she goes there all the time during school."

"Run and fetch her, will you, Zack?"

"Sure, Pa." Zack was off the wagon and out of sight in a few seconds. He'd not only grown taller, but he was faster as well.

In a couple of minutes he and Becky reappeared, and we set off for home.

Uncle Nick was right. Everything was fine after we got home. The incident before breakfast blew over and no one mentioned it again. I reckon making plans with the minister must have settled things in Pa's mind, because he didn't seem to be annoyed at things Katie did after that. He told her that he and the minister had set the date, and she nodded her approval.

"There are many things we will have to discuss, Drummond," she said.

"I reckon," said Pa. "We got two weeks."

"Which isn't long," persisted Katie.

Pa nodded. There were no more fusses after that.

Two nights later, I found myself lying in bed awake. Gradually, Pa and Katie's voices reached my ears from the other room. Nick was already out in the barn. Everyone but me was asleep, and I guess they thought I was too. I figured they were talking about some of those things Katie said they needed to "discuss." I just lay there, not paying much attention, just hearing the low sound of their voices.

But suddenly I realized they were talking about me! I immediately strained to listen.

". . . going to be eighteen next year . . . time a young woman gives thought . . . future comes sooner than . . ."

It was Katie's voice talking, but I could only hear pieces of what she said. When Pa spoke I could make out his deeper voice clearly.

"There's plenty of time for all that later."

"I can tell you from my own experience, Drummond," Katie answered back, but again I only heard some of her words, ". . . goes by quickly . . . those years with my aunt and uncle . . . now here I am over thirty . . . lost opportunities . . . just now getting married . . . time we thought about . . . she's marrying age, Drummond."

What! Katie talking to Pa about marrying me off already! I quickly forgot my resolve to be nice to her and the prayers I'd been praying for her, and tried to listen more intently.

"I ain't gonna have Corrie getting married any time soon," said Pa, and I breathed a sigh of relief. "Besides, she ain't of a mind to be marrying just now anyway. She's got writing to do and maybe teaching. She asked me about college a while back."

". . . good thing to have dreams . . . realistic too . . . life in the West . . . need a husband . . . chasing foolish fancies . . ."

"It ain't so foolish. She's written for that paper of Singleton's, and she's helping the Stansberry lady with teaching. Corrie's no ordinary young lady, I tell you. She had to grow up in a hurry when her ma died, and I figure she can do just about anything she sets her mind to."

Oh, Pa! I was so proud to hear him say those words!

"Yes, well . . . discuss it again . . . don't have to settle Corrie's whole future right . . . still think it wouldn't do any harm to look . . ."

"I'll tell you again, Miss Kathryn. I may be making you my wife for the young'uns sake. But what becomes of Corrie is for her to decide."

Pa's voice had a finality to it, and I could feel that he believed in me! Just hearing those words made me so happy!

"Yes, well, that's fine . . . we'll see what comes

291

. . . did want to talk to you also . . . the other children . . . school clothes . . . won't do for them to be chasing around . . . rags don't befit the children . . . was it that lady called you — a leading citizen?"

"I ain't no leading citizen and my kids ain't dressed in rags."

". . . only thinking that . . . do have the money, Drummond, to present a better face . . . your family and you . . . people think of you more highly if . . ."

"I ain't out to impress no one, or my kids neither."

"About Zack . . . he's —"

"He's nearly grown, too, just like Corrie. I ain't gonna be putting no harnesses on him, neither. He's a good boy, and —"

I didn't hear the last of Pa's sentence. How I wished Zack could have been listening right then!

". . . agree . . . wonderful young man . . . only feel I would like . . . suitable . . . with that young Indian —"

"Little Wolf?" exclaimed Pa. "He's a good kid, too, and harmless."

"He *is* an Indian, and I don't want him around here . . . don't know what might . . ."

"His father trains horses up over the hill! Got a good stable. Them two boys is like brothers. They're talking about riding together some day, racing horses even. And I ain't gonna be telling Zack he can't do something like that. He's got his heart set on it, and that's a good enough thing."

Pa's voice had an irritated sound to it again. I guess Katie knew it, because she didn't say anything more about either me or Zack or getting the young'uns better school clothes. They kept talking for a long time, but settled back into less disagreeable topics. I finally went to sleep with plenty of thoughts still floating around inside.

Like I said before, things would never be the same again. In less than two weeks that lady sitting out there would be Pa's wife!

CHAPTER 31

A TALK WITH PA

The very next day, when we got home after school, I could tell Pa was being quieter than usual. There'd been lots of things running through my mind all day, from listening to Pa and Katie the night before. I couldn't help it. I was worrying again.

I'd been writing, of course, but I wanted to talk to someone about it too. Because of other things I was thinking about, I knew I couldn't talk to Mrs. Parrish.

Maybe part of me knew that there were things on Pa's mind. I suppose that's what drew me out to the barn that afternoon. I knew he was there and I knew he was alone, and I hoped maybe we'd be able to talk a little. We hadn't for a long time.

When I walked in, I expected to see him shoveling out the stalls, or raking up straw, or fixing or building something. Pa was always busy with his hands. But instead he was just standing there, leaning against a saddle slung over a rail, a piece of straw in his mouth, staring out the window toward the woods across the creek. Just standing there still, not doing anything, not moving.

"Hi, Pa," I said.

He didn't seem startled. It was almost as if he expected me. He turned around slowly. I'll never forget that look on his face — not a smile, but neither was it serious. It was almost a look of relief. I had the feeling he was glad it was me instead of Katie.

"Hi-ya, little girl," he said. He hadn't called me that since before he had left New York. I'd forgotten all about it. For a second I was six or seven again! But the present jumped right back at me a moment later.

He didn't say another word right then, but when I was close enough, he stretched out one of his great long arms, put it around me and drew me into a close hug for several seconds. When he released me and I stepped back, our eyes met, and I could tell we each knew what was on the other's mind.

It was a special moment with Pa. Right then, despite what he'd just called me, I knew he was looking into my eyes as a grown-up, as someone he cared about, and as someone he needed. Even men, I knew, needed someone to understand, needed someone to feel things with, and at that moment I knew I was that someone for Pa.

"Won't be long now, huh Pa?" I said with a smile.

"Yeah," he sighed, letting out a long breath. "Week from Sunday, I reckon."

Again it was quiet.

"Quite a gal, Miss Kathryn, wouldn't you say?" he said. He was making conversation, not asking my opinion.

"You're right there, Pa," I said. "She's got what folks call spunk."

Pa laughed. "Yep, that's a good word for it — spunk! But you can't help kinda liking her though."

"Yeah," I agreed. "I reckon most anybody'd like Katie Morgan once they met her."

"What about you, Corrie?" Pa said. "What do you think? Do *you* like her?" Now he *was* asking my opinion.

"Of course, Pa," I said. "I like her okay."

"You figure she'll be a good step-ma to the young'uns?"

"I reckon. They all seem to like her a lot. She's friendly and nice to everybody."

Pa thought for a moment.

"And what about you? You think you'll be happy with her being *your* step-ma?"

"I don't know, Pa," I answered. "It has been kinda hard for me to get used to, I suppose. But I want you to be happy and do what you think's best. And anyhow, like Katie said, I'm getting older and I won't be around that much longer."

"What makes you say that?"

Suddenly I realized I'd said too much. I felt my face redden, but I couldn't take back the words.

"I heard you and Katie talking last night, after

I was in bed. I'm sorry for listening, Pa. I couldn't help it."

"What'd you hear?"

"Oh, about her thinking I oughta get married pretty soon, before I got too old and turned into a spinster, I suppose."

Pa shifted his weight uneasily. I could tell he was embarrassed that I'd eavesdropped.

"She had no call to be saying those kinds of things, and I straightened her out too, I want you to know."

"I do know, Pa," I said. "I want to thank you for those nice things you said. I felt so proud that you thought that about me. I didn't know you knew me so well — you know, about the writing and teaching and things I want to do."

"I ain't such a dense ol' goat as I look, Corrie Belle!" Pa laughed. "And I've had a talk or two about you with that Parrish woman too. She thinks mighty highly of you."

I nodded. Pa bringing up Mrs. Parrish just complicated everything in my mind.

We were both quiet for a minute. Pa left the saddle he'd been leaning against, and walked over toward a bale of straw. He looked like he was going to sit down, but then he just gave it a kick and shuffled along farther.

"I don't know, Corrie," he finally said. "There's just something wrong."

He let out a big breath I could hear clear over where I was halfway across the barn. Then he turned and walked slowly back, kicking at the loose straw with his boot on the wood floor. "You know what I mean, Corrie? You can just feel when things ain't quite right. She's a nice enough young woman, and I doubt a fella'd do better writin' off blind like I done. But I can't help thinkin' of Aggie. And Miss Kathryn just ain't ever gonna be like a 'mother' to my kids. She's more like Nick — like a younger sister or something. I just don't know that I can ever get so I love her the same as your ma."

I knew now wasn't the time for me to say anything. Pa wasn't a talkative man as a rule, but when stuff started coming out of him, like I'd only seen it do a time or two before, it came out like a river instead of a trickle! I was glad Pa felt he could be that downright honest with me.

"I know a marriage can be a good one without all that being in love sort of thing. It ain't that I'm expecting anybody to be my wife like your ma was. But when I look in Miss Kathryn's eyes, there just ain't nothing there that pulls me and says 'This here's the woman I want to be like a new ma to my kids.' Nick and she do okay together, though they can squabble too . . ."

Pa paced to the window of the barn and looked out.

"There they are now, walking down to the creek, Nick helping her with that second pail of water."

He turned back toward me.

"You see what I mean, Corrie. It's different

298

with me. Sometimes I think Nick oughta get himself a woman like that. He's always needed someone to hog-tie him and keep him outta trouble. But I want a woman who knows what she's about and keeps her distance a mite more'n Miss Kathryn seems to be able to."

He stopped, then looked up at me, almost as if he was wondering if I was still there or if he'd just imagined me and had been talking to himself all this time.

I smiled. "Couldn't you — couldn't you maybe talk to her again, Pa? Or do you think maybe it's . . ." I fumbled for words. I didn't know what I was trying to say. I didn't know what Pa wanted me to say. My words just kind of ended in the middle of nothing.

But Pa just kept on going. "That's it, don't you see? There just ain't much I can do. I'm a man of my word. Besides that, I figure I'm probably blamed lucky to find a woman like Miss Kathryn who's willing and able to throw in with an ol' gold miner with nothing but a big cabin already full of kids and kin. What else is a man my age gonna do, anyway?" He stopped suddenly and gazed out the window again.

"Well, you remember what Rev. Rutledge said about trees crossing our path," I said.

"Yeah, I remember, Corrie," he said slowly after a long thoughtful pause. "Matter of fact, the Reverend was making a lot of sense to me that day. Half the time I can't make heads or tails of what he's talking about. But I did un-

299

derstand what he said about the trees."

"Me too," I said. "I guess we both got trees falling in our way."

"Maybe it's the same tree," said Pa with a sly smile.

I laughed. Quickly his face sobered up again.

"The one thing the minister didn't say, though," he added, "is what you're supposed to do when the tree falls and you can't go no farther. Sometimes after the tree has blocked one path, it takes a while tramping around in the brush to find the new one! You understand what I'm driving at?"

I smiled again. "I think I do, Pa."

He looked into my eyes like he had when I'd first come into the barn, then he looked me over from head to toe.

"I meant what you heard me say last night. You ain't an ordinary young woman by a long stretch!"

"Thank you, Pa." I knew my eyes were getting wet, but if you can't cry at a time like that, what's the use of tears, anyhow?

"No, sir. And I love you, Corrie, love you a lot."

I put my arms around his waist and hugged him. It felt so good to have his arms reach around and hug me back.

CHAPTER 32

ALONE WITH THOREAU

Pa'd been having me take one of the small wagons into town with Snowball every morning to get us all to school, so he wouldn't have to take us in and come back. We left Snowball and the wagon with Marcus Weber for the day, then he'd have her all hitched and ready for us when school was out.

The day after my talk with Pa, about halfway up the hill toward home, a rider on horseback flew past us. Then just as we were driving up to the cabin, back he came toward town.

"Who was that, Pa?" Zack asked as we got down, glancing back along the dust just settling back down onto the road.

"Friend of your uncle's," said Pa.

"What'd he want that he didn't want to hang around for?"

"Oh, nothing. He just thought he seen one of them polecats Nick fleeced in that poker game back in the fall."

"That fella Hatch?" said Zack.

"No, no, it weren't Hatch," said Pa. "Who was it Hammond thought he seen in town?"

301

"Barton," said Uncle Nick, sauntering toward us.

I looked at Zack and shivered. I remembered *that* name!

"But even if it was Barton," Uncle Nick went on, "I didn't wind up with any of his money. He ain't got no call to have a grudge against me."

"Yeah, but them kind o' lowlifes stick together," said Pa. "I think Hammond's right. You oughta lay outta sight for a few days. Them kind never forget."

"Naw, what could Barton have against me?"

"Hatch mighta sent him."

"Hatch ain't got the brains to think o' something that clever!" said Uncle Nick, glancing at Zack with a smile and a wink, enjoying his own wit.

"And I ain't sure *you* got the brains to keep outta trouble when it comes looking for ya!" shot back Pa. "Where'd Hammond say he saw him?"

"East of town, out by the church building, kinda hanging around that new livery of Markham's."

Pa thought for a moment. "Well, I don't like it. You lay low and keep away from town. We'll keep a good eye out for ol' Hatch for a few days. Like I say, you get varmints like that together and you can never tell what kinda mischief they'll pull."

When we went inside, we were kinda quiet — all except for Uncle Nick, who kept joking and making light of the whole affair. Pretty soon Pa and Nick headed back up to the mine. Katie was working at cutting up some potatoes.

I wanted to be alone, so I fetched my book and went back outside and wandered along the stream. After Mr. Hammond's visit I wasn't exactly of a mind to go for a long walk in the woods, but I did want to get out and away from everybody, even just a *little* away.

So I went up past the mine, waved to Pa, walked across the board Pa'd put down across the creek, and went just a little farther up, not quite out of sight of where Pa was working. I felt safe there, but alone at the same time.

I'd brought my journal and pen with me. I don't reckon I'll ever think of my journal writing again without thinking of Mr. Thoreau. His *Walden* was just about the finest piece of journal writing I could imagine. He's a fine writer, and what he thought of to write about! He must have had some active imagination. I hadn't read much of it at all yet, but I found myself opening it to different parts, and wherever my eyes fell, on any page, whatever he was talking about was so interesting to read!

To write like that — what a dream that would be! I wanted to start right then making everything I put down in my journal better and better.

But it's not just the writing, it's how Mr. Thoreau taught himself to watch and listen and observe all the stuff going on around him. Most folks are too busy, and their lives are too noisy, ever to see the little tiny things. But Thoreau watched bugs, listened to grass growing, heard the sounds of the sky, and paid attention to every little thing. Yet from those little things he seemed to know so much more about life's *big* things too — as if the little things held secrets to big things!

When I read in *Walden* a quietness and an aloneness came over me. More than the fact that Mr. Thoreau *was* alone when he wrote it, I felt quieter and still just from reading it.

Most folks seem to like lots of noise all the time — they want to be talking and laughing and doing things. But sometimes I wanted to be still, to be quiet, to think, to be alone. I wanted to see the world more like Thoreau saw it. Most of the time I figured other people didn't understand that. They thought I was in a sad mood or didn't like talking to them. Every once in a while, when we were having a recess or before or after school when there was some time, I liked to wander off to that little fir woods where Becky had been the other day. I liked all the other kids, but there were some moods that I couldn't share with other folks, and I just had to think and walk and listen to the woods and the water and the sky and the animals to make it all come out right. Reading Mr. Thoreau's book satisfied that part of me that needed aloneness every once in a while.

In one place he talked about a tree he'd planted:

The sumac grew luxuriantly about the house, pushing up through the embankment which I had made, and growing five or six feet the first season. Its broad pinnate tropical leaf was pleasant though strange to look on. The large buds, suddenly pushing out late in the spring from dry sticks which had seemed to be dead, developed themselves as by magic into graceful green and tender boughs, an inch in diameter. . . .

I didn't even know what the word *pinnate* meant, but I liked how he described watching that tree grow. I really sensed from his telling about it that the tree was *alive.*

We'd planted some of the seeds Katie had brought us already, south of the house where Pa said we could start a little fruit orchard. So after I read this, I determined to pay attention to every detail as those trees grew from seeds to seedlings to trees, watching them bud and flower and bear fruit in the springtime, then go dormant in the fall.

In another chapter of his book, a chapter Mr. Thoreau called "Solitude," he said:

I have never felt lonesome, or in the least oppressed by a sense of solitude . . . I find it wholesome to be alone the greater part of the time. To be in company, even with the best, is soon wearisome . . . I love to be alone. I never found the companion that was so companionable as solitude. We are for the most part more lonely when we go among men than when we stay in our rooms. A man thinking or working is always alone, let him be where he will. Solitude is not measured by the miles of space that intervene between a man and his fellows. . . . Society is commonly too cheap. We meet at very short intervals, not having had time to acquire any new value for each other. We meet at meals three times a day, and give each other a new taste of that old musty cheese that we are. We have had to agree on a certain set of rules, called etiquette and politeness, to make this frequent meeting tolerable. . . . We live thick and are in each other's way, and stumble over one an other, and I think that we thus lose some respect for one another. Certainly less frequency would suffice for all important and hearty communications. . . . The value of a man is not in his skin, that we should touch him.

I guess I don't understand all of what Mr. Thoreau says, and I don't agree with all that about being alone, because I like people and I like to talk and be with them. I certainly don't fancy the idea of going off to live alone for two years! But still I like what he says, and I don't want to forget it. The danger seems to me being altogether one way or the other, so you can't be learning in different directions in your life.

Maybe that's another reason I liked his book, because I wanted to grow in *lots* of ways — not just as a teacher or a writer or a woman or a Christian, but in *all* those things, and lots of other ways besides.

Thoreau wrote more in *Walden* about being alone, but also about how much he loved nature and the world:

I am no more lonely than a single mullein or dandelion in a pasture, or a bean leaf, or sorrel, or a horse-fly, or a bumblebee. I am no more lonely than the Mill Brook, or a weathercock, or the north star, or the south wind, or an April shower, or a January thaw, or the first spider in a new house. . . . The indescribable innocence and beneficence of Nature — of sun and wind and rain, of summer and winter — such health, such cheer, they afford forever! And such sympathy have they ever with our race.

But the favorite passage I discovered those first days of reading in *Walden* was about ice forming on Walden Lake. Maybe I was drawn by the intricate detail of the things he noticed. Once we get slowed down, and get our minds so they're paying attention, a whole new world is suddenly there to discover that most folks never see. But God made that little world as part of the world of men and women. And I can't help wondering if we can't understand all God wants us to if we only see the big things.

When I read this passage, I couldn't help thinking of Mr. Thoreau himself. I could hardly believe a grown-up man being so still, so quiet, having so much time just to watch and listen, to see how thick the ice is, to lie down flat on the ice — it must have been cold! — and just stare through the water. Just thinking of him doing it made me laugh, but I'm glad he did, because his writing about it showed me a little of how I ought to look at the world.

I tried to imagine knowing the world like Thoreau knew that pond, or knowing another person that well. Or myself! What would it be like to be able to look inside my *own* thoughts and feelings like he did that frozen lake?

That's how I want to know God someday too — the little things about Him as well as the fact that He holds all the power in the universe. The same God that designed water to skim over with something hard and shiny called ice when it gets to just the right coldness, is the God who makes a thousand thunderstorms. The same God who made the little bug and the sand he scoots on, is the God who made me. And I don't want only to know the thunderstorm God, I also want to know the God who cared enough to make bugs.

Here's what Mr. Thoreau wrote about the ice:

The pond had in the meanwhile skimmed over in the shadiest and shallowest coves, some days or even weeks before the general freezing. The first ice is especially interesting and perfect, being hard, dark, and transparent, and affords the best opportunity that ever offers for examining the bottom where it is shallow; for you can lie at your length on ice only an inch thick, like a skater insect on the surface of the water, and study the bottom at your leisure, only two or three inches distant, like a picture behind a glass, and the water is necessarily always smooth then. There are many furrows in the sand where some creature has travelled about and doubled on its tracks. . . . But the ice itself is the object of most interest, though you must improve the earliest opportunity to study it. If you examine it closely the morning after it freezes, you find that the greater part of the bubbles, which at first appeared to be within it, are against its under surface, and that more are continually rising from the bottom; while the ice is as yet comparatively solid and dark, that is, you see the water through it. These bubbles are from an eightieth to an eighth of an inch in diameter, very clear and beautiful, and you see your face reflected in them through the ice. There may be thirty or forty of them to the square inch. There are also already within the ice narrow oblong perpendicular bubbles about half an inch long, sharp cones with the apex upward; or oftener, if the ice is quite fresh, minute spherical bubbles one directly above another, like a string of beads. But those within the ice are not so numerous nor obvious as those beneath.

I like Thoreau's way of observing and describing. He went on to tell what happened when the ice got thicker and harder to see through, and how he'd break it to see what would happen, and what happened to all the different kinds of bubbles when the ice got thicker. The first thing that comes to my mind now when I think of him or of *Walden* is a picture of Mr. Thoreau stretched out on that freezing cold ice!

On that particular afternoon when I'd been reading in his book and writing down some of these favorite passages in my own journal, thinking about how I could be more observant and a better writer, I finally got tired of reading and writing and put the books down. I stood up and stretched my arms and legs, sucked in a deep breath, and looked around me.

There wasn't any ice, and there wasn't likely to be any for a long spell. But I thought to myself maybe I could still do what Mr. Thoreau did and see some other tiny things that God had put around me.

I was standing on the edge of the woods, about twenty yards away from the stream that wound down to the mine where Pa and Uncle Nick were still working. I looked up. Overhead the pine trees were tall and mostly filled up the blue of the sky. Then I looked down at my feet. Pine needles. Dead, fallen pine needles by the thousands — maybe the millions — were scattered all through the woods.

I thought about looking at them closer, like Mr. Thoreau did with the ice. So I lay down on the ground, flat, with my elbows in the grass and dirt and my head propped on my hands about six inches from the ground. And I just stared at the earth.

Then I picked up several of the pine needles and examined them. They were in little clumps of three, held together by the most curious stuff at one end that easily ground away to a tan powder when you rubbed it between your fingers.

Why did God make it so that three needles were hooked together? I wondered.

What a great notion, to have the needles die every year and fall from the tree when new ones come. And what a nice carpet they made for the forest floor! I scooped through the grass and pine needle carpet with one of my hands. The pine needle mass was two or three inches thick! To have gotten that thick, they must have been falling right in that spot for years and years — maybe hundreds, or even thousands of years. And yet probably no person, no human being had looked right *there* at *those* pine needles ever since God made the world. That little spot of ground might have been sitting there for thousands of years, just waiting for me to come along on this day and lie down and play with the ground with my fingers, and wonder about the things that came to my mind because of it!

I got up and brushed my hands off on my dress, then went back to the rock where I'd been sitting and wrote about the pine needles in my journal.

I don't suppose I'll ever be a Thoreau, I thought to myself as I read over what I wrote a few minutes later, *but I reckon I have to start somewhere.* More than likely Mr. Thoreau never figured a girl from California would be reading his words when he first wrote them in his journal either. That's just how I felt when reading over *my* journal nine years later to make a book out of things I wrote. I never dreamed anyone else would ever see them. And I knew what Mr. MacPherson would say the minute he saw this chapter about ice and pine needles and my thoughts about Mr. Thoreau's *Walden.* He'd say, "Get rid of that kind of stuff, Corrie! People want to hear what you *did* and what *happened,* not always what you're thinking about. You're too pensive for your own good!"

I had to ask him what "pensive" meant, and he said it meant a person who was always losing himself in thinking and pondering things. So I told him that's why I kept a journal, because I liked to think to myself on paper. He just humphed and shrugged, muttering something about young women and their "unhealthy cogitations" — whatever that was. But he didn't need to worry, because plenty was going to "happen" before long.

In the meantime, my afternoon with Thoreau and *Walden* and my journal was over and I walked back across the creek. I'd completely forgotten about the apprehension I'd felt a couple of hours before.

As I approached the house, I saw Katie with Becky and Emily off toward a clump of oaks that bordered the clearing where the cabin stood.

"What are you doing?" I asked, walking up.

"Watering my grass," said Becky.

"And my moss," added Emily.

"It's starting to green up real nice," said Katie. "I think it survived the trip."

I said to myself that I'd have to make a point to come back here alone. It would be interesting to study the two little growths up close, like Mr. Thoreau would, and see if there *was* any difference between the green, growing things of Virginia and California.

CHAPTER 33

THE NOTE

The next day at school I was more "pensive" as Mr. MacPherson would say. I was thinking about Pa and Katie and the wedding coming up just nine days away, and I suppose I was seeing lots of things through different eyes too, because my mind was full of *Walden*. So I wasn't paying heed to things like I should have been.

After school I couldn't find Becky. Pa had gone to town that morning, so when I didn't see her around after school, I vaguely remembered Pa saying something at breakfast about "if any of you wanna ride home with me . . ."

My thoughts were occupied with other things. So when none of us could find Becky anywhere, I figured Pa had fetched her without any of us seeing him, and I loaded the other kids up in the wagon and headed home.

We rode up and there was Pa. But he'd been home for two hours and hadn't seen anything of Becky. Then we started realizing we had something to worry about.

Pa immediately started to saddle Jester.

"I'll go back in, Pa," I said. "It's my fault for leaving her."

"Naw, it's okay, Corrie."

"We could both go," I suggested. "It'll make it easier. We'll have to check all around town and one of us'll have to ride out to Miss Stansberry's. Becky could be anyplace."

Pa thought for a moment. "I reckon you're right. We'll ride in on Snowball and Jester, then we'll split up if she's not still around the school someplace. You go to the Stansberrys' and I'll go see Mrs. Parrish. One of them's sure to know where the little tyke is."

Five minutes later Pa and I were galloping toward town.

Four hours later we returned, just the two of us. No one in town had seen Becky. She had disappeared.

We were silent all the way home. We'd talked to everybody we could think of. I don't know what Pa was thinking, but I know he was worried. I was praying.

A couple of times he muttered something about what a fool he had been to think bringing Katie here would change things, and mumbling about troubles following him for the rest of his life. I suppose we were both blaming ourselves for what happened.

It was pretty silent that evening. Inside the house it might as well have been a tomb.

Katie tried to cheer everybody up, and a couple of times I thought Pa was going to yell at her to shut up and let us all be sad in peace. But finally she realized she wasn't helping and quieted

315

down on her own. Pa just sat there, his feet up on the table, and she didn't even say anything about the dirt.

Just as it was getting dark, we heard a horse galloping up outside.

Pa jumped to his feet and ran out the door, leaving it wide open. Every one of us followed him.

It was Sheriff Rafferty.

"You find her?" shouted Pa as the sheriff reined in his horse.

There was no reply. Rafferty slowed to a stop, then dismounted, threw the rein over the rail, and walked toward Pa. It was clear from his face he didn't have good news. He was holding a piece of paper.

"Sorry, Drum," he said. "All I got's this." He handed Pa the paper. "Weber found it nailed to a post outside his livery in this envelope with your name on it. No one saw how it got there. He brought it to me."

Pa grabbed it, fumbled hurriedly with the envelope, and unfolded the paper. As he read, a sickening look of dread spread over his face.

You'll get yer daughter back, Hollister, when you fork over $50,000. The loot's mine, I'm jist gittin' what's comin' to me! An' jist in case yer not lyin' about not knowin' where it is, I figure yer mine's worth plenty. So you jist git the money, or fifty thousand in gold, or the deed to yer place. It don't matter to

316

me. Try to find the little girl, and I'll kill you and her both! If there ain't no money by next week, we're leavin' yer brat to the wolves. They'll find her in less than two hours! And then I'll grab another o' yer kids and we'll go through this all again. So pay up, Hollister, fer yer own good! I'll git word to you where to take it.

"Krebbs!"

Pa's voice held sounds of wrath and despondency and self-blame and hatred. He walked a few steps away, one hand on his head, the other at his side with fist clenched.

"We gotta do some serious talking, Drum," said Sheriff Rafferty.

Pa turned back around to face him.

"There was also this," the sheriff went on, pulling another envelope from his pocket. "This one had *my* name on it. I guess they figured if they couldn't get you one way, they'd put me on your trail."

Again Pa slowly opened the envelope and took out a folded paper. It was an old, half-torn, yellowed and ragged warrant for Pa's arrest.

"Well, I reckon it's all caught up with me at last," said Pa with a sigh. "You better come on in, Simon."

Pa led the sheriff inside. The rest of us followed and closed the door behind us.

CHAPTER 34

THE REFUSAL

The minute we were inside, Pa ordered all us kids into our rooms, but he didn't pay much attention, and we left the doors open. We were all ears, hanging on every word that followed.

"What's this all about, Drum?" asked the sheriff. "I know your kid's in trouble and we'll do what we can. But I'm a sworn lawman and I got a duty too. So I'm asking you, is this warrant on the level?"

"It's a pack of the darndest lies that — !" I heard Uncle Nick exclaim. But Pa's voice cut him off.

"No it ain't, Nick, and you know it."

Then he turned to the sheriff. "I suppose you could say it's on the level, Simon. But there's always two sides to these things."

"Well, I'm listening, Drum. You're my friend, and I figure I owe you the benefit of the doubt. But if this warrant's in effect and they're still looking for you, then — well, then I don't know what! It's my job, you know, and friend or not, I gotta —"

"I understand what you're up against, Simon," said Pa calmly. "How about if I tell you what happened. Then if you figure you gotta take me in, I'll go with you peaceably — as long as we get Becky back first. After that, well maybe it's time I faced the music and quit hiding from my past. That's what I got me a wife for, 'cause I always knew something like this might happen."

"Sounds like a straight deal to me," replied Sheriff Rafferty.

"And you gotta let me and Miss Kathryn get done with the wedding first too," added Pa. "That way, I'll know the kids are gonna be safe."

"When is it?"

"Week from Sunday."

"Agreed, Drum. Now get on with it."

Pa heaved a deep sigh. The room was completely silent for a minute or so, then he started.

"Well, you know how when I first came here I didn't let on my name was Hollister. I went by Drum plain and simple, and let folks think that was my last name."

As Pa spoke I tiptoed to the open door so I could peek out just an inch. I saw Mr. Rafferty nodding his head.

"And Nick, too," Pa added. "Most folks around here still call him Matthews."

"You in this too, Nick?" said the sheriff, glancing up at Uncle Nick.

"Never mind him," said Pa. "If you take me in, you gotta be satisfied with that. You ain't got no warrant on Nick, and I want to know he's around to keep the mine going, for the kids' sake."

The sheriff seemed to chew on his words a while, then looked over both Pa and Uncle Nick.

"For a man sitting trying to explain to a lawman why there's a warrant out on him, you seem to be putting lots of conditions on what I can and can't do."

I thought at first that he was being serious, then I wondered if he was joking with Pa. But nobody laughed, and I never did know.

Pa just shrugged. "I don't figure you got much choice," he said. "You ain't gonna get my story otherwise. And you and I both know that if I decide to fight, you'd never take me in. I got too many friends in these parts. So I don't see that you got much choice."

"Just go on with your story."

"Well, that's the reason when we came west, why we — why *I* didn't use my real name. That's an old warrant, before we got caught. We were part of a jailbreak, and after that the law mostly figured we were dead, which was why we thought we'd be safe. But I reckon technically, seeing as how we escaped, that warrant would still be valid."

"What were you in for?"

"You're not gonna like hearing it."

"It was a bum charge — a frame-up!" said Uncle Nick.

"What was it, Drum?" said the sheriff again.

"The worst, Simon — bank robbery and murder."

The sheriff let out a low whistle. "That's bad," he finally said.

"Nick's right, though," added Pa. "We'd been riding with the gang, that much is true. So I reckon you could say we were accomplices on the robbin' part. But we weren't nowhere near any killin'."

"And you were part of a break?"

"Yeah, we busted out, along with a bunch of others. We didn't cotton to the notion of dangling from the end of a rope for something we didn't do, so when we had the chance we lit out and came out here."

"And so who's this fella Krebbs who's been bull-doggin' you these last couple of years? He got something to do with all this?"

"He's part of the original gang that pulled the job. He and several of the others got away clean. Krebbs always figured we had the loot. So when he heard we'd busted out, he got a whiff of our trail, and he's been tracking us ever since."

"You got the money, Drum? If you do, turning it back in would go a long way toward proving to the law your intention of living straight from now on."

"Come on, Simon!" said Pa in disbelief that he would even ask. "Look around! Look at my hands. Look at how hard me and Nick work up there in that mine every day. You think we'd have been bustin' our backs all these years if we had that fifty thousand stashed someplace?"

Rafferty gave a half-shrug and nodded thought-

321

fully. "Probably not. But I had to ask."

Pa settled back in his chair, waiting for what the sheriff would say next. I glanced over at Katie. She hadn't said a word the whole time. I wondered what she was thinking — probably that she'd gotten herself mixed up with more than she'd bargained for!

"Well, Drum, your story makes sense. I've always figured you for a man of your word. So I'm inclined to believe you. But I think you better tell me the whole story. It's dark now, and those varmints obviously have your young'un someplace we won't find tonight. We got time, so I want you to start at the beginning."

Pa let out a heavy sigh, and launched into the tale that none of the other kids but me had heard. I'd tried to explain things to them, but I was glad they were hearing it from Pa's own lips. I wanted them to know how it had really been between Ma and Pa, and why he'd had to leave us without any word.

Twenty or twenty-five minutes later he was done. He didn't shed tears this time, like when he'd first told me the story. But I knew it had been hard for Pa nevertheless. There were still hurts he felt from what he'd done.

There was a long quiet in the room.

Sheriff Rafferty was the first to break it. The next sound we all heard was the ripping of the warrant in half.

"I believe you, Drum," he said. "Like I said, I figure you for a man of your word, so I'm

322

gonna pretend I never saw this."

I could almost feel the relief that spread over Pa's face.

"Now we gotta get your little girl back," said the sheriff. "What do you want me to do, Drum? You got fifty thousand?"

Pa laughed, a bitter laugh that didn't have any joy in it.

"Are you kidding?" he said. "Fifty thousand? It might as well be a million! Me and Nick's got maybe $3,000 in the bank. Here we figured that was real good for a year's work, more'n most men see in their lives. Now it looks like nothin'!"

"You want me to round up some of the boys and get together a posse?"

"And do what?" said Pa. "We ain't got a notion where they are."

"With enough men and enough time, we could find them."

"We ain't got time! And like he said, Krebbs'd just kill Becky, then snatch one of the others. I know him. He's a mean one. He won't stop till he's got the money. The way I figure it, I gotta pay him or we'll be runnin' from him forever."

"How we gonna raise fifty thousand, Drum?" said Uncle Nick. "There ain't nobody in this town who's got that kind of cash."

"There's one, Nick."

"You don't mean that lowdown —"

"That's right — Royce."

"Royce'd never give you that much money!"

"Not *give* . . . loan. That's what bankers do, they loan money."

"How would you pay him back?" asked the sheriff.

"If Nick and me put away $3,000 in a year, all we need to do is work a little harder. Zack's getting to be a man. He can help. We can make five, maybe ten thousand a year outta that mine. We could have Royce paid back in five years!"

"Work harder!" groaned Uncle Nick.

"For Becky, we'll put in fourteen hours a day up in that pit!" said Pa. "And you'll be with me! Besides," he added after a little pause, "I don't see what choice we have. We don't know where they are. Krebbs'll kill Becky if we don't give him the loot. You know him, Nick — you know he'll do it sure as the sun shines. And the only way to get that kind of money is from Royce. It's all we *can* do."

"There's the claim," suggested Katie. "What about that?" For the first time since she'd come, her voice sounded timid.

Pa shook his head. "We can't do that, Miss Kathryn. The mine and this claim's all we got. Leastways, if we pay him, after five years the mine and the cabin and the land's still ours. No, we'll pay him."

Pa's voice had a decisive sound to it. No one said anything else for a little bit. Then Sheriff Rafferty got up out of his chair.

"Well, I reckon you'll be coming to town in the morning to see Royce," he said. "Come and

324

see me when your business is settled. We still want to do our best to nab this bushwhacker."

He shook Pa's hand, then left.

The next morning bright and early we all rode to town.

Everyone wanted to go, and with Buck Krebbs on the loose, Pa was in no mood to argue. He told Katie to keep Tad and Emily with her near the wagon. I guess he figured Zack and I were big enough to take care of ourselves. Uncle Nick stayed with Katie, I went to Mrs. Parrish's office to see if she'd heard anything, and Pa went to the bank to see Mr. Royce.

The whole town was abuzz with talk of Becky's kidnapping. Mrs. Parrish knew everything, and the minute I walked in she ran toward me and embraced me. I told her what Pa was doing.

A few minutes later I saw Pa through the window walking out of the bank and back toward the wagon. I rushed outside, not even thinking to close the door.

Pa was walking toward the wagon. Katie was still sitting in it with Tad and Emily. Uncle Nick was on the ground leaning against one of the wagon wheels. Zack was behind the wagon kicking a rock in the dirt. I ran up just as Pa got there.

He just looked at Uncle Nick and shook his head.

"What?" exclaimed Uncle Nick.

"He turned us down," said Pa. "He laughed in my face. I said, 'Have you heard about my daughter?' and he said, 'I heard something to that effect, and I'm sorry, Hollister, I truly am, but fifty thousand is a huge sum of money.' I told him we were good for it, and that's when he laughed."

Pa couldn't help sounding angry. But there was more desperation in his voice than bitterness or hatred.

"The oily scoundrel's probably in on the whole thing!" cried Uncle Nick angrily.

"I thought of that," said Pa.

"He's nothing but a double-dealing snake!"

"A snake who's the only one around here with money."

"You told him we'd work it off?" asked Uncle Nick, calming a little.

"Yeah. I even said we'd sign over the mine as collateral for the money. That's when he laughed again. 'A hunk of ground for fifty thousand?' he said. 'And when the mine plays out a year from now, where does that leave me? No thanks, Hollister. Far too risky an exchange! Look, I'm sorry about your kid. But this is business. And this would be a bad loan, pure and simple. Any banker in the country would turn you down flat.' That's when I walked out. I couldn't listen to another word. But I could feel his gloating eyes on my back. I knew the rascal was smiling inside, getting his revenge on us for spoiling his little scheme last year."

Pa was silent. He and Uncle Nick both stared at the ground, trying to decide what to do. I hadn't noticed at first, but now I saw that Mrs. Parrish had followed me out of her office. She was halfway across the street and coming toward us.

Pa didn't see her. All at once he lifted his head and said to Uncle Nick, "Nick, you go over to Rafferty's. Bring him to the title office. You and me's gonna sign over a quitclaim on the mine to Krebbs. It's the only way we'll ever see Becky again."

Without another word, he walked off down the street in the direction of the Miracle Springs Land Office.

CHAPTER 35

THE OFFER

The moment Pa headed off, Mrs. Parrish changed her bearing across the street so that she would intercept him. They were only about twenty feet from the wagon when she stopped him.

"May I have a few words with you, Mr. Hollister?" she said.

"I've gotta get down to the title office, ma'am," replied Pa, still walking.

"If you would just spare me a moment or two," she persisted. "What I have to say may affect your plans."

"You know about Becky?" said Pa, stopping and looking directly at Mrs. Parrish.

"Yes. I know everything. As I came out of my office a moment ago I could not help hearing of your conversation with Mr. Royce."

"A skunk!" said Pa.

"I would not want to disagree with you, Mr. Hollister." Mrs. Parrish paused a moment. When she continued, her voice was different than I had ever heard it sound before. It almost had a quiver to it. "Perhaps you would allow *me* to help you."

"You, ma'am?"

"Yes. Please — I want to help. I can't bear

the thought of you giving up the mine."

Pa stared at her intently. "Just what is it you aim to do, ma'am?" he asked. "I want you to know I appreciate that you're fond of my kids, but right now, just how do you figure you can help?"

"Let me give you the fifty thousand dollars."

Pa's face clearly showed the shock he felt from her words.

"You . . . you . . . would *do* that, ma'am?" Pa half-stammered.

"If only you'll let me." Mrs. Parrish was now looking Pa deeply in the eye. "Please, say you'll let me help, won't you, Drummond?"

Pa didn't know what to say. He looked down at the ground, scuffling in the street with his boot. I knew he was thinking real hard. I couldn't help remembering what he'd said once when Mrs. Parrish had offered to help one time before: "I ain't takin' no handouts from a woman!"

"I know it would not be an easy thing for you to do," Mrs. Parrish said. "And there would be no way to keep it quiet. But to save your daughter, and the mine . . ."

She let Pa finish the thought for himself.

Finally he looked up, but still said nothing.

"And for the future of your upcoming marriage!" added Mrs. Parrish. "I'll not only be doing it for you and your children, but also for your bride." She glanced toward Katie and the rest of us. "Think of it as my wedding present, just a little early."

At last Pa spoke. As he looked at her, his face showed that he'd been conquered.

"You've got that kind of money, ma'am?" he asked quietly.

"I can get it."

"No handout — it'd be a loan?"

"Of course."

"I'll pay you back every cent — with interest!"

"You just name your terms, Drummond," she said with a slight smile, "and I'll satisfy your every request."

Pa shook his head and sighed.

"Then I'll go along, I reckon," he said.

"Fine! You do whatever else you need to and meet me in my office in an hour." Mrs. Parrish turned and started to walk away.

Pa stopped her. "Ma'am," he said, "I really am much obliged to you."

She smiled, then crossed the street back to her office, while Pa turned in the direction of Sheriff Rafferty's office.

In a few minutes Mrs. Parrish came back out of her office carrying a small parcel of papers. She did not even look across the street where I still stood by the buckboard with Katie and Zack and Tad and Emily. She walked straight to the bank and inside.

Pa and Uncle Nick didn't come back for quite a while. Fifteen minutes later Mrs. Parrish walked out of the bank. I had wandered up the walk in that direction, but when she came out she headed straight back to her office without saying a word to anyone.

After she'd closed the door of the bank behind her, I saw Mr. Royce come to one of the windows, then spread the curtain aside with his hand and watch her as she walked away. He had a gleam in his eye and a horrible look of triumph. Mrs. Parrish wasn't carrying any papers.

An hour later Pa came back. He went over to Mrs. Parrish's — alone.

After a minute he and Mrs. Parrish came out together. They walked to the bank and inside. Ten minutes later they came out again, Pa carrying a large leather bag.

Mrs. Parrish went back to her office, and Pa went down to the sheriff's. When he came out his hands were empty. He came straight to the wagon, called to us, then he jumped up onto the seat. We all piled in. He yelled to the horses and we were off toward home.

"What do we do now, Pa?" asked Zack.

"We wait," said Pa.

CHAPTER 36

THE PLAN

We didn't have to wait long.

Sheriff Rafferty came riding up in a cloud of dust just about an hour after noon. "This is it, Drum!" he shouted, dismounting as his own dust overtook him, and running toward Pa with a letter in his hand.

Immediately everyone swarmed around. Mr. Jones was there now too, both to share the anxious waiting with his friend and to help if he could.

"A kid rode into town a few minutes ago and delivered this to me," the sheriff said. "I didn't know him. Told me he lived down by You Bet. Said a stranger gave him five bucks to ride to Miracle and give this letter to the sheriff. The kid said he said sure, the man gave him five dollars and the letter, then rode off. That's all the kid knew."

Pa took the letter and read it out loud.

Give this letter to Drum Hollister. It's fer him.

Hollister, I hope fer yer kid's sake you got the loot. Put it in a coupla saddlebags an' ride out the trail to Deadman's Flat over the

Chalk Bluff Ridge. Go a quarter mile past Steephollow Creek. There's a road off left with a sign — To Negro Jacks — stuck to a tree. Behind the tree's a dead stump, half-hollered out. You throw the saddlebags in there! Don't try findin' us cuz we ain't there. We ain't nowhere near there, but we'll get the loot an' when we does we'll let the girl go. If you ain't got the cash, you sign over yer deed on yer claim to Buchanan J. Krebbs an' put that in the saddlebags instead. Do what I says, Hollister! Remember the wolves!

"Well, let's go!" said Pa. "Where's the money, Simon?"

"Hold on just a minute, Drum! Let's talk this out a spell. There's still a chance we can figure out where these guys are. We don't want to give them the money if we don't have to."

"I thought we had all this settled!" snapped Pa. "There ain't no other way but to do as Krebbs says."

"Well, I ain't so sure," said the sheriff. "I been thinking while I rode out here — if we could just figure out who's in it with him —"

"Somebody's in it with him for sure," interrupted Uncle Nick. "Krebbs can't read or write his own name! He's the dumbest —"

"That's right!" said Pa. "I plumb forgot. He couldn't have written these two notes."

"Barton!" said the sheriff. "He's had schooling.

333

I've run into him a couple of times. Saw him reading a newspaper once. He could have done it. And Hammond saw him the other day, probably watching the school from across the way by Markham's place."

"He must've seen Becky going off toward the woods," I suggested.

"Barton's from Dutch Flat," Mr. Rafferty went on, hardly noticing my idea. "And I know ol' Negro Jack. His place ain't four miles from there!"

"I bet that polecat Hatch is in on it with 'em!" said Uncle Nick.

"Krebbs always had a way of smelling out the lowlifes around a place," said Pa. "I don't doubt but what you're right, Nick. I'd wager plenty that Dutch Flat's where they're holed up."

"Okay, now we can't go riding in there with twenty men," said Mr. Rafferty. "They'll kill the girl."

"They'll be hiding her someplace safe," said Uncle Nick.

"What'd he mean about wolves?" asked Mr. Jones, speaking for the first time.

"Oh, nothin', Alkali," said Pa. "It was just some threat they made in their first note."

"What threat? What'd they say?"

"They said if we tried anything they'd high-tail it outta there and leave Becky where the wolves'd find her."

"And they's down by Dutch Flat, ya say?"

"That's how we got it figured," answered the sheriff.

"Well, there's a pack o' wolves that's seen sometimes down jist south o' there. Ya heard o' 'em — on Frost Hill."

"So if they were hiding her away someplace —" began Mr. Rafferty, but Uncle Nick's voice cut him off.

"The cave!" he cried. "They've got her in ol' Hatch's cave! That's it, I tell ya, Drum! When that ol' cuss had me there, I could hear the wail of wolves and he kept tellin' me he was gonna leave me there to get eaten by 'em."

Everyone was quiet, thinking hard.

Sheriff Rafferty turned and walked away, slowly, looking first at the ground, then up at the sky. It only took him about two or three minutes.

Suddenly, he spun around and strode back to where the rest of us were standing.

"I think I've got it," he said. "I think we just might be able to save Becky *and* keep our hands on the money. Now look here, Drum — just in case they've got somebody watching us, you'll ride out like he says, alone, with the saddlebags and the money. But we'll follow, about five or ten minutes behind you. You dump the bags, but we'll keep half our men there. If any of them come to get it, we'll ambush them. Meanwhile, the rest of us will circle back up across Chalk Bluff Ridge and down on the other side of Dutch Flat. Isn't that where Frost Hill is, Jones?"

"Yep. Ya come down off the ridge, across Bear River."

"And where's the cave?"

"Right there, Squires Canyon."

"Okay, we'll split up, half guarding the money, half circling back behind the cave."

"I'm riding to the cave," said Pa. "She's my girl."

"Fine by me. But you'll need help," said the sheriff. "They'll have a guard, but probably only one or two men. If you and two or three of the boys get the drop on them, you should get her fine. One of you ride back to Miracle with the girl, the others ride back up the ridge to where we're waiting at Deadman's Flat. Once the girl's safe, we'll send the money back to town, then all the rest of us'll ride on to Dutch Flat and see if we can smoke out this fella Krebbs."

"What if they come for the money and see you there before I've got Becky out?" asked Pa.

"They couldn't get anyone to the cave before you got there. You'd have a lead on them. And they'll never figure us to know where they're hiding her."

"That may be," said Pa seriously. "But if anything goes sour, you give them the dough, you hear?"

"Fair enough," said Sheriff Rafferty.

There was a pause. The men looked around at each other, anxiety and determination on all their faces, as if to say, "Let's get this done!"

Finally the sheriff drew in a deep breath and said. "Well, if we're agreed, I'll ride into town. Several of the men have already volunteered to help. Nick, Drum, Alkali, you men round up whoever you can on this side of town — Shaw, Hammond, whoever might be willing, I'll get the money from the safe in my office and be back here with the men in, say, an hour."

Pa nodded.

Just as the sheriff was in the saddle and wheeling his horse back down the road, Pa glanced around.

"Where's Zack?" he said.

"He rode off," said Emily.

"Tarnation!" exclaimed Pa. "Which way? Did you see him, Emily?"

"Over the hill by the mine, I think, Pa."

Just then the door opened and Katie walked out.

"Zack said to wait till you were through to tell you this," she said. "He said to tell you he went to get Little Wolf, and not to worry about Becky."

CHAPTER 37

THE RIDE

Pa ran to the barn.

"Blue Flame's gone!" he yelled.

He ran back. "Nick, Alkali," he said, "you round up whoever you can, like Rafferty said. I'm gonna ride after the sheriff and see if I can catch him and tell him to be back sooner'n an hour if he can. Otherwise, I'll try to cut Zack off across the ridge if those two ride that direction and through Miracle on their way to wherever they're going. I think I know where!"

Pa was already mounted and on his way as he was yelling out his instructions. "Fool kids!" he said to himself as he galloped after the sheriff. "Liable to get themselves killed, along with all the rest of us!"

Within two minutes everyone was gone, and it was just Katie and me and the two younger ones. Suddenly I realized we were alone, and I remembered the sheriff's words about wondering if they had someone watching us. Buck Krebbs was sure familiar enough with our place!

I went inside to show Katie where Pa kept his rifle and I asked her if she knew how to use one. She said she did. Knowing Katie, I wasn't surprised.

Mr. Jones got back first. He had Patrick Shaw and his eighteen-year-old son Caleb with him. Uncle Nick was next with two other nearby miners. All the men had rifles.

Pa and the sheriff came about twenty minutes later. Altogether they brought another six or seven men. Zack wasn't with them.

I begged Pa to let me go. I promised to stay behind and out of the way.

"Not even if *you* had fifty thousand dollars, Corrie! I got two kids out there already, and that's two too many."

"About the money, Pa," I said. "I think Mrs. Parrish might have done something awful to get it."

He looked down at me from where he sat on his horse, wanting to ask me what I meant but knowing there was no time. Sheriff Rafferty was already explaining the plan to the men.

"Don't worry, Corrie. I aim to do my best to get it back."

He reined his horse around, joined the others, and after a few last-minute words, Pa took the saddlebags with the money and sped off over the hill to join the trail running east. The sheriff and the men waited about five minutes, then followed.

The rest of us went inside.

Everything was still and quiet for three hours. We heard nothing more until we heard a horse outside. It was Little Wolf, alone. The first thing

I noticed was the blood on his arm.

Frantically I ran to him, shouting out questions. And between Little Wolf's story and the information we got later that night, I found out all that had happened.

Pa rode east, then south across Washington Ridge, by Fowler Spring and Sailor Flat, over Buckeye Ridge, across Chalk Bluff Ridge and down into Deadman's Flat. The whole time he was watching out, but never saw a soul. That was about an eight- or nine-mile ride.

He got there all right, found the Negro Jack sign, and tossed the saddlebags in the hollow stump. He said he didn't think Krebbs had anybody there yet; they probably didn't figure Pa'd be so quick getting the money. So Pa sat off to the side and waited, but he didn't think anybody'd been watching or trailing him either. In ten minutes Sheriff Rafferty came with Uncle Nick and the rest of the men.

They split up. Pa took Mr. Shaw, Miss Stansberry's brother Hermon, and Marcus Weber with him. Everyone else hid in the woods nearby waiting to see if Krebbs or anybody'd come for the saddlebags. Pa and his three men took off west, up on top of Chalk Bluff Ridge, then followed the ridge trail southwest so as to come around and down on the far side of Squires Canyon where the cave was.

Before they were even halfway along the ridge, right by Red Hill spring, they saw a rider coming toward them. Quickly they got off their horses and led them off the trail, drew their guns, and got ready for a fight. But when the rider got closer they put their guns away. It was Zack.

In the meantime, when we'd all been back at home, the minute Zack heard what Pa and the sheriff planned to do — and he had a big grin when he was telling about it! — he sneaked around the back of the cabin, gave Katie his message, and got Blue Flame out of the barn as quietly as he could. He said he knew Pa would say no if he asked, so he just didn't ask. Little Wolf knew the woods better than any five men in Miracle put together, and he figured the two of them would have the best chance of rescuing Becky if she was in the cave. He saw Pa heading for town looking for him, but by that time he was way up on the side of Buck Mountain.

By the time Pa and the sheriff and the rest of the men were gathering at our place, he and Little Wolf were already crossing Scotts Flat halfway to Gold Run. When they got to Gold Run, they skirted the edge of town, rode up toward Dutch Flat, and turned off the road before they got to Blue Devil Diggings, so as not to be seen by anyone riding south out of Dutch Flat. They tied their horses, then walked slowly up to where Zack and I and Pa'd been before. Zack remembered the area pretty well and he knew from there they'd be able to get a good look down into the canyon and at the cave.

Sure enough, there were two men standing outside the mouth of it.

They slipped up closer, quietly, until they were within earshot.

The two men were Hatch and Krebbs.

"I'll be back this evening," Krebbs was saying. "If they ain't brung the loot yet, I'll bring ya some grub."

Hatch said something, but Zack didn't hear what it was.

"That ain't none o' yer concern, ya old buzzard!" Krebbs said. "You jist do what I says, an' you'll get yer cut. You stay put right where you are, and if anybody 'ceptin' me comes around here, you blow their heads off. Ya got me, Hatch?"

Again Hatch said something.

"I know there ain't nobody gonna come. There ain't no way they gonna find where we got the kid if they had a year. But I want somebody here anyway, an' that's what I'm payin' you fer."

With that, Krebbs turned and rode off up the far end of the canyon.

Zack and Little Wolf spied out the area a bit more. They figured the horses were best where they were, not far from where we'd tied them when we rescued Uncle Nick. Then they set about a plan to lure Grizzly Hatch away from the cave.

For Little Wolf, that wasn't so difficult, though it took them twenty or thirty minutes to get into place — Zack behind a boulder above the cave, Little Wolf down in the canyon, about fifty feet in front of it. When Zack signalled that he was ready, Little Wolf began making sounds to get Hatch confused — throwing his voice, making animal sounds, then a call like a wolf.

But Hatch wasn't as easy to fool as Buck Krebbs had been. His beady eyes spotted Little Wolf almost as soon as the first bird-call was out of his mouth.

The first sign that he'd been seen was the explosion of Hatch's shotgun. If Little Wolf hadn't been mostly behind a tree, it might have been worse. As it was, some pieces of buckshot found his leg and wrist.

"I see ya, ya redskin varmint!" cried Hatch. "Let that learn ya not to come around here!"

Little Wolf started down the canyon, then looked back. When he saw Hatch wasn't going to follow him, he knew he had to try something else. He pulled an arrow out of his quiver and let one sail toward Hatch, thunking into a pine tree about five feet away, exactly where he'd aimed.

That made Hatch mad, which was just what Little Wolf wanted.

"Why, you no good animal!" screamed Hatch in a rage. "You won't take a warning! We'll see if a belly full o' buckshot is more to your liking!"

He tore down the hill after Little Wolf.

Little Wolf started to run, and for the first time he felt the pain in his leg. He tripped and fell just as Hatch released the load from the second barrel. It flew over Little Wolf's head, ripping a six-inch piece of bark off a Ponderosa pine.

If he hadn't fallen just then, Little Wolf would have been dead.

He jumped to his feet and flew down the canyon limping, hearing Hatch cursing behind him and fumbling to reload his gun. Within seconds Hatch was after him once more.

In the meantime, Zack scrambled down the hillside, went inside the cave, and found Becky. She was dirty, hungry, and afraid, but her spirit wasn't broken. Zack said her first words to him were, "Hi, Zack. I was just getting ready to escape."

He signalled her to be quiet, untied the ropes around her hands and feet, then picked her up in his arms. Cautiously they left the cave. Zack looked all about, heard Hatch yelling a hundred yards away, then made a dash with Becky down the hill into the canyon, then up the other side just like I'd done with Uncle Nick. Halfway up the opposite side, he heard the sharp report from Hatch's gun again. He jumped in terror, nearly throwing Becky to the ground, knowing the danger his friend was in. But he continued on up the hill, finally put Becky down, and hand in hand they ran the rest of the way to the horses, where they fell onto the ground in exhaustion.

Twice more Zack heard Hatch fire. Every time he wondered if he'd ever see Little Wolf again.

Then came a long silence lasting five minutes or more. From far down the canyon came another shot. Almost the same instant, there was a rustle in the brush behind him. Zack turned. There stood Little Wolf, his face pale, sweat and dirt on his forehead, but smiling broadly.

"I finally managed to get the old goat chasing his own tail," he said out of breath, "but he was not so easy a prey. He is a man of cunning, despite his look of a crazy old fool."

"You're hurt!" said Zack.

"Yes, I am hurt, but not badly. He is not so bad a shot either," Little Wolf added with a tired smile, "for a man on the run. But, little one," he said, kneeling down beside Becky, "you are safe and well?"

"Yes, Little Wolf," said Becky. "Thank you for saving me."

"Your brother is the one with courage. He came to me and told me we must save you."

"We have to get out of here," said Zack. "Come on, Becky. You and Little Wolf have to get home."

"Where are you going, Zack?" asked Becky.

"I gotta get to Pa."

"Let me ride the Chalk Bluff Ridge," said Little Wolf. "I know it like my own hand."

"No," insisted Zack. "You must get home and out of danger. Your father must tend your wounds. But first, take Becky to Mrs. Parrish in Miracle. She will know what to do. Might be nobody's at our place. Then you go to your father."

Little Wolf looked into Zack's face, so much younger than his own. "I will do as you say," he said. "I am too weary to argue, and perhaps you are right."

Little Wolf mounted his pony, and Zack handed Becky up in front of him. "Be careful until you are past Gold Run," warned Zack.

Little Wolf rode off. Then Zack mounted Blue Flame, worked his way north, past Blue Devil Diggings, back across the Bear, and up Chalk Bluff until he regained the trail on the ridge. Then he swung Blue Flame northeast and made for Deadman's Flat.

CHAPTER 38

THE FIGHT AT NEGRO JACK'S

When Pa and Zack met on the trail, there wasn't time for Zack to do much explaining. Pa'd have to wait to hear the whole story along with me and everyone else.

All Zack said was, "Becky's safe! She's on her way back to Miracle with Little Wolf."

The next moment, Pa, Zack, Hermon, Stansberry, Marcus Weber, and Pat Shaw were riding like the wind back to rejoin the sheriff and the rest of the men.

Even before they'd started down off the ridge toward Steephollow Creek, they could hear the gunfire.

They rode in from the north, the way they'd come from Miracle earlier. Pa could tell as they approached that Rafferty and Uncle Nick were pinned down. But they still had the entrance to Negro Jack's covered, so Pa figured the money was still there. Otherwise Krebbs and his men wouldn't be hanging around fighting.

Krebbs had a man watching after all, Pa discovered later, who had taken off for Dutch Flat the minute the sheriff and his men rode in. By the time Little Wolf had outsmarted Grizzly Hatch back at the cave, Buck Krebbs and his men were riding north out of Dutch Flat for a showdown.

Pa and the others came down slowly off the ridge, hoping to keep from being seen. When they got in a position to outflank Krebbs and his men and get a good bead on them, they opened fire.

The surprise of the attack must have helped because the rocks and trees they'd been hiding behind were no longer any good. Now they had to move to protect themselves from their exposed positions, and while they were scrambling back in retreat, the men with the sheriff were able to get higher up on the hill and gain a better vantagepoint.

The exchange of gunfire went on for ten or fifteen minutes, but neither side was any closer to being able to send someone in to snatch the saddlebags without being seen and getting shot.

I guess Zack was feeling heroic, because for the second time that day he slipped away without Pa's seeing him.

Suddenly, the next thing Pa knew, there was Zack, behind a small boulder, not fifteen yards from the *To Negro Jacks* sign. Immediately Pa knew what he was trying to do. At almost the same instant, Pa saw Buck Krebbs about the same distance away from the stump on the other side, behind a thick fir, hidden from Zack's sight.

"Zack, no!" yelled Pa, standing and shouting through his cupped hands.

But it was too late. A sharp crack from a Winchester exploded through the air. The slug ripped through the calf of Pa's right leg and he fell to the ground. The same instant Zack made his dash for the stump. He laid his hand on the leather saddlebags, when an evil voice froze him in his tracks before he could make good his escape.

"Don't do it, boy!" said the voice. "Let go o' the bag."

Zack looked up.

There was Buck Krebbs ten feet away, a sneer revealing black and yellow teeth. In his hand was a revolver aimed directly at Zack's head.

For two or three seconds both stood dead still, staring each into the other's eyes, weighing the odds, asking himself what the other might do.

Lying on his belly seventy-five feet above them, blood oozing from his leg into the grass and dirt, Pa had slowly pulled his pistol from its holster and was now drawing it into position. Wincing in pain, he grasped the gun in both hands and stretched out his arms in front of him, squinting as he gazed down the black steel gunbarrel.

Suddenly, Zack clutched the saddlebags and darted toward the nearest tree.

The split second it took for Buck Krebbs to refocus his aim was too long. As his finger began to squeeze the trigger to liberate the bullet that would end Zack's life, Pa's .45 sounded from above.

The gleam went out of Buck Krebbs' eye. He crumpled to the ground where he had stood, shot dead through the heart.

With the money gone and their leader dead, Barton and the rest scattered to the hills. It was over.

Sheriff Rafferty and Uncle Nick jumped out of their hiding places and ran down the hill, congratulating Zack, then tending to Pa's wound. The slug hadn't hit either a bone or an artery, but it was a nasty gash and the slug was still in his leg. They had to get him home and to the doctor's without delay.

CHAPTER 39

THAT NIGHT

That afternoon Doc had to come out to our place to tend *two* patients.

After leaving Becky with Mrs. Parrish in town, Little Wolf had ridden to our place instead of home, like Zack had said. He wanted to see if we were there, to tell us Becky was safe and where she was. But by the time he arrived, he was so weak and faint that he couldn't go another step.

I ran toward him yelling, "Where's Becky? What happened? Are Pa and Zack safe?"

Little Wolf told me later he didn't hear a word I'd said. The moment I reached him he half-fainted and collapsed off the side of his pony into my arms. It was all I could do to keep from toppling over with his weight!

All he was able to whisper was, "Becky . . . safe . . . with Mrs. Parrish . . ."

Katie saw through the window and rushed out to help me. We carried him inside, found his wounds, and dressed them as best we could.

He must have been hit more than just that first time. It looked to me that he had a dozen little pieces of shot scattered in his leg and arm, and his clothes were covered with blood. It was no wonder he was faint!

When we got him laid down, I reminded Katie about the gun, told Emily to lock the door behind me, and said I was riding into town to get the doctor and see how Becky was.

I got back in about half an hour. Doc's buggy was about fifteen minutes behind me, and by the time he had most of the shot out of Little Wolf's leg and ointment and bandages on the wounds, Uncle Nick and the sheriff were riding in. So he started right in on Pa.

By evening Pa was on the mend too. Doc gave Pa two or three glasses of whiskey, and after it had taken effect and Pa was half-asleep, he dug the slug out of his leg. I could hardly stand it. I thought I would throw up a couple of times. There was more bleeding, and Pa yelled out. But when it was over, Doc said the wound was clean. He dressed it, and told Pa to stay off it for a couple of weeks.

"Stay off it, Doc?" Pa exclaimed, wide awake now after the painful surgery. "I can't lay around for two weeks!"

"Then all I can say, Drum," replied the Doc, "is keep your weight off it if you can. Use a cane or a crutch or something. The more you use it, the longer it'll take to heal."

Little Wolf wanted to go home, but he was even weaker than Pa. He had not only lost blood, the exertion from the long ride had worn him out and he remained pale all day. Doc said we should keep him at our place at least overnight.

"Keep him in bed, warm, and get as much of that soup down him as you can. I think I got all the shot out. He'll be much stronger to-morrow."

Zack rode over to his place to tell his pa what had happened.

Not long after the Doc left I suddenly remembered about the money.

"Pa," I said, "what about the money and Mrs. Parrish?"

"You're right, little girl," said Pa, rolling over in the bed and facing me. "I plumb forgot."

"I'm scared of that man Royce, Pa."

"What's he got to do with it?"

"Mrs. Parrish got the money from him, Pa."

"From his bank. Outta her account, like anyone else. I went with her to get it."

"Pa, I think there's more to it than that." It was the first chance I'd had to tell him about seeing her go to the bank with those papers, and the look on Royce's face afterward.

Pa was already half out of his bed by the time I finished. "Why, that woman!" he said, "I hope she ain't gone and done nothing foolish! Here, Corrie, help me with this leg!"

He was already struggling to stand.

"Pa, the doctor said you had to —"

"Never mind the Doc! I gotta get that money back to town."

"Lay back down, Drum," said Uncle Nick, who had wandered over to see what the commotion was all about. "I'll take it to her."

"No, this is something I gotta do myself. What's gotta be said's something nobody but me can say."

"I'll take in the money with a letter from you," suggested Uncle Nick.

"Don't you understand? That woman saved our hides, and this place of ours too! You don't thank somebody for that with a letter. Besides, she may have just —"

He stopped, fumbling to get his arm through his coat sleeve "Well, never mind that — we'll just hope it's not too late."

He grabbed the single crutch the Doc had left him, grabbed his hat, and made for the door. "Somebody come and help me up the horse. Nick, where's them saddlebags?"

Uncle Nick brought him the money and boosted him on top of Blue Flame, who was still saddled from Zack's ride to Little Wolf's father's. Pain filled Pa's face from his swollen leg, but there was no talking him out of what he knew he had to do.

"Can I go with you, Pa?" I asked.

Pa looked down at me, thought for a moment, then shrugged and said, "I don't reckon there'd be anything wrong with that. Sure, come on."

I flew into the barn and saddled Snowball as fast as I could. I didn't want Pa to think of some reason for changing his mind.

It was well into evening when we rode into Miracle Springs, but the June sun still had another hour of life left. The town was quiet. A few people

354

who saw Pa ran over to greet him with smiles and shouts and congratulations, but Pa just kept walking Blue Flame straight down the dirt street, hardly so much as acknowledging the well-wishers who came out to greet him. He had a determined look in his eye and he rode straight for Mrs. Parrish's.

When we got there, he dismounted without any help, although when his legs hit the ground his face twitched from the pain. He slung the saddlebags over his shoulder, stuck the crutch under his armpit, then said to me, "Corrie, I know you like to be around all that's goin' on so you can write everything in that journal of yours. But this here's somethin' I gotta do alone. So you just wait here."

He went inside and I waited.

Fifteen minutes later he came back out, without the saddlebags. His face was wearing a look I wish I could describe, but I could write for two pages and not get it right. I'll have to be satisfied to remember it in my mind.

He didn't say a word. As he was getting on the horse, I saw Mrs. Parrish come to one of the windows and pull aside the curtain and look out, just like the banker had done.

I smiled and gave a little wave. But she didn't seem to notice. I guess she wanted to make sure Pa got on his horse okay. When I glanced over again a moment later, she was no longer there.

As we rode back through town again, word must've spread around that Pa was there because now all sorts of folks were out on the streets. Riding there beside him, I felt like we were in the kind of parade I've read about in New York City! Everyone was shouting and calling out things to Pa as if he was some kind of town hero. And this time he was laughing and returning the greetings and waving back. I guess whatever had been on his mind before was taken care of now.

I couldn't help but think it seemed a mite strange. Here all these folks came out to see Pa, treating him like he'd saved the town from destruction. And back home where we were headed a houseful of folks were celebrating Becky's rescue, and there was food and good smells and lively talk, and everybody was feeling happy. And yet back in town Mrs. Parrish was all alone, and nobody even seemed to know that *she'd* been the real hero of the day. It didn't seem just fair that she wasn't part of the celebrating.

Just then we saw the minister walking down the sidewalk. He waved, and we waved back. But Pa had stopped to talk to the sheriff for a minute, so Rev. Rutledge kept going without pausing for a chat. He was walking in the direction of Mrs. Parrish's. I was glad. Maybe she wouldn't have to spend the evening alone after all.

As we continued on our way a couple of minutes later, I glanced back for one last look at Mrs. Parrish's house before we turned up the street that led out of town. She was on the porch with Rev. Rutledge. It looked like she was explaining that she was just leaving, because he turned around and walked away.

Mrs. Parrish went out toward the little stable beside her house where Marcus Weber was standing waiting for her, holding the reins of a saddled horse. She was carrying the saddlebags Pa had brought her.

Mr. Weber helped her up, then she dug in her heels and went flying away out of town to the south. I turned back, and Pa and I rode north past the last of the buildings, and up the hill toward our place.

The rest of that night was spent in celebrating, waiting on the two invalids in the cabin, and hearing all the stories there were to tell — starting with Becky's version of events, then Zack's and Little Wolf's, then Pa's.

"But I'll tell you something," said Pa as he finished his account of the gunfight at Deadman's Flat, "when I crawled to my feet and stumbled down the hill to see if Zack was safe, and I saw Buck Krebbs lying in the dirt, there wasn't any joy in my heart."

It was a somber way to end a day that had turned out better than we might have hoped the night before.

"No sir, a dead face is an awful thing to see, especially when I knew it was my hand that took his life. God forgive me, I had to do it, else he'd have killed Zack for sure. But don't any of you kids ever think killin's a right thing. It's a dreadful thing, I'm tellin' you! Buck was our enemy, but I'll never forget that look on his dead face, and I pray God can do somethin' better with him now than he was able to down here. He was a bad man, but that don't make killin' him a pleasant thing."

We all went to bed late that night with plenty to be thankful for, and also a lot to think about.

I didn't know if it was a right thing to do or not, but I couldn't help praying for Buck Krebbs one last time. I remembered the Bible verse that said we were to pray for our enemies.

Maybe it was too late, but I figured I ought to do what the Book said. So I did.

CHAPTER 40

PREPARATIONS

The next day was Sunday.

Little Wolf felt much better and went home. I figured we'd all stay home, but Pa insisted on going to church. His leg was still swollen, and there wasn't any way he was going to do much walking, crutch or no crutch. Four of us together carried him to the wagon, where he lay down in the back on some blankets. Uncle Nick drove the wagon, and the rest of us gathered in back around Pa. Even Katie went with us, sitting up front beside Uncle Nick.

It was a fun ride to town, although Pa didn't say much. Buck Krebbs was still on his mind, I could tell. Maybe he felt he needed to make peace with God and himself over the killing, and he figured church was the best place to do it.

But the service hardly fit Pa's mood. Everybody cheered when they saw us pulling into the meadow in our wagon, and they all ran toward us, hugging and shaking hands and showing their happiness that everybody was safe. During the service Rev. Rutledge thanked the Lord for his protecting hand over Becky and Zack and Pa and everyone else that had been involved.

When church was over, after the last song and prayer, Rev. Rutledge stood up in front and said, "I have one final announcement. I realize it is probably unnecessary, but in case there are any persons present who do *not* already know — next Sunday, one week from today, after the morning service, at one o'clock in the afternoon, you are all invited to attend the wedding of our own Drummond Hollister to Miss Kathryn Morgan, newly arrived from Virginia."

Several of the men whooped and turned around to give Pa a wink or a few words. Katie smiled pleasantly at the women who glanced at her. But if anything, the minister's announcement seemed to dampen Pa's mood all the more.

Pa stayed in bed the rest of Sunday and all the next day. Doc came out again on Tuesday and pronounced the swelling reduced.

Pa hobbled around a little Tuesday afternoon, then went back to bed. His spirits were depressed, I could tell — probably from not being able to get up and be about and working. He never was one for sitting still doing nothing.

On Wednesday Mrs. Parrish rode out in her buggy to fetch Katie and me. From the very first word of the wedding several weeks ago, Mrs. Parrish had taken it upon herself to see that Katie had a new wedding dress for the occasion. Now it was time for the final fitting and last minute alterations, and she asked me to come along to Mrs. Gianini's. "Women get together, and men get together," she told me, "before weddings. And this is *our* chance!"

Mrs. Gianini was all business, fussing with pins and her tape, and muttering this and that about the hem and sleeves and lace and veil and ribbon. The dress was of light blue, with a high neck, and wide, loose shoulders and upper arms. The bodice was close-fitting, and below the waist the dress filled out with several petticoats underneath. The buttons and lace were of pale yellow, as was the cummerbund around the waist and the bow tied in back.

"It's beautiful, Mrs. Gianini," said Katie after she had put on the dress for the final time and stood in front of the mirror. "So beautiful! I never expected anything like this out here. I don't know how you did it, but this style you and Almeda chose doesn't make me look so round."

"We wouldn't have our Drummond Hollister's bride with anything less," said Mrs. Parrish, smiling at Katie, a smile that seemed to have a hint of sadness in it, though her voice never betrayed it. "He's a 'leading citizen,' remember."

As she gazed over the bride-to-be, the look on Mrs. Parrish's face reminded me of how she looked at me sometimes. Her eyes were so full of love, almost motherly, but not without that look of pain that I never quite understood either. She had done so much for me — and for Pa. And now she was having this dress made, probably at her own expense, for Pa's new wife whom she barely knew. I couldn't help thinking what a selfless woman she was.

361

"You look lovely, my dear," Mrs. Parrish added, standing back and regarding Katie as Mrs. Gianini took in a last tuck about the waist, then pinned it in place. "I know Corrie's father will be proud when he sees you coming down the aisle on Sunday."

"Won't he already have seen her in the dress after we get ready and drive in?" I asked innocently.

All three of the women laughed together.

"Oh no, Corrie!" said Mrs. Parrish. "Don't you know, a bride and groom must never see one another on their wedding day until the moment when she starts down the aisle." They laughed again.

"My ma always told me I wasn't the marrying kind," I said. "I reckon she was right. But how will Katie and Pa not see each other?"

"Oh, Katie will spend Saturday night with me, of course," replied Mrs. Parrish. "We'll get her all ready right here. You and Becky and Emily shall help me! And we'll have to get you three all dressed up too. Your pa will be so proud to see all his women looking so beautiful!"

As always, Mrs. Parrish's enthusiasm was catching. Pretty soon all four of us were laughing like little girls. I was so happy that Katie and Mrs. Parrish looked like they were going to be friends! I couldn't have stood it if Mrs. Parrish couldn't be at least a little bit like part of our family!

When Mrs. Parrish and I happened to be alone in another room for a few minutes, I asked her

362

about the papers and Mr. Royce and the money. She opened her mouth as if she was about to reply, then thought better of it and stopped herself. A strange look came into her eye.

Then she said, "Corrie, what happened with the money is between your father and me. I know you and I haven't kept secrets from one another. But this time I'm going to have to do just that. It is not that I don't want you to know. But if the story's to be told, I want your father to be the one to tell you. You see, it's his secret now, not mine. So that means it's his to share or his to hold on to, as he sees fit."

By Thursday Pa was a lot better, although he was still acting quiet. His leg still hurt a lot, but he was able to hobble around pretty well.

Friday morning came, and Uncle Nick didn't show up for breakfast.

"Zack, run up to the mine and fetch him, will you?" said Pa.

But Zack came back alone a couple of minutes later. "He ain't up there, Pa."

"Anybody seen Nick today?" Pa asked the rest of us.

No one had.

Still nobody had seen him by the time afternoon came. By evening Pa was getting fidgety, and starting to mutter. Uncle Nick didn't come home that night.

Saturday Pa was furious.

Here it was the day before the wedding, and Katie and I had lots of things to do. Mrs. Parrish was out twice to our place, and Katie and I went into town with her for an hour in the afternoon. Through it all Pa was ranting about Uncle Nick's disappearance.

"The hare-brained idiot's gone off again!" he kept saying. "Probably drunk someplace, losin' away every dime he's got to some gambling shyster!"

Saturday night came. Still no sign of Uncle Nick.

"That numskull!" Pa said over and over. "His sense o' timing's about as lame as his smarts with cards!"

"What are we gonna do, Pa?" I asked.

"What do you mean what are we gonna do? There ain't nothin' we *can* do! We don't know where he is. The loco fool is gonna miss the wedding!"

Mrs. Parrish rode out one last time, this time to get Katie and take her to town for the night.

"You all sleep well tonight!" Mrs. Parrish said as they got ready to leave. "Tomorrow's going to be an exciting day!"

Then she turned to Pa and said in a more serious tone. "Mr. Hollister, do you need anything? Any help with, you know, with your brother-in-law —"

"I appreciate your thoughtfulness, ma'am," Pa replied. "But I'll be fine." It was the gentlest I'd heard Pa talk in two days. "Alkali's comin' out in the mornin'. He'll help me get dressed and all."

"And don't you worry a thing about the younger children, Mr. Hollister," she said. "You just get everybody to town, and I'll make sure everybody knows what to do. You'll be very proud of your family, Mr. Hollister."

"Thank you, ma'am," said Pa.

They each gave a little wave, then Mrs. Parrish and Katie were off toward Miracle.

The rest of us went back inside and got ready for bed, everyone listening, I think, for the sounds of Uncle Nick's horse riding up.

But we all fell asleep without hearing it.

CHAPTER 41

THE BIG DAY

Most of the town showed up for the wedding.

Just the fact that Pa'd written for a mail-order bride was curious enough, so lots of folks were interested. And I don't suppose it's all that usual for a man to get married with five of his own children sitting in the front row watching!

But most of all, Pa was a highly respected man around Miracle Springs. It wasn't just that he had friends. It was more than that. I suppose Pa represented what a lot of folks wished for themselves. Here was a man who'd come to town running from the law, using an alias, with nothing to his name. Now Miracle Springs was celebrating its first wedding with him! At least with Sheriff Rafferty he'd been cleared. He had a family, a good claim, and a chance to settle down.

Maybe they were proud of Pa. Maybe some envied him a little. But whatever their reasons, almost everyone piled into that little church that Sunday afternoon. They'd brought in extra chairs from the Gold Nugget, but some of the men still had to stand up in back.

Even with all the people, there was one less than there should have been. My mind kept turning over the question, just like Pa had said as he glanced around at the cabin and up toward the barn and mine one last time: "Where in tarnation's Nick?" And now we were sitting silently in the church, thinking the same thing.

At last Pa and Rev. Rutledge stood up in front. Pa looked so handsome in his black suit. The music started to play — it was Miss Stansberry at the piano in the back of the church.

I turned around to look.

There stood Katie in the gorgeous dress. Slowly, an inch at a time, she began to walk up the aisle between the chairs.

Softly the music played, the only other sound the faint rustle of Katie's dress as it moved along the floor.

My eyes scanned so many faces in that second. Half the town's saloon girls were here, dabbing their eyes with pink and white handkerchiefs, as if "ol' Drum gettin' hitched" spelled the end of all the wild nightlife of Miracle Springs.

Katie was about a third of the way down the aisle now. I suppose she looked pretty. People say that brides always do. I didn't really notice her face.

I turned back to the front. Rev. Rutledge stood tall, with a nice minister-looking smile on his face. Pa beside him was just staring, not smiling at all.

Miss Stansberry started through the processional song again.

You could hear the sounds now of people starting to turn around and watch as Katie approached Pa. She was almost beside me now, still walking slowly. More handkerchiefs came out of hiding. Right behind me I saw that Mrs. Parrish was holding one too. I caught her eye and she tried to smile, but I saw a look of sadness in her face.

All heads turned with Katie, back toward the front of the church, where she had just about reached Pa's outstretched hand. But amid the noise of turning and looking and the piano's tones there now came another sound — faint at first, then steadily louder.

It was a horse galloping up. Louder it came, until it was right next to the church building.

But instead of gradually fading away in the other direction, the skidding hoofbeats and whinnying of the horse caught us all by surprise. Glances began to scatter about the church at the sound of a rider dismounting and the loud booted clomping of footsteps coming up the church stairs two at a time.

The music stopped. Katie turned around.

Suddenly the door flew open and crashed against the back wall.

There in the open doorway stood Uncle Nick!

His face wore three days' growth of whiskers. His clothes were filthy, he still had on his hat, and the dust from his hasty approach seemed to billow into the room on his heels.

He stood there a split second, taking in the scene. Then he ran forward halfway up the aisle, and shouted: "Drum, you blamed fool . . . you're marryin' the wrong woman!"

Instantly the church was in an uproar.

Katie's mouth was hanging open. Rev. Rutledge stood stock-still in consternation, not knowing what to do. Pa stared at Uncle Nick for just a second, his face growing red with fury.

Then he strode forward toward him as fast as his bad leg would let him hobble. He looked as if he was fixing to knock Uncle Nick's block off!

"Just a dadburn minute!" cried Uncle Nick. "Hear me out, Drum. After what I got to say, well, then you can do what you like! Don't you know by now, you ol' goat . . ." and as he said it, he ran the rest of the way up the aisle and stopped just beside where Mrs. Parrish was sitting, ". . . this here's the woman you oughta be marryin'!" He grabbed her hand and held it in Pa's direction before the shocked Mrs. Parrish could think to withdraw it.

"She's the woman who loves you, you idiot! You're so blind you can't see the nose on the front of your face!"

Uncle Nick dropped Mrs. Parrish's hand, went the rest of the way down the aisle, took Katie's hand, and added — as if to end the discussion — "Don't you know Katie's the woman *I* got *my* eye on?"

Now the commotion *really* erupted!

Everyone was half out of their chairs and balking and stirring about. Pa was still standing there where Uncle Nick had left him, speechless. I glanced behind me quickly. Mrs. Parrish was staring down into her lap and quietly weeping. She was still holding her handkerchief and not even bothering to use it.

Realizing what a stir he'd caused, and maybe embarrassed at his outburst, Uncle Nick by this time had run back outside. Katie went after him. Rev. Rutledge was scurrying about trying to restore some semblance of order, but he wasn't succeeding too well.

I think everyone knew the wedding was over — for right now, at least. Some folks walked outside, others still sat looking around bewildered. Some of the ladies were uttering comments along the lines of, "Well, I never —" and "Gracious sakes, in all my days . . ."

"Wait! Wait, people — please!" Rev. Rutledge shouted, trying to be heard above the chaos and confusion. "Take your seats until we get this all sorted out! . . . Mr. Hollister!"

But Pa was moving slowly away from Rev. Rutledge now, limping toward where I was sitting. He didn't hear the minister calling his name. I don't think he was aware of the church quieting, and the turning of every eye upon him to see what he was going to do. He was coming toward the row where all of us kids were sitting, but he wasn't looking at us. His eyes were fixed on someone else.

By the time he got to Mrs. Parrish, the church was quiet again.

Pa stopped.

I reckon she could sense he was there. After a moment, Mrs. Parrish slowly looked up. Her eyes were all wet. Pa stood gazing down on her with the nicest, most sheepish, half-embarrassed smile I could ever have imagined on his face.

She half-laughed, but it was sort of a half-cry, too. Her handkerchief quickly went to her eyes, and she glanced away. But only for a second. She looked right back at Pa, and her eyes found his.

"Mrs. Parrish, ma'am," said Pa sort of timidly, "I reckon there's a thing or two you an' me oughta be talking about."

"Yes, Mr. Hollister," she said, nodding, dropping her gaze and smiling softly. "I think you are right."

Pa reached out his hand. She took it, rose to her feet, and joined him in the aisle while everyone sat and watched them.

As they started toward the door, Mrs. Parrish said, "But don't you think, *Drummond* — " She said his name slowly, and though I'd heard her use his given name a time or two before, now it suddenly meant so much more as she said it. "Don't you think that it's finally time you started calling me Almeda?"

Even from where I was sitting in the front pew, I could see the back of Pa's neck getting red.

"I reckon you're right, ma'am," he replied.

Mrs. Parrish looked up into Pa's face with a most radiant smile. I could tell that she loved him. I think she probably had for quite a while.

They walked through the open door, outside, and down the stairs. I could hear Pa's uneven footfall as he struggled down the steps. Inside the church it was dead silent.

Suddenly I was on my feet. I ran back to the door and looked out.

Pa was limping across the meadow next to the church with Mrs. Parrish beside him. I could tell they were talking, but their voices were much too soft and far away to hear. Mrs. Parrish slipped her hand through Pa's arm and looked up at his face every so often.

Nobody else was around, so nobody ever heard what they said to each other. I asked them both, more than once, to tell me what they'd said.

But Pa would only reply, "That is one conversation, Corrie Belle, that ain't never gonna find its way into your journal!" It was a good while before he said any more. But seeing the two of them like that was a sight I will never forget.

Behind me, the noise of commotion was rising again. Now it grew even louder than before. The wives didn't know whether to be scandalized at the proceedings or happy. The men were all telling their versions of "I knew ol' Drum would . . .", or "Did I tell you the time when Drum . . ." Some of the saloon girls were still crying. Others were laughing and making jokes and already heading for the door to leave. I suppose Alkali Jones said it best. His only comment was, "Well, if that don't beat all!"

I don't know where Katie and Uncle Nick had gone, but now Uncle Nick came back into the church, more calmly this time. Katie was right behind him. He put up his hands and tried to get everyone's attention.

"Hey, you all — quiet down!" he called out, motioning with his arms. "I got somethin' to say!"

Pretty soon most of the folks' eyes were on him.

"Well, I reckon I done it, huh?" he said, "I made a plumb nincompoop outta myself!"

Everyone laughed.

"But the way me an' Katie's got it figured is that Drum looks to be a mite too occupied right at the moment —"

More laughter and some shouts from a few of Uncle Nick's rowdier friends. "And it seems a shame, with Katie comin' so far an' all, an' all you good folks comin' here today — well, it seems a shame to put such a colorful pretty wedding dress an' a church full of guests to waste. So we figure we oughta go on ahead with this here wedding. An' since Drum's busy, I'll take his place! Katie says none of you'd object . . . and *she* don't object, neither!"

Now the place really erupted with shouts and cheers, and finally a round of applause.

Rev. Rutledge had a look of astonishment all over his face. But everyone else seemed to agree that the idea made all the sense in the world.

" 'Course Katie'd like me to get cleaned up just a tad," said Uncle Nick when he could be heard again. "So if you folks don't mind waitin', I'm gonna hightail it home an' shave off some o' these whiskers an' throw on some clean duds, an' I'll be back inside an hour. That oughta give you time to round up Drum and tell him about the change in plans!"

A wave of laughter swept the room. Uncle Nick turned and ran out the door. Several seconds later we heard the galloping hoofbeats like those that had started the uproar. They quickly died in the distance.

Everyone started milling around in little groups, and slowly filed outside. Katie marched through the crowd to where Rev. Rutledge was standing and spent about five minutes with him, making whatever arrangements she had to, I reckon. Then she came over to me and the other kids. Even if she wasn't going to marry Pa after all, she was still going to be kin, so I guess she felt it was her duty to see to us. She knelt down and explained to Tad and Becky and Emily what had happened, and told them she was going to be their Aunt Katie.

And an hour and a half later, as we all left the church for the last time that day, that's exactly what she was.

CHAPTER 42

WONDERING ABOUT THE FUTURE

Uncle Nick and Aunt Katie went to San Francisco for a honeymoon.

If I thought the town was buzzing before, now there wasn't *anything* more the subject of conversation — from the school to the Gold Nugget to the General Store to the groups of men standing around the streets — than what Uncle Nick had done at what was supposed to have been Pa's wedding! Those folks who hadn't attended were kicking themselves for weeks!

I suppose the one person who wasn't thrilled with the sudden way everything had gone topsy-turvy was Rev. Rutledge. He went through the wedding ceremony with Katie and Uncle Nick with a smile on his face. And I think down inside even he could see how much better it was for Pa to walk down the aisle — still in that handsome black suit, with Katie on his arm — to give her away to Uncle Nick, than it would have been to marry the two of them.

Still, the change was bound to affect his fortunes probably as much as anyone's, and nobody saw him much for several days.

All us kids were positively *dying* to know what was going to happen next. That night we pestered Pa with question after question. But he wouldn't say much. There was a kind of crafty smile on his face, but he just kept saying, "We'll see, kids . . . we'll see."

He did make more than his usual number of trips into town during the next few days, and he hardly went up to the mine at all. Mr. Ashton and Marcus Weber ran the Mine and Freight Company mostly by themselves for the next week.

I knew Pa and Mrs. Parrish were trying to figure a lot of things out. They'd had their differences. They had both had another wife and husband whose memories they still loved. And they both had homes and businesses they didn't want to give up. But neither one of them would let on a word about what they intended to do about all those things.

And when they finally did say — well, that was another whole story!